ELLE HARTFORD

Love and Ghosts at Hideaway Lake

First published by Phoenix & Kelpie Press 2026

First edition

ISBN: 979-8-9948255-1-8

This book was professionally typeset on Reedsy.
Find out more at reedsy.com

"To see and to be seen. That is the truest nature of love."

-Brené Brown

~~~

"Far safer through an Abbey—gallop—
The stones a'chase—
Than moonless—one's own self encounter—
In lonesome place—"

-Emily Dickinson

Contents

Author's Note

Welcome to Beyond! I love writing these books, and I hope you'll enjoy your time here.

Now: as you read, you'll find some references to a summertime investigation in Helenia, and several criminals. Those events are recorded in the book *Labyrinth of Crime,* part of my Alchemical Tales mystery series. You **don't** need to have read that to make sense of this story: this tale is very different, and Sakura will catch you up on anything you missed.

That said, if you're into cozy mysteries and think you might like to read *Labyrinth,* please be aware there are some **spoilers** in this book. You won't find out the actual answer to the mystery, but you'll find out one of the extra people who was involved in the crime.

And of course, you'll know who Saki falls in love with in the end! ♡

Hideaway Lake

Prologue

Sakura

There are a few things I have to tell you for this to make any sense.

The first is that I'm a shadow witch.

The second is that I run a café in a small town called Belville, and I'm pretty good at it (aside from getting up in the mornings).

The third is that one of my best friends is an alchemist named Red, and she tends to get into trouble. She can tell you all about that herself in her own book. But for now, suffice it to say that when I tried, last summer, to throw her a celebratory girls' trip before her upcoming wedding, in a beautiful and very popular ancient city called Helenia, no less, what we ended up doing was getting embroiled in local disappearances and helping the police bring down several criminals.

The fourth is that a judge later ruled that one of those

criminals, a fancy business owner, should not be allowed to hold on to, nor to profit from, any of her property gained during the time of the crime.

The fifth is that said business owner then decided to leave her unfinished "divine health resort" to *me*.

SOLVE THE MYSTERY

Spa Hallow

FIND YOUR DIVINE SELF

MINOTAUR
ENTERPRISES

Chapter One: Legends

Sakura

I'm not a particularly health-conscious person. An accident in my youth left me with fairy-made legs from the knee down and a firm conviction that as long as I have most of my body parts and they're working sort-of properly, I'm fine. It also helps that my interests tend to run to love and food rather than, say, running marathons.

Nor am I a person who attaches much significance to matters of divinity.

And I'm not a big fan of resorts, either.

But on this particular winter day, I was tired and confused and disappointed in myself enough to admit that maybe a resort was what I needed. *Maybe.* From the main street in Helenia, I looked up, up, up. (I'm also not a particularly tall person.) Helenia is famous for being an island surrounded by

1

sparkling blue waters and featuring one *very* large, hopefully dead volcano. The city itself is plastered to the volcano's side, a bunch of cobblestone streets and white buildings with tile roofs and terribly steep staircases, all spread out along the crescent-shaped harbor behind me.

And we were headed all the way up that dead volcano in a glorified chair lift.

Tourists of all stripes were waiting patiently in line, filling up gondola after gondola and being whisked into the air. Whisked at a rumbling, mechanical pace, in any case. On my last trip to Helenia, I'd missed this tourist attraction. Serene beaches and restaurants boasting live music were more my speed. But, this trip wasn't about my enjoyment—it was business.

One glance at my companion was all that was necessary to confirm *that*. Bertram was tall, thin, and as straight-backed as the clipboard he carried close to his chest. He'd been talking nonstop. I was starting to wonder if his presence was some sort of test. Or if perhaps this "inheritance" was all some kind of elaborate revenge.

"Work on the extension of Gondola Line A is now complete," he was saying. "So access is no problem. This was Phase One of the Spa Hallow plan, you understand—there has to be a way for the construction supplies and machinery to *get* there, of course."

I frowned. I understood that a resort wasn't viable unless people could get to it, but I'd figured that it was supposed to be, you know, divine and untouched and nature-y. Not something that required heavy equipment to create. "Machinery?"

"Obviously. It takes a lot of heavy equipment to create perfection," Bertram said with a matter-of-fact nod. His perfectly curled brown hair brushed his perfectly tan forehead, and I had to wonder how much machinery *that* had taken.

"But . . . why?" I turned and looked at him properly now. His collared shirt, a pale pink which I approved of, had been ironed. Was *he* the one ironing his shirts? Was he the one who'd been in charge of ironing the resort into shape, too? He certainly seemed to know a lot about it, for a business assistant. I was pretty sure that was how he'd introduced himself. When he gave me a perfectly bland, blank look, I explained, "I figured the resort site was chosen because it already *was* perfect? 'Divine,' wasn't that the word?"

"Right, sorry," Bertram said, with a sort of bob and weave of his head which seemed to be his approximation of a chuckle, "it's 'divine' because of the pond. Technically, a reflecting pool. It's a creation most likely ten to twelve centuries old of rough-cut local stone, with an unknown depth. One hundred feet wide by three hundred feet long, extending back toward the mountain peak. It takes up the majority of the . . . plateau, I believe the geology people called it. You hadn't heard of it before? The tourist brochures call it 'The Gods' Reflecting Pool.' You'll hear locals refer to it as Hideaway Lake. Of course, you'll also hear them talk about a monster, but—"

"Ohhh," said someone else—someone new. One of our fellow gondola-riders was leaning over my shoulder: not a difficult feat. It was an elf with a sun-screened nose and wide, excited eyes behind their heart-shaped pink sunglasses. Somebody clearly not bothered that winter in Helenia was nowhere near as balmy as the popular summer months. "Are you talking about The Lake at the Edge of the World?"

I joined the elf in eyeing Bertram. *Was* he?

And here I'd thought I was in for a bit of respite after the disastrous way I'd left things in Belville.

"Ah, some people do call it that, of course," Bertram admitted. This time it was a head dip, not a bob and weave. So he wasn't amused by the name: he seemed to dislike it. Too dramatic, most likely. "Only the more *sensational* divine pilgrimage tour packages," he added, proving my point.

"I heard it was under private ownership now, and no tours can go there," the elf said helpfully. "Are you saying you know one that does? My friends and I are *dying* to see the monster!"

"I hope not," I replied, projecting my voice up to make space for myself the way my height could not. I've found a light tone works best for getting people's attention, and the touristy elf was no exception. I had their full attention for the first time as I went on, "You heard right, and the site is closed. If you want to get to it, I'm afraid you'll have to time-travel back to the summer and make yourself instrumental in the capture of a wealthy criminal. Probably argue with her too—that's probably what did it," I added under my breath. *Note to self: pick fewer arguments?*

But when I know I'm right, I have a dangerous habit of expressing it.

"Oh." The elf looked about as confused as I was. I'd taken one look at Bertram and carefully stowed my confusion away as soon as I'd arrived, though.

"The gondola is docking now for the cliffside carving and outlook," said assistant said, in his firmest, snobbiest tone. Maybe he hadn't appreciated my flippant tone regarding his previous employer.

The elf was being tugged away with the crowd disembarking, but they paused for just a moment and turned back to me. "*Can you time-travel?*"

"Not that I know of," I replied. Fully resisting the urge to face palm. "Have a nice tour. Bye!"

If only it was so easy to get rid of this new assistant!

This time, though, Bertram waited until the gondola was empty except for himself and me. He nodded at the driver at the head of the cabin. He didn't even say words, just nodded. What was this? A new language of head movements? I refused to adopt it.

As the gondola lurched back into the air—have I mentioned yet that air travel and sea travel try my stomach?—Bertram reestablished his grip on his clipboard. "As I was saying, the reflecting pool is the center of . . . a considerable amount of local legend. It's unfortunate, though of course, it also adds to the appeal of—"

"Like what?" I interrupted.

Bertram had to tilt his head down to look at my face. I waited until he said, with a new, very faint tone of strain emerging in his voice, "'Like what,' what?"

"The legends," I said, giving him a cheerful smile this time. "What are the legends? Why are tourists and locals talking about monsters?"

"Ah," he said. I got the feeling he was longing to rifle through his clipboard. Had he really not expected me to be interested? "There are . . . numerous legends, of course. But there has never been a confirmed sighting of any monster, and most accounts can't even agree what it looks like. It's all nonsense, I wouldn't bother with it if I was you. They say it can sense your deepest fears—patently ridiculous. The other legend you'll hear is that somewhere on the opposite side of the pond is a staircase, also made of stone, which ascends to the peak of Mount Hallow and, from there, to the realm of the gods.

But we really can't take any of this—"

"Is there?" I asked sweetly. He was dismissive of the monster but cagey about a staircase, and I wanted to know why. When Bertram opened and closed his mouth several times with no success, I took pity and added, "Presumably someone has climbed to the top of the mountain to look? Sounds like it's been there a long time. Surely the thought has occurred to some enterprising soul."

"Of course, of course," said Bertram, clutching his clipboard so hard his knuckles went white. "The fact of the matter is, it's just a small bit, ah, dangerous. But people have been to the top of the mountain. Of course. We assume that must be the case. As you say, it's been there . . . a while."

"Making assumptions doesn't sound like good business practice," I said, my voice now bordering on saccharine. I'll be the first to admit I have a certain villainous streak. Bear in mind that you're not meeting me on my best day, won't you?

"Right, yes. That's true," said Bertram. "But, ah, the problem is, we don't have any verifiable reports from anyone who's made it to the top. Just—rumors."

I let him think about that for a moment. While he stewed, I turned to look out the gondola windows again. The breeze was chillier now, and we were a truly dizzying distance from the harbor. But it didn't matter: there wasn't any need to look behind us. The view in front of us was more than enough.

The trees were beginning to thin out. A ridge rose above the treetops—a ridge that was clearly our destination. We were close enough to it that the mountain peak was totally obscured for a moment. But then we rose just enough, and it popped into view, sharp and imposing against Helenia's perfect blue sky.

Belville was also set on a mountain—not quite so high up, though. Had you asked me if I wanted to purchase *more* property, my first thought wouldn't have been more mountainside land . . . it wouldn't have even been my twelfth thought. But even I had to admit that this was gorgeous. It looked exactly the way it *ought* to look. Rugged, quiet, and ancient. Not a place for business after all.

"You're saying no one's made it to the top and come back," I mused, looking at that mountain peak.

"That's correct. Actually," said Bertram, quite suddenly, "it's not just that. There were also reports while building the gondola station—some of the workers were spreading rumors. I wouldn't have bothered you with them, but you'll probably hear it soon enough. People think the site is haunted."

And that was the moment that the gondola cleared the ridge, and the "site" was in full view. The lake really was a perfect reflection pool—it was glorious—but I saw instantly why people called it "Hideaway Lake." The mountain wasn't mirrored in it. Not even a rough reflection. Instead, the lake was pristinely, calmly blue. The trees waved gently in the wind, a wind that carried the smell of crisp water and the barest suggestion of alpine snow.

It was love at first sight. This site could be as haunted and full of monsters and stairs as it wanted to be. I wasn't going to change a thing.

Chapter Two: Butterflies

༄

Marcus

Waiting comes naturally to me.

And, because I have lived in Helenia for hundreds of years, so does knowledge. My acquaintance at the airship station informed me that a shadow witch had arrived. I'd long known of the court's decision and the strange bequest. I was familiar with the land concerned, as well.

The site looked much as it always had, aside from the new gondola station perched on the edge of the cliff. *That* was a modern monstrosity of wires and glass. I suppose all these things must be. But I knew it was only a drop in the bucket compared to the all-inclusive resort that had been planned.

I stood contemplating the station in silence. The late winter sun was warm on my shoulders, and the birdsong from the forest surrounding the pool was quite pleasant. Normally, I might have come up here to walk among the trees and see the new shoots of early flowers rise from the dirt. Such meditations were my primary solace—had been a singular source of contentment for months. A time when I could will myself back into waiting.

But now, knowing that the waiting would soon become something else, there were butterflies dancing through my veins.

The gondola docked smoothly, and two figures alighted on the wooden deck. They were shaded by a narrow roof, but the construction was open-air, without walls; I could see her very clearly. Her white hair shone softly in the shadow. Her bright blue eyes were weary, tired, but otherwise she had not changed.

Naturally, neither figure had expected to be met with any person in such a remote location—let alone me. Though I was watching her, I was aware that the second figure saw me and jerked half a step back.

"*Pluto?* Why are you here?"

That he knew me by name was not surprising, but merited thought. I glanced at him and recognized an employee of Minotaur Enterprises. The memory came back reluctantly. He'd been sent to me in search of magical artifacts, years ago . . . A notable effort, as most of Helenia had believed—and still believed—that I ran an illicit market of ancient items. Where once I was thought to be a lord of the underworld, now I was rumored to be a lord of crime. To some, it didn't matter. Either they knew better, or they didn't know enough.

Industry leaders were often the latter, and this assistant had been no different. I nodded an acknowledgment and returned my attention to *her*. "I have business with Sakura."

She had her hands on her hips, the yellow fabric of her skirt flaring out just past her knees. The look on her face said she was choosing her words. I tucked my arms behind my back. I had no idea what she might wish to say to me after six months, and my hands were shaking.

"Oh," said the assistant, meanwhile. "Right. The business with the ghost? Or the monster?"

I will admit I am considered something of an authority on ghostly matters in Helenia, by those who know more than the rumors of illegal trade. But I had not heard of any such concerns at the resort. If I had, I might have tried to meet Sakura *before* she reached the gondola.

"I'm not here on business," she declared, her lips pursed.

This appeared to catch the assistant by surprise. I let him ask his questions, studying the exchange.

"What?" he asked first.

She turned to him and crossed her arms. Though she was considerably shorter than both him and me, she was by far the most intimidating of us. "I'm here to rest. It *is* a resort, isn't it?"

"Not yet," he sputtered. "There's the construction—Phases Two through Thirteen—to go over, and the marketing plans— the Spa Hallow brochures—we'll need approval to go ahead with leveling the forest, and then of course there's the legends you wanted to know about—and the ghost—"

He was looking at his clipboard as he spoke. He didn't see how her chest was swelling, her expression indignant.

But the magic I had seen her wield so adeptly last summer was gone. Curious. I had no doubt she still *had* it, but she didn't seem to be using it—not even to shift her pink luggage, which was settled chaotically at her feet.

11

"Bertram," she interrupted at last, in a sweet tone which with her was dangerous, "Take the afternoon off. In fact, take the next few days off."

"What?" he asked again.

"Go home. Go out. Whatever you like. Your sole job right now is assisting me as I take ownership, right? And as your new boss, I'm saying, scram. Give me a few days to think. If I hear another word about phases or machinery, I'm going to curse your clipboard. Okay? This gondola can give you a ride back down, right?"

"Yes," he admitted, uncertainly. "But—you can't stay up here?"

"It's mine, isn't it?" Sakura replied lightly. "I see a cabin over there. A worker's cabin, I take it? Excellent. You have the keys? Good. Leave them with me, and go back to town. Enjoy your evening," she added, more kindly, as he complied. Bertram the assistant was packed back into the gondola and headed down the mountain before he could think of another word to say.

And then she turned back to me.

"Marcus Antoine Pluto." Her arms were still crossed as she regarded me, the new keys dangling from her fingers. My heart lurched. To use a person's full name was rarely a good sign. Among magic users it could even be dangerous, as they used the knowledge to cast powerful spells over each other. But the hold Sakura had on me was no spell.

As she stood at the edge of the station, steps above the ground, her face was still in shadow. I had to look up to meet her gaze. It was not encouraging; but then, I had done very little worthy of encouragement.

"Listen," she continued matter-of-factly, the lightness gone.

"I'll hear what you have to say, but I have to warn you. I—I'm not the same person I was six months ago. Things are different now. Like I said, I'm not here on business. I'd rather it wasn't brought up."

The falter in her voice broke my heart. What had happened to her since summer? I should have tried to reach out to her: I felt that very keenly. But I had been too shy then, and I was too cowardly now.

Not a becoming look for someone long-lived enough to know better. I dropped my gaze to the bare ground at my feet.

"I'm not trying to be mean. I just need you to understand." Sakura's voice had softened, though she didn't move. That was good. If she came near me, I felt I might break apart.

Last time I saw her, she kissed me.

And now she wanted to talk about anything else.

In fact it was clear she *needed* to talk about anything else. Something must have distressed her, indeed; and while I couldn't ask about it, I reminded myself that I could do as she wished. "Sakura," I said. "Please be careful. No doubt you know it as well as I do, but—I suspect some ulterior motive in bequeathing you this place. It is not a popular project in town. The idea of leveling ancient forests alone is bound to create protest. And the idea that it might be haunted—"

"Do you know anything about that?"

She was looking at me keenly. Even when I had been the one hidden in shadow, I felt she could see everything about me. She knew that I dealt with the spirits of those passed on. Somehow, she'd seen through every shield and known the whole truth of my existence the day that we met. The mask of divinity I used to obscure my expressions had never worked on her. She saw everything, though I did not understand how, nor why it held her interest. With dark hair, dark eyes, and dark gray skin, I was never the one of my siblings who stood out.

"I had not heard anything," I admitted. "But I do not consider the idea unlikely. This site has been home to many temples and refuges over the years. Many are fascinated by it."

"Many could be fascinated by the money behind it," Sakura pointed out.

A salient point, and one which I could not argue.

Sakura sighed, and I glanced back up at her, watching her shoulders fall. "For the record, I agree with you," she said. "I doubt this was some kind of 'thank you' for everything that happened—not that it was only *me* who did the investigating, but anyway. The question is *how much* ill intent there is here. Maybe it's some kind of weird vengeful scheme, sure. Or maybe it's just a matter of suffering through lectures about development from Bertram for a few days. Who knows?" She shook her head, her short hair swinging past her neck. "Is that all you came to say?"

I did my best to hold her gaze, helpless.

"Right, sorry." She smiled, just barely, rueful, sweet. "I did just ask you not to bring anything else up. Okay, um—thank you, for going along with that. Like I said, I don't mean anything against you . . . it's just, I have a lot to sort through at the moment. But don't worry. At this point, I *dare* a ghost or scheme to try to mess with me, honestly."

"Do you truly intend to stay up here?" I asked.

"I do." The look on her face said she would take no more argument on that fact. "And the first thing I'm going to do is sit down and make a cup of tea."

Chapter Three: Noises

❧❧❧

Sakura

I made it all the way to the cabin at the edge of the woods without once tripping or looking back. I had to, because I could feel him watching me. (I did manage to drop a suitcase at one point, but I recovered it quickly.)

I paused on the little wooden porch, fiddling with the unfamiliar keys. Maybe it had been rude of me not to invite him in? But gods above, this cabin, while large enough to have been visible from the gondola station, was far too small to house the both of us. Seeing him in person again was enough. The thought of being with him in an enclosed and *private* and probably very cozy and intimate space was . . .

I dropped the keys, and cursed myself.

Look, all this would have been lots easier if I had been using my magic, sure. But I wasn't going to risk it, not with him still

17

standing near the station, waiting. He hadn't protested at me leaving, but he was going to make sure I got inside my new accommodations, I knew that much. He was old-fashioned that way.

That's the thing about gods. They're inevitably behind the times.

Still, it was kind of nice. If I wasn't such a ball of chaos, I would have appreciated it. But as it was, I didn't much like the idea of someone witnessing me bang my knees on my suitcase and try literally the same key twice in a row, scratching the lock on the old door.

Through a combination of gritted teeth and silently threatening the door with everlasting curses if it didn't let me in—neither of which probably worked, but I was doing my best—I finally got the lock to turn over. Without risking so much as a wave over my shoulder, I chucked my bags inside and hopped after them.

Gods. I don't ever *hop.*

I stood there recovering for a long moment. My back to the door, my eyes squeezed shut. I wanted to cry, but reminded myself I hardly had the right. I'd ruined a lot of peoples' days lately. I couldn't complain if my own was not going well.

Then something else inside the cabin scratched.

My breath caught in my throat. I hadn't even bothered to look around. Was something else in there with me? Some*one* else?

I listened as hard as I could. All I could hear was the air wheezing in my chest. Though the afternoon was bright outside, the cabin was dark inside, shaded by the porch and layers upon layers of dust. I considered my options.

Then—and this will tell you a lot about my priorities—I

inched to the right. There was a window beside the door, overlooking the porch and, beyond it, the lake. I peered out and could just barely see the station through a layer of dirt. Empty. Marcus was gone.

With a full-body sigh of relief, I whirled around, lifting my arms, letting my magic *free.*

I don't know how it is with normal Witches—not really. Or with sorcerers or fairies or deities either, when you think about it. There are a lot of ways to be magical in Beyond, but all I can really speak for is my own way. And it's a pretty unusual way—shadow witchery, I mean. Normally, kids who have magic go to schools and learn and follow lots of rules and then take posts being official Town Witches or scholarly sorcerers or what have you. Shadow witches just kind of . . . hang out on the edges. Some choose to, and some—like me—never had a chance to be anything else. It can make people uneasy, using magic that's a little bit wild. I mean, fair enough, honestly. I'd had my share of mishaps.

Oh, but actually *using* the magic. As my hands rose through the air, sparks flew around me, scattering out into the cabin, filling the space. Illuminating what was hidden. It was a feeling like nothing else. Like expression, like safety, like *connection* all at once. For a moment as the unspoken spell flared, I was completely at one with my new home-away-from-home.

And I was fairly certain that there wasn't another person in it. Ghostly or otherwise.

No, there was just me, and my bags toppled over next to my feet. The main room I'd come into was square, and housed a small unfinished coffee table, as well as a ratty old couch on the back wall. The wall to my right was taken up by a large, lovely hearth. To my left, past the front door, was a long, narrow kitchen that extended to the back corner of the cabin, where another dusty table stood on uneven legs, accompanied by a similarly listless chair. There was a very dubious ladder at the back of the living room, and a door that led to a shadowy tub-shaped thing which I hoped signaled functioning plumbing.

Hmmm. So far, so good.

To be honest, I'd packed my bag without thinking about *where* I might stay when I got to Helenia. In the back of my mind I'd half assumed that the resort would be mostly finished, and I'd be taking up temporary residence in some boring, off-white generic hotel room. This was infinitely better in comparison. But it still needed quite a bit of work.

I set about making the space livable. Shadow magic draws power from the emotion of the witch using it—that's why it's called *shadow*: in order for it to really work, you have to face a lot of your own feelings—like jealousy, anger, or shame— that we usually prefer to keep hidden. Our "shadow self," the less acceptable or glamorous bits. I had *plenty* of angsty power to draw upon at that particular moment, but it still wasn't the kind of magic that can simply create *something* from *nothing*. (Very few magic practitioners can do that anyway— the exception would probably be creation deities. But we're trying *not* to think about deities right now, you know.) So, while I could use magical energy to locate a broom and shove it across the floors, and do the same with rags and a bucket of soapy water for the walls and windows, I still had to do some things myself.

I sat on the floor beside the front door, not bothering to move my luggage before I tugged the main compartment open. I often travel with candles, and I *always* travel with tea and my favorite cup, complete with glass stirring stick topped with a little butterfly. I put the candles on the mantel above the living room hearth, promising myself I'd go back outside and gather some wood later.

By now the kitchen was reasonably clean, and much brighter. Turned out, the filmy curtains above the sink had completely torn off during my over-zealous magical cleaning. No matter: a new set of curtains was just another thing on the list.

The list?

I caught myself, watching my thoughts as I rifled through cupboards and found an old copper pot. Washed it and filled it in the rough stone sink. Settling it on the old stove, lighting the burner with a little spark, I realized that I *was* making a list.

New sofa, with nice fluffy cushions. Proper chairs for the dining nook. Pretty curtains. A living room rug. More tea cups and a teapot . . .

I bit my lip. And proceeded to make tea directly in the copper pot, like an absolute heathen, just to make a point to myself.

This wasn't a holiday and it wasn't starting over in a gorgeous new place. It was . . .

Penance?

I turned away from the word. Listen, *in general,* I am good about facing my emotions and dealing with them head-on, so that my magic doesn't get away from me. *In general.*

Life wasn't feeling very *in general* right now. And since I was alone on top of a mountain and no one else could conceivably get hurt—any further—by my actions, I decided to ignore the knot in my chest for a little while longer.

Instead, I sat down on the one chair and pretended it wasn't at an angle. I sipped my tea from my special cup and pretended I didn't miss my cafe. And then I stood up and steeled myself to go back out into the woods, like I *often* had to gather firewood, and it was no big deal.

I mean, it's just sticks, right?

Living in Belville had spoiled me.

I locked the cabin door carefully behind me, then took an actually good look around the porch this time. The roof extended down over the space, blocking the sun. A *very* unreliable-looking railing at each end connected the front beams to the sides of the house. I was not a carpenter, not by any means, but my brother was. All I'd have to do was invite him out here and his big-sibling instincts would kick in, and surely . . .

No.

Biting the inside of my cheek firmly, I strode down off the porch, stumbling across the one uneven step. A path created by many work boots rather than by design led to the station, another led down along one edge of Hideaway Lake. I took the second, and turned off again to go around the cabin, into the woods.

I quickly ran out of any path. This slowed me down a little. I am not, by nature, a hiker; my main experience with the forest in Belville was watching it from the comfort of the main road in and out of town. It seemed odd to simply walk into the trees, like I hadn't been invited.

But there wasn't any other option if I wanted heat in my cabin tonight. Normal Witches have lots of magic-fire spells, but their spells require ingredients and preparation. Shadow magic is more innate and instant. It doesn't need words or bits and bobs, but it *does* need constant monitoring. It is not, in short, a responsible way to maintain fires.

My magic shimmered around me as I stepped between the trunks. Sort of an anxious habit—not one I'd used in years. But the cloak of black sparkles reassured me now. Everybody's magic has a color unique to them, a shade or an undertone or dual sparkle that marks them out. Mine is black, not because it's shadow magic, but just because . . .

Well, I'd spent a lot of years wondering about that, to be honest. Shadow magic can be any color: it's just magic like anybody else's. The color reflects the person, not the energy itself. I'd long ago embraced my black sparkles: they reminded me of spooky things and fearlessness. But these past few days . . . let's just say I was feeling it more in an "old crone warning off others" sort of way.

Something snapped to my left. A branch. Right? I turned to look, a little dazzled by the sun streaming through the trees. Behind me, there was that scraping sound again, and the scattering of dry leaves.

I whirled, hands up. My magic flared around me. There was nothing.

I sighed, and shook my head. If an unhappy criminal had sent me out here to get haunted or eaten by some kind of forest monster, they had another think coming. All I had to do was focus. Although—well, the other thing about magic is, there are a lot of low-level things you can set up. Like charms that can be bought and used by non-magic users, or glamours like the one I used to change how my shoes looked: after years of use, those were basically ingrained in my fairy-made feet. But in this case the most useful would be wards:

shields, really, which most magic-users put on themselves each morning with just a word or two, or a special amulet, or some grounding practice.

I hadn't been doing that lately. Which was probably another reason I was so jumpy . . .

I tripped over a branch submerged in dead leaves. Remembering that *that* was why I was out there, I leaned down to collect it. It was dry and scratchy—and about as long as my entire cabin, something I realized as I tried to lift it. Apparently, it was more dead tree and less branch. I dropped it, but then realized I could snap some branches off it. Easier than reaching up to branches still on trees!

I'd snapped two, then three, and was getting the hang of this when I heard the echo.

I tested it. Yep, there was no doubt. Each time *I* snapped a branch, something *else* in the forest was snapping something just out of sight.

Surely that wasn't normal forest animal behavior?

I clutched my bundle of sticks. Would it be enough? Should I head back to the cabin?

Nonsense. Nothing was going to run me out of the forest.

I walked back to the edge of the trees again, though—better safe than sorry, in this case. I looked for more fallen trees there, keeping one eye on my sunlit surroundings. But I never *saw* anything. Just leaves on the ground, the occasional thorny bush, tree trunks . . .

I'd wrestled a particularly thick tree branch off of the forest floor, and was feeling very proud of myself, when something just behind me snorted.

As I've said before, I don't *hop.*

I did, however, shriek. I managed to keep hold of my

sticks—just barely. Again I whirled around, magic reaching out through the trees. But nothing was there—how was nothing there? I'd heard it right behind me!

Something *whooshed* overhead, and I was officially done with being in the woods. Pride and stubbornness be cursed!

I clutched my sticks to my chest and began walking, *very* quickly, back to my cabin. Running was unwise, given how uneven the ground was. But I was almost there. Something was crunching behind me. The sun was setting already— when had that happened? My cabin wasn't too far away, but it was quickly becoming shadowed.

That was when I realized that my cabin apparently had a back door.

The thing behind me that I somehow couldn't sense but *knew* was there let out another snort, and I forewent being wise as well as being proud. I sprinted for safety.

Chapter Four: Coffee

Marcus

"I'm surprised at you," said Quinn Doyle. He leaned back in his chair, casually finishing off an almond croissant. "All night, staying down here in town? Then again, maybe I *shouldn't* be surprised. You do have a talent for holing yourself up."

"I do not," I said. My own croissant and coffee were untouched. I had shown up at Quinn's house at daybreak: not very polite nor very practical, as I knew he kept odd hours and slept late whenever he could. However, I hadn't been able to help myself. When he answered the door alert and awake, I'd thought I was in luck. But instead, all he'd done so far was insist we go out for breakfast and then persist in making fun of me.

"You do," he said, with confidence. "How many times have I seen you since summer?"

"I haven't been doing much business," I protested.

"You're making my point," Quinn returned. Then he settled his chair back on all four legs and leaned over the table, smiling at me. "But you didn't have to wait for business to come by, you know."

"I was planning to come by when I knew you were leaving," I said, rather stiffly.

"Ah, yes, your contacts." Quinn settled back again, his smile becoming thoughtful. "I still find it hard to believe you have such a network, and yet you do not *do* anything with it."

I dropped my gaze and poked at my croissant. Quinn Doyle was someone whose opinion I greatly respected. This was not a common occurrence. He'd lived in Helenia for several years, and had built himself a practice as a consulting detective. When buyers would contact me looking for ancient artifacts, I would often ask him to look into them. Despite the rumors to the contrary, I took pains to make sure my business—such as it was—operated for the general good.

Quinn himself was a young man, pale-skinned and dark-haired, with gray eyes which often seemed to be laughing. Though his taste in clothes was old-fashioned for the time, running to button-down shirts and tailored vests, he was invariably well-informed and could disguise himself with ease. Sometimes he seemed so very much younger than I, full of curiosity and energy. Sometimes, he seemed far older, old enough to scold me for something I'd done—or neglected to do.

"Eat it, don't poke at it," he told me, when I did not speak. "Even *you* need to look after yourself, you know. Especially if you think you're in for another epic showdown."

Quinn, in his capacity as detective—and as my friend—had

been involved in Sakura and her friends' investigation as well. He'd decided shortly after that he would leave Helenia, but had yet to go. The thought occurred to me now, as he watched me slice a piece of croissant and eat it with knife and fork, that perhaps he had been waiting for this. For me. I glanced up to meet his gaze. "Do you think such a thing is likely?"

"Not as much as you do."

I swallowed. "In any case, the point is that I won't be involved. But if you—"

"Hold on," Quinn interrupted with ease. We sat at the front window of a café just off main street Helenia—far more his environment than mine. Even surrounded by tourists and diners, he was relaxed. We'd been seated here long enough that the café had filled up, and the street outside was busy with shoppers. "Run it by me again," he insisted. "Why aren't you involved?"

"She doesn't need me to be," I said, hiding my face in my coffee cup. The coffee itself was terrible. Perhaps because I had let it sit untasted for so long.

"I got the impression last summer that she might want you to be," Quinn said, his gaze steady on me no matter how much I attempted to hide.

"She said things have changed," I replied.

Quinn gave me one of those skeptical looks, at which he is particularly skilled. His dark brows came together in the middle, and his lips were pursed.

"I didn't ask her to explain. And I don't want you to either," I went on hastily. One can never be too certain with a detective. "I just thought perhaps it would be best if you . . . took a look into this ghost business."

"Ghost business," Quinn repeated, still skeptical.

29

"If she wanted you to," I added.

"Right. Never mind the fact that *you* are the one with the power to—"

"Not here," I interrupted, glancing around anxiously. After centuries of living, it wasn't like me to be so self-conscious. Perhaps I *had* been too reclusive in the past few months. Nevertheless, I enjoyed the measure of anonymity which my reputation in Helenia granted me. The rumors were so exaggerated that they obscured me and my actual abilities in uncertainty. If asked, every single person in the café would report a different version of my "crimes," and give a different description of my supposed appearance.

"Very well." Quinn's face remained vaguely amused. "How do you propose we ask her permission for the 'ghost business' investigation, then?"

I hadn't thought that far ahead. I possessed the ability to transport myself and Quinn to the resort, of course, but I did not believe it was ethically sound to do so uninvited. Waiting for her yesterday had been an imposition as it was. But I had been hopeful then.

"Hmmm." Quinn smiled. Though I do, in fact, cloak my appearance, and have been told that my expressions rarely vary, Quinn was one of those who was sharp-eyed enough— and familiar enough—to follow my unspoken thoughts. "I thought as much. You don't want to go see her yourself. What if *she* came to see you?"

"What?" The pastry I'd swallowed dissolved into butterflies at the thought.

"Or if, for example, she *happened* to see you while on her way to see something else. Like coffee," Quinn suggested.

He was the one seated with the clearer view of the window,

and there was only one reason he would be suggesting such a thing. In fact—I realized in an instant—this must have been the reason he insisted upon the café nearest the gondola station in the first place. I rose, but was unable to speak before he put out his hand.

"Don't run off," he said. "It's going to be fine. I'll do the talking."

"But—"

"Stay. Consider it a personal favor. You owe me after neglecting me for months," Quinn declared, standing as the force of his suggestion guided me to sit once more. I remained there, staring at the half croissant left on my plate, as he hailed someone coming in the front door.

"Saki, over here! Remember me? Ha! Come and sit with us after you order. This place is always packed!"

Saki. Her nickname. He said it so easily. Like everything else. The lightness and familiarity of it filled me with a longing I'd never felt before, in my long life. Even after she'd collected her order and joined us at our little table, I had barely regained control of myself. I tucked my hands discreetly under the table.

Her blue-eyed gaze lingered on me a moment, but I could not tell what she was thinking. At last she turned to look at Quinn, her expression relaxing into a crooked smile. "Fancy meeting you here."

"Fancy indeed," he replied solemnly, before breaking into a similar grin. "But I'm afraid you'll find that the fare is anything but. This place is mostly packed with tourists who don't know any better."

Sakura sipped at her cup, a confection of milky coffee and whipped cream, and set it back down before making a face,

31

sharing her impression with us. "I see what you mean." She tried her muffin next, which seemed to be more palatable.

"Of course, it must be near impossible to travel to other cafes, given the excellence of the Pomegranate back home." Quinn was watching me, not her, as he said it. He saw what he wanted, no doubt: I startled. I knew Sakura owned her own cafe, but I had not realized this was its name.

But Sakura herself simply yawned before taking another large bite of her muffin and declaring, "It's too early in the morning for flattery. What are you two doing here? Is this an ambush?"

She glanced at me again. My face flushed, and I looked out the window.

"Purely a friendly coincidence, at the moment." Quinn rocked back in his chair, looking over her. She was as flawlessly put-together as always. The scarlet ribbon in her hair matched her dress perfectly, and its overall top over a close-fitting soft white sweater and white petticoats was entirely appropriate for the chilly morning. Her appetite was fine: the muffin was already nearly gone. What Quinn hoped to see, I couldn't imagine. He went on, "How's the new place?"

"Actually . . ." I could feel her gaze pulling back to me, and I met her eyes, alarmed to see a flicker of concern there.

"What happened?" I asked her.

"Nothing exactly." Sakura contemplated her empty plate, then looked up with a self-deprecating smile tugging at her lips. "Well, I made an utter fool of myself, is all. I'm not sure there was anything there. But I thought I heard—noises. In the woods. I don't suppose you two know if that fits with the rumors?"

"Until recently, the only rumors I'd heard were ones about

a monster in the lake," Said Quinn. "I never heard of it going into the woods before. Frankly, I always thought it was a children's tale. That monster's supposed to grant wishes, not go around making noises. What did you hear?"

"Why were you in the woods?" I asked.

She focused on me. "Did you think I ought to go back to my cabin and stay there quietly until called for again?"

I faltered. That was assuredly *not* what I had thought, and yet—I could offer no defense. "I—I only thought—it could be dangerous."

"We've been over that," she retorted, heat creeping into her voice. "I'm not worried about dangerous."

And yet, once again, she hadn't used magic since seeing us—not even to hold her coffee aloft as she navigated the crowded cafe.

I didn't say that, though. Just filed it away, confused. "Yes, but—"

Quinn broke in, addressing himself to Sakura. "You're being a bit hard on him, don't you think?"

She sighed as she slumped in her chair. "Probably. I'm sorry, Marcus." The emotion of hearing her speak so familiarly rendered me speechless. I could only nod as she went on, "I had a rough night, I can admit. Like I said, I'm not worried exactly, but—I want to know what's going on. The sooner I figure it out, the sooner I can . . ."

"Yes, do tell," Quinn suggested. "What *will* you do?"

"I haven't decided yet," she said, recovering herself. "And to that end, more information would help. So. What do you know?"

"Aside from the basic legends of wish-granting lake dwellers and gods on the mountaintop, nothing in particular—yet," Quinn told her lightly. "We just happened to be talking about it, though, didn't we, Marcus?"

I frowned at him.

She glanced at me, opened her mouth as though to say something, then thought better of it. Her gaze fell to the rest of my croissant.

Without thinking, I offered her the plate.

Her eyes flicked back up to mine, curious. I shrugged.

She smiled at me sweetly, a gesture of thanks, and then picked up the croissant and began eating again.

Quinn let his smug smile linger on me, letting me know he'd been watching. I turned resolutely to the window again.

"If you came to town because you'd like to hire the illustrious services of Helenia's premier consulting detective," Quinn said airily, as though nothing had occurred, "you're in luck. I happen to be free at the moment."

"Oh, do you?" Sakura looked amused, and rather suspicious—as well she should. "Perhaps you could take him a message, then."

"One point to you," Quinn declared, laughing, acknowledging the joke at his own expense.

Sakura grinned. "Actually, I came to town to get some food. I hadn't realized before I went up there that the ice box would be empty. And—maybe some curtains."

Quinn's gaze on me was speculative. "Marcus could carry—"

"I have an appointment," I interrupted.

For a split second—did her gaze fall?

But the moment was gone. She turned to Quinn. "Well, if you're up for it, I suppose I could give you a ride up to the resort, give you the tour, and see what you think. But the gondola won't take general public up there, so you'll have to wait for me to do some shopping first."

"I can do more than that. I can guide you through the market," he promised.

She laughed. "As long as the shops you suggest are better than this one."

"I'll do my best."

I had gone very still. Forgotten. An easy feat, for someone with a slippery relationship to time.

But she pulled me back. As they rose, she set her hand on my arm. Only for a moment—for the briefest moment. Her fingertips were light and warm. "You can come by if you remember anything," she said.

As she left, I sighed, very softly.

The trouble was that I remembered *everything*.

THE HERMETIC HERALD

Local Detective Strikes Again!
Quinn Doyle was instrumental in the recovery of local university student, says Officer Herakles. Many suspected the student, 21, had been lured into the Underworld after their partner suddenly passed away... [cont. pg 3]

Town Hall Says: New Fines for Businesses That Don't Shovel Snow
Page 2

Is Spring Coming? Forecast Grim

Development in the Business World: Vera Speaks Out

Chapter Five: Capture

✦⁘✦

Sakura

Listen, I know what you're thinking.

Well—if you're thinking, *how did she survive the terrifying snorting in the woods,* we're not talking about that. Let's just say it was a sleepless, sheepish kind of night.

Now, if you're thinking, *why invite that poor man to your cabin when you're clearly trying to avoid him (though not succeeding at it), that* I can understand.

The answer is, there's a flaw in your logic, and the flaw is me. I'd spent all night (all the bits where I wasn't hearing snaps and scratches in the walls and stomps in the woods outside) reminding myself that I'm pretty much a one-person kind of gal, and that *one person* is me.

But it wasn't fitting quite right.

The truth is I love *love,* and I used to adore setting all my

37

friends up. But since I'd let everybody in Belville down, and sort of run off to come to Helenia, and used this silly spa as a cowardly excuse to return to the scene of my crime and yet *still* not proven capable of dealing with my feelings like a mature adult, I wasn't feeling too confident about love. Least of all, with a man so sincere and gentle. Not that I would try to match him with someone else. Because yes, alright. Basically, I've been head over heels for him since the day we met.

Gods, I love that man. And I am *not* going to let him get stuck with me.

But I'm also not going to resist the urge to invite him over? He just looked so distant, I couldn't stand it.

Enough said. I let Quinn distract me for a little while with his chatter about Helenia and which shops to go to, which to avoid. We went to a market of covered stalls set just a few blocks of main street, the sort of place where locals outnumbered tourists—a rarity in Helenia. I still wasn't letting myself think of this as anything long term. I promised myself I wasn't filing away everything he told me.

But I did purchase several sets of curtains with cheerful yellow flowers sewn all over them. They came from a stall on the street corner bursting with all kinds of fabrics, sold by a gnome who reminded me of a friend back in Belville. I made Quinn wait while I went back and also bought a set of matching tea towels, a pair of rose-colored bath sheets, some fresh soft bed sheets, and a deep blue quilt patterned with stars. It was *cold* on the mountain, after all, even though I had managed the fireplace quite well.

Quinn carried the tower of folded linens with good humor. He obviously had some kind of plot up his sleeve. I knew that he was a good friend of Marcus's, and I knew, too, that whatever Quinn was plotting was probably on Marcus's behalf, but it couldn't be something Marcus had asked for. Marcus might have asked him to investigate, but I doubted he'd have done anything more. Therefore, I didn't feel a bit remorseful about giving Quinn a hard time.

Once I'd filled the bag on my arm with soaps, local cheeses, bread, eggs, and winter veggies—all the essentials—I let him lead the way back to the gondola. We passed right by an antiques shop with a set of lovely tea pots and charmingly mismatched china cups in the window . . . but I resolutely carried on. Besides, we had enough to carry already.

Quinn waited until we were alone at the resort, the gondola driver cheerfully returning to tourists and cliff carvings, before saying anything important. At least he was discreet that way—unlike Bertram.

Who had yet to make any kind of appearance, come to think of it . . .

But I marked this down as some good luck, and focused on the present. Quinn stood on the station platform, looking out at the lake. It was perfectly still—the reflected sky was a perfect copy, just as real as the *real* one. But the mountain peak, though visible in real life, was hidden away in the lake.

"So all they managed to finish so far is the station?" Quinn asked, looking around keenly.

I shifted the bag of food in my arms. Silly as it sounds, I'm not really used to *carrying* things. But even though he wasn't Marcus, and he was probably plotting something annoying, I didn't want to risk magic around anybody. "I guess so? That's all Bertram got out yesterday, before Marcus scared him. Well, actually, *I* scared him. He'd been talking my ear off the whole ride up about bringing machinery up here to create 'perfection,' and as soon as I saw this place, I couldn't stand the thought of him and his buddies *developing* it."

"Marcus did mention he came up to meet you." Quinn gave me a searching look, and I ignored it. He went on, "I have to admit, I'm glad to hear you say that. That's how most residents in Helenia feel—not that they have any particular say in what you do, since the land is legally yours. Including, I understand, the mountain peak itself?"

"Yes, but I didn't ask him how much *around* it is," I noted, frowning to myself. I was thinking of those woods. "I guess a map would be handy at some point. But for now, it's basically just what you see."

"And what a view!" Quinn smiled as he looked across the pool again.

Apparently, blankets and towels were a lot lighter than vegetables. Or people without magic just become used to holding things? Either way, I was done with it, myself, so I stepped down from the station and began walking to my cabin. Er, to *the* cabin. To the first in what was a row of four or five cabins that stretched out along the edge of the pool, actually.

"Have you been in those?" Quinn asked as he caught up with me. Curse him and his long legs! Was everyone in Helenia tall?

"I haven't," I admitted. "One was enough, yesterday. But I have a whole ring of keys."

"We can try them today, then," he decided. "If you're up for it?"

"That is the point of you investigating." I looked up at him, curious. "Do you actually expect to find anything? A ghost or some such thing? Or are you just here to cause trouble?"

"I thought I was here to carry towels," he replied. But I knew to wait him out. "Somebody will have told you that this place is supposed to hide a staircase that leads to the home of the gods? Yes. Did they also mention how many people have fallen to their deaths trying to find it, climbing all over the mountain?"

I bit my cheek. The idea was unfortunate, but not surprising. "No, that hadn't come up yet."

"Then there's the folk beliefs that this place is especially sacred to the goddess Diana, she of moonlit nights and remote forests, will turn those who offend her into cursed animals," Quinn added.

Remembering those snorts, I suppressed a shiver. "I'm aware of Diana, but not the finer points of her mythology."

"Why should you be," Quinn agreed. "Now, there's also a rumor or two around town that the surveyors for this very project unearthed some ancient tomb hidden in the mountain, and aroused a vengeful ghost."

"What?" I shook my head: trust Bertram not to bring *that* one up! "Is there any proof of any of these?"

"Of course not. That's the fun of rumors." Quinn beamed at me as we reached the porch, and he held back while I began the trial-and-error practice of unlocking the door. I really needed to mark the appropriate key somehow. As I went through the routine, he kept talking behind me. "One of the surveyors' secretaries swears that equipment was stolen, and that they heard 'monstrous' noises in the woods. But what that means is up for debate. A ghost might make noises just as well as a monster, of course, or some poor offender who was turned into one . . ."

41

"What kind of noises?" I asked, as the door finally opened.

"Rampaging footsteps, howls, the usual cries of distress," Quinn said. He followed me into the cabin and was clearly looking around with interest.

I did my best to focus on the kitchen and putting away my food, keeping my voice light. "Just the footsteps? Not—snapping or something like that?"

"I'm not privy to the finer details," he remarked. "Not yet, that is. You have to understand, I haven't been investigating the stories—just keeping an ear open to local gossip. You never know when you'll come across something useful. Marcus would be happy to provide you with any artifacts you might like to spruce this place up, you know. He has a very fine ever-burning cauldron, and a few protection spells . . ."

This non sequitur withered and died as I turned to glare over my shoulder at Quinn, who had remained in the living room. "I'm not moving in."

"Aren't you?" He asked, glancing innocently at the towels over his arm.

Curse him. To beat me at my own game! I sighed as I finished tucking away the cheeses and eggs. "Even if I was, I wouldn't take his relics from him."

"But that's the point, isn't it? He sells them. He likes helping a cause."

"I'm not a—" I stopped short. "Did you hear that?"

"I did," Quinn said, dropping his annoying arguments and setting the linens on the counter. "A scratching?"

I shushed him, and sure enough, the sound came again.

"I think it's coming from the bathroom," I whispered. "It's right on the other side of the wall from the sofa, back there."

"So the door there goes outside?" He was looking at the back door I'd discovered last night—discovered, burst through, realized was unlocked, then reinforced with several magical locks. It now looked like it might guard the entrance to a bank vault (if the vault was wooden and old and leaning slightly to one side).

I coughed a little. "Um, yeah, that door goes outside. I wouldn't worry about it."

Quinn glanced down at me. The scratching noise happened again. "What else has happened?"

"Something rifled through my tea," I admitted, still in a low whisper. I gestured to my precious tea tin at the end of the counter, which I'd found tipped over that morning.

"And that wasn't enough for you to use your magic on whatever it is?"

"I can't catch it," I retorted.

"You could try now. It sounds close."

"No! That's a terrible idea," I protested. "Can't you deduce what it is, or something?"

"Not without investigating," Quinn said. He rolled up his sleeves. Obviously, he was about to break into the bathroom. I didn't bother arguing further, but I did plan to follow—just not *too* closely, just in case.

I had to hand it to him: he knew how to walk quietly over the rough wood floors. That was no easy feat. The scratching came again, and it was making me more antsy every second. It was terribly hard not to use my magic, like forcing yourself to walk through the forest with your eyes closed. But I couldn't risk it going haywire.

Quinn paused at the bathroom door, sheltering under the spiral staircase that I'd fashioned from the old ladder the night before (I don't do ladders, but the cabin's lone bedroom was on the second floor—or rather, in the attic). The bathroom door was ever so slightly ajar, and the scratching was louder than ever. Quinn noticed the bucket I'd used to clean yesterday on the floor nearby, and silently lunged for it. I didn't understand this in the least. What was he going to do? Hit the ghost over the head with it?

He put one finger to his lips, then leapt into the bathroom bucket first.

There was a loud clatter, a scuffle, and then—a bleat.

A bleat?

I was just about to ask him what in *Beyond* he was doing when a small white form came barreling out of the bathroom. Neither it nor I had any time to think. It hit me square in the legs, and we both crashed to the floor.

And the next thing I knew, I was on my butt, eye to eye with a small, very confused-looking goat in my lap.

"Solved the case," Quinn declared as he emerged from the bathroom. But, with a rueful glance at the empty bucket in his hand, he added, "Didn't catch the culprit, though."

I sighed. "I think *I* did."

CLASSIFIEDS

Experienced secretary seeking new
employment. Adept in office spel
magic, and schedule managem
Contact Emmie Bea at 12

Ghost hunters for hi
Well-versed in po
and mor

Chapter Six: Up and Up

Marcus

I waited for a while after they left the cafe, collecting myself. Though I did not, strictly speaking, have an appointment to keep, I knew that if I lingered I might meet someone else. Someone else with a penchant for coffee and possibly running into Quinn.

And in the meantime, I could dwell in the memory of her touch . . .

"Pluto?" The voice pulled me back to the present.

I nodded as the young police officer sat beside me. "Officer Herakles."

"Not often I see you here," he said, coffee sloshing from the sides of his tall cup. The lapel of his blue uniform was crumpled, and there were ink stains on his large fingers—Herakles was part giant, and had to slide the table back to fit in the space Sakura had left. He did this, as I had seen him do everything, with the sort of gusto which did credit to his name.

It was one of the facets of life in Helenia which fascinated me. Though many of the deities and heroes of myth had long since moved on, either in this world or the next, people in Helenia continued to name their children after legendary figures. Herakles was currently my favorite.

If I could, indeed, be said to have favorites.

"Nothing wrong, is there? Seen Quinn?" he asked me cheerfully. "Just starting a shift, myself, and thought he might have a tip about this latest Town Hall business."

Business. A word, I reflected, which could have so many meanings.

"Quinn is consulting with Sakura, who has come to look over the property at Hideaway Lake," I told him.

"Oh. Oh, *I* see," said Herakles, with a wide, easy smile. "You wanted a word, did you? Make sure everything's on the up-and-up?"

I hesitated. "In a purely unofficial capacity."

"I get it," the officer assured me. "You're worried. I would be too. The whole thing is a head-scratcher. Would've thought it was just a trap, myself. But don't worry! The judge took care of all that. I was at the trial, watching, you see. There were all sorts of requirements. Chief says it was unusual they got to bequeath the property at all, but since it wasn't to a relative the judge didn't mind, and rumor is Town Hall doesn't want the responsibility. On account of all the monster-hunters and mountain expeditions and what have you."

"Hmmm." I was not surprised to hear that Helenia's government did not want the site.

"Too famous around here for its own good," Herakles observed, summing up the situation. "Needs someone strong-willed to look after it. I figured Sakura was a great choice. You don't think so?"

I watched him down his coffee. "She hasn't made up her mind."

"Takes time, I guess. If anything comes up up there, just let me know," Herakles offered. "But knowing you two, I'm sure you'll be fine. Tell her I said hey, alright? And tell Quinn I want to see him, too!"

The officer was gone, and in his wake I mused. He clearly assumed Sakura and I were close. It was a new but not unpleasant feeling—or it might be, if only it were true.

This time, however, I did not give myself the chance to dwell. I knew where I wanted to go next.

Business in Helenia was inevitably a personal affair. In a city with so much history, every venture had a legacy, every avenue had been explored. The most powerful meetings were the ones in home offices behind gated courtyards. Though the head of Minotaur Enterprises herself had been exiled from Helenia for her role in the summer's crimes, I knew that her home had not yet been sold, and that it must be the center of operations for her remaining assistants as they tied up the loose ends.

I appeared on a side street at the eastern edge of town. To my back was the harbor view. In front of me, a mansion, its front door mere steps from the street. Modern construction: a conviction that money is only as good as the amount of jealousy it provokes. The windows were wide and glittering, the statues flanking the door caked in gold, but the protection spells woven into the plaster walls were lacking.

Nevertheless I dealt politely with the staff and the remaining secretary, as is my habit. They had no share in their employer's guilt. Bertram Paige, however, might be another matter.

I was let in to see him in his former boss's office, a room wide enough to house a home, full of gilded edges and lined with windows overlooking a terrace decorated with imported plants.

When he looked up to see me standing there, his expression changed from annoyance to fear.

"I *told* you, I don't want to be—oh—it's you. Why are you here?"

I tilted my head to one side. His tone was neither polite nor conciliatory. There were heavy circles under his eyes. "I have business to discuss with you."

"Yesterday you said the same thing about Sakura." Bertram pulled a clipboard off the desk, using it to shield his chest. His gaze darted around me, as though she might appear. "Did she come too? I was planning to see her later today—I just had some things to go over, I thought she'd like time to settle in—"

I wasn't particularly impressed by his plans for the day, and he seemed to sense as much, because his words faded. I cleared my throat. "What I have to say today is for you, Bertram."

While I'd been holed up in my house overnight, as Quinn put it, I'd made a point to go through my records. I keep notes of every sale I make—even the ones that fall through. There are so many people in Helenia these days, too many for me to remember everything I'd like to. But now I remembered everything about my previous encounter with this particular young man.

"I'm only following instructions," he protested. "To the letter. You can read them yourself."

"Yes," I agreed, "I would like to do so. Please have a copy made for me."

His knuckles on his clipboard were white. More than likely, he had not expected me to call that bluff. He did business the same way his predecessor had: more show than substance. But unlike her, he didn't have the fortune and prestige of a successful string of bakeries and other ventures behind him.

"Well—I'd be glad to of course—but I'm not sure the lawyers would like it," he said.

"Aren't you?"

I watched him calmly. Perhaps it's the rumors; perhaps it's the magic I've become accustomed to wearing; but in any case, I find that my presence is often enough to put pressure on those who would otherwise be uncooperative. It's a power that I'm not averse to using in some instances.

Bertram was growing smaller behind his desk. He had no way of knowing that I had dealt with several of the lawyers handling Minotaur Enterprises personally, nor that I was on friendly terms with Officer Herakles. But he knew that his boss had sent him to me: not for an ancient urn or good luck charm, but for one of the tools I used myself, the key that allowed me to travel from one place to any other in the blink of an eye. A key I kept on my person at all times. Teleportation artifacts were rare, and mine was not for sale. Bertram had watched as I refused every exorbitant offer. Sometimes I think that to refuse money scares the business-minded even more than divine power does.

"Well," he said, drawing out the word, "I suppose in this

case . . . since you're a friend of Sakura's . . ."

Fortunately, he was rifling through the drawers of the desk, and didn't see my expression flicker.

He drew a sheaf of legal papers from a drawer. "I can ask the secretary . . . She's very busy at the moment—we're all very busy. There's so much to get settled, I'm sure you understand. We can have it sent to you in a few days . . ."

"I'm sure you are very busy," I echoed. There had been no visitors in the house aside from myself, and the secretary—a pleasant fairy who introduced herself as "Emmie!"—had not even bothered to check a calendar before ushering me to this office. Bertram wanted to put me off, and I would not have it. "I will wait on this spot until the copy is made."

"You can't just stand in my office." Bertram looked, not exasperated, but scared.

As well he should be, making such claims. I held his gaze. "*Your* office?"

"Well—just for now—just while we close things up," he muttered. "I'll go get that copy for you."

"Bertram." The young man stopped in his tracks before he got to the door. "Please ask Emmie to handle it, provided she has the time. You, remain here with me. There is one other thing I would like to say to you."

He was clutching the papers so tightly that Emmie had to smooth them out. But she did accept the task cheerfully and strode off to perform her spell, leaving her fellow employee with me.

I strode toward him, one step at a time. "Bertram Paige," I said quietly. "Is there anything else—anything not in those documents—that you would like to tell me about this resort, and its exchange?"

He quivered but he held his ground. "No. You'll—you'll read all about it. That's all there is."

"I see." I watched him. There was something—a flicker of something unexpected in his eyes. Perhaps he had more backbone than his behavior up to this point had suggested. Perhaps in my concern, I was pushing him too far. I relented, stopping a few steps from him, returning my voice to its usual pitch. "I appreciate that there are proper ways to do things, particularly in business. It is not my habit to bully those with work to do, Bertram, but I hope that you can appreciate my interest in this matter. Should my . . . friend find herself in any danger, I will cease to consider this a matter of business. Do I make myself clear?"

Bertram broke eye contact for just a moment. He shut the door beside him and turned back to me. "Is it true you're a god?"

A question many acquaintances inevitably asked, but not one I had anticipated in this circumstance. After a moment's hesitation, I chose my answer. "What I am at present is nothing compared to what I will be capable of if this goes poorly."

"I just asked because maybe you could convince her." Bertram took two quick steps forward, surprising me once more, though I held still. "If you know her, you must have realized how stubborn Sakura is. I learned it myself yesterday. I thought I could convince her just with the proper reports, like you said. But she's not going to listen to me—I see that now. Maybe she'll listen to *you*. Maybe *you* can convince her—it's not safe for her to stay."

To hear him say her name was, I realized, extremely unpleasant. But I controlled myself. "Why not?"

"Everyone who finished Phase One came back saying the project is haunted," Bertram whispered.

I crossed my arms. "Explain."

"That's just it! They wouldn't say. But we did almost lose someone. One of the workers. At night, the ones who stayed to keep watch said that ghostly lights were flying over the pool. She went out to investigate them, and she was lured away. They found her the next morning with her magitech torch still on, unconscious at the edge of the woods. It got so bad no one would stay overnight. We barely got the station finished. Everyone who went up there came back saying that it's a holy site and it's not supposed to be disturbed, and that if we go on, we'll keep paying the price."

I nodded to the desk. "Get a piece of paper. Write down her name and occupation, as well as the name of the construction companies and suppliers you've dealt with so far. Please."

Bertram moved as if to do so, but hesitated. "But if you can just convince Sakura of the danger . . ."

"She deserves the full picture," I said. "Are such details not part of your work?"

"Of course." He crossed to his desk and began scribbling the information on his clipboard. As he was finishing, Emmie knocked and opened the door, handing the copied file to me with a smile on her face. The rose gold sparkle of her magic was still rising from the copied ink.

"Thank you," I said, accepting the papers with a nod. I took Bertram's note as well, and held his gaze one more time. "Is there anything else?"

He glanced at the papers, then at me. "No. I hope you have better luck than I did."

His voice sounded unusually sincere. I mused on it as I took my leave, finding my way out of the newly made mansion with my prize tucked under my arm.

When I got to the street, I slipped from that neighborhood and into my own garden. It was a simple feat, one I performed without thinking. I was still mulling over what Bertram had to say. He was not a person I admired, but it seemed he might have reason to worry. Should it become public that his previous boss's pet project was "haunted," he may find it difficult to find further employment in Helenia. Though the city was a modern one, it was also superstitious.

I considered my newly-acquired paperwork. I would take it to Sakura, of course—but she would be busy with Quinn just then, and . . .

And I *am* a terrible coward at heart. Even my lovely garden was cold comfort. A dark snake fled the sunny stones as I walked down the path, and I felt too much kinship with the creature. The stone guard dog keeping watch in front of my door wagged her tail at me, though; she loved me still, despite my weaknesses.

My house was quiet, a refuge. I moved through it until I reached the library, and there I lost myself in considering the documents Bertram had given me.

In doing so, I lost track of time—as often happens. It was dark outside before I looked up. It took me a moment to realize what had drawn my attention: a bell on the mantelpiece—a bell whose counterpart I had long ago given to Quinn.

GUIDELINES FOR GHOST MEDIATORS

HAUNTING CATEGORIES:

1. MINOR / COLD SPOTS AND NOISES
2. CONFIRMED / MULITPLE SIGHTINGS
3. SERIOUS / OBJECT MANIPULATION
4. MAJOR / INTENT TO SCARE
5. DANGEROUS / CONFIRMED HARM

Chapter Seven: Collision

Sakura

For the second evening in a row, I was running wildly through the forest. This time I didn't have an armful of sticks, which was good, but it was pitch dark outside, which was *not* good. Quinn was a few steps ahead of me and I still didn't dare draw on my magic. I just put my head down and did my best to keep my balance over the uneven ground.

Which worked fine until I ran right into Marcus.

Let's not pretend I didn't know exactly who it was, okay? I knew very well. Immediately. Only one person in my life wears black buttoned shirts and smells like cedar smoke. Only one person in my life is immovable enough to not only stand in someone's way, but then also refuse to even step backward when run into. His arms surrounded my shoulders at once, and he was so solid and gentle I could have cried. I tucked my head into his chest and wrapped my arms around his back and clung to him like a barnacle.

A barnacle with a recently-adopted goat, a horrible detective, and a woods monster to worry about.

"Glad to see you're thinking of *me!*" said terrible detective yelled at us.

"What is the danger?" Marcus asked me.

At that, I knew I had to get a grip on the situation. Not a physical one—my hands were still twisted in Marcus's shirt—but someone needed to call the shots. I lifted my head. "We saw things chasing us. We caught a goat this morning but that isn't it now. We have to stay together. Quinn, get back here!"

"I'm the one who rang the bell," the detective grumbled, his voice growing louder as he jogged back to us through the dark. "You should have caught *me*."

"You probably set the whole thing up," I protested on Marcus's behalf.

Something behind us *yowled.*

Marcus's hands on my shoulders tightened, his chest rising as his breath quickened. "That does not sound like a set up," he observed.

I agreed with him, and the last thing I wanted him to do was let go, but I had an idea, which was more than either of the pair of them could say, apparently. "Marcus, you can shield us," I reminded him. "If you put up a shield, and we all stand back to back, maybe we can see what it is. And maybe—catch our breath and figure out where we are."

Before I'd finished talking, he conjured up a bubble around us, a shimmer of silver energy that came out of the ground and closed securely over our heads. Reluctantly, I slipped my arms from him, and turned to look out at the woods around us. He remained right next to me, his arm pressing into my side, as if reassuring himself I was there.

Unfortunately, so did the detective. He took his place at my other side, grumbling again. "Trust a shadow witch to think we should *see* the scary monster and not just, I don't know, *go inside*."

"You're the one who's supposed to be investigating," I retorted.

"Can someone tell me, calmly, what has happened?" Marcus's voice sounded strained. "Why do you two not know where you are?"

My new goat bleated. Probably annoyed at being in Quinn's arms. Rightly so.

"And why have you got a goat?" Marcus added.

Poor man.

"Give me Lulu," I demanded. Quinn handed her over. I was freezing now without Marcus's arms around me, and still half tempted to kick Quinn out of our bubble of protection—something I could hardly do if he had my new pet with him. I snuggled the little white goat into my chest, keeping my eyes on the woods as I told Marcus, "She came with the property. She was in my house, I mean, she was in the cabin all last night keeping me up. I kept scanning for what was making noise, but I was looking for *humanoid* things, or taller things at least, so I never caught her! Then she wouldn't go into the forest by herself, which I think was a good idea on her part because she can't possibly be wild—"

"There *are* wild goats in this area," Quinn interrupted from over my right shoulder. "Tell her, Marcus. Maybe she'll listen to you!"

"—and there's something lots worse than goats out there!" I concluded.

Lulu bleated again, this time obviously in agreement with me.

For a moment we stared into the woods. It was so dark, even with the faint light of the protection spell, that only tree trunks like ghostly bones were visible amid the gloom. Twigs snapped. I took a tiny step closer to Marcus.

"I still don't understand," he said. His hand found my elbow, and Lulu snuffled at his fingers. The fact that she was so content to be held only proved my point. Quinn was a heartless detective for ever suggesting leaving her out in the woods.

"For the record, I didn't say we should just leave the goat out here," he piped up.

I was riled up, and I snapped back. "You wanted to use her to lure out the monster!"

"I did not! Marcus, please. You know I wouldn't do such a thing. I just *said* that as long as you were determined to bring her—"

"If we'd have left her, she'd have got into my tea again!" Obviously.

A huge shadow whooshed overhead and between the tree trunks before I could see what it was.

"Please," Marcus said. "One at a time."

"Make Quinn do it," I said irritably. "He thinks he's the rational one."

"Quinn," Marcus sighed, "what have you done?"

"I didn't do anything," Quinn protested. Lamely. "I carried towels. I rode the gondola. I looked at the view. When Sakura let me into the first cabin, which she has taken possession

59

of—whether she admits it or not—"

"No editorializing!" I suggested. Something whooshed overhead again, and I added, "Maybe we should lower our voices."

"Because we *want* to lure this thing out?" The supposed detective asked.

I wanted to glare at him, but I didn't dare stop watching the woods. "Well, as long as we're *here!*"

"When you went into the cabin, *what?*" Marcus broke in.

"When Sakura let me into the cabin she's definitely not taken up residence in, we both heard scratching noises and I subsequently caught a goat," Quinn replied.

"Hey! *I* caught her!" I corrected. I did my best to keep my voice low, but Lulu bleated loudly in agreement. Something flickered behind the tree trunk in front of me.

"We caught a goat," Quinn continued. "It had apparently made itself at home in the cabin. Sakura asked me what I thought it was doing here, and if it had been left by one of the workers, to which I said—"

"Is all of this detail necessary?" Marcus asked.

"You'll see why," I told him, straining my eyes to see another flicker.

"To which I said, miniature goats are fairly common in the forests on the island, though they usually have brown or tan coats, not white. Sakura pointed out that the goat appears house-broken, though I still consider that an unlikely coincidence, and proceeded to name the goat Lulu. I knew then that she wasn't going to try to re-home it—"

"Editorializing!" I whispered.

"My apologies. Did anyone else see that light? Just there." Quinn pointed slightly to his left, and both Marcus and I leaned over his shoulders to watch, waiting to see if anything appeared again. Lulu shuffled in my arms. Quinn went on, in a very quiet, hoarse voice, "I also knew that 'baby goats,' as they are sometimes called, though they are, in fact, adults, are sometimes kept as pets. But to do so requires some equipment, namely food and water bowls, bedding, and most especially, a *leash*."

"She's been fine, stop complaining," I told him. "There! I think I saw a flicker again."

Marcus's hand on my elbow tightened, and my heart skipped a beat. "I was told this is necessary?" he prompted.

"Yes, *because*," Quinn whispered, as we all stared hard at a tree some distance away, "I suggested that if the goat had been abandoned, its owner had most likely lived in one of the other worker's cabins, and that we could test this theory by searching each one for evidence of goat habitation."

I would have scoffed, but this time I didn't just see a flicker, I saw an actual light. Hovering off the ground, eye level for me, as big as Lulu's head. I nudged Quinn and Marcus.

"Sakura insisted on bringing the goat to see if it recognized anything," Quinn went on, his voice barely louder than breathing as we all leaned in. "Which was, as I informed her at the time, preposterous, because how would you know? We spent all afternoon searching the remaining cabins, and Miss *Lulu* never developed a capacity for speech. By the time we were done, we *should* have returned to the first cabin to eat, but then Sakura said—"

"I didn't say!" I hissed. The light wobbled between two trees, blinking out and then bobbing back into view. Marcus had moved his hand to my shoulder, and it was only the tightness of his grip keeping me still.

61

"*Sakura said* she needed more firewood, and I wanted to investigate anyway, so why not go into the woods?" Quinn editorialized from between clenched teeth. "Never mind the fact that neither of us had a map or compass, nor any kind of prepared location spell. May I remind you that I have never been to these woods before?"

"That's it? You've been lost since sundown?" Marcus murmured, his eyes still on the light. By now we were all watching it fully. Any ideas about the security of standing back-to-back were long forgotten.

"It's more than that," Quinn admitted quietly.

I knew then that he was going to be too much of a wimp to say it. So I jumped in. "*Quinn said* some monsters are known to prefer goats! And that Diana is known to have favored deer, which are very like goats, if you squint a little, and who *knows* how good this monster's eyesight is. And then while he kept going on and being mean about it, Lulu got scared and ran away, and we had to chase her all the way back to the reflecting pool, but on the mountain side, and Quinn eventually grabbed Lulu but then he tripped and fell over and this humongous shadow popped out of the trees and howled at them, and then we all had to run *back* into the woods and that's when he *finally* called you!"

Of course, I hadn't realized that Quinn *could* get in contact with Marcus like that, not on the fly. But that had definitely been his one good idea of the day. Marcus was much better than Quinn to have in a situation like this. Probably because Quinn had already annoyed me by having schemes and suggesting we sacrifice my goat to an ancient moon deity, but even more so because Marcus was incredibly careful. I realized then, standing separated by only a layer of magic and a few yards from a floating light in the woods, that I had placed a *lot* of trust in Marcus, and I didn't even regret it.

"This isn't the thing that chased you, then?" he asked after a moment.

"No," said Quinn, *quite* irritably, "and I've seen about as much of it as I need to. It's a ball of light, it's hovering. Do we really need to keep standing out here?"

"So much for investigating! Don't you want to know what it is and what it wants?"

"It could just be a phosphorescent sphere of moss in the wind, for all we know!" Quinn hissed back. "I say we either go and face it up close, or we turn around and go home!"

That was a surprise. I thought *I* was the reckless one! The way he phrased it, too—that *face it* went straight through my heart, and I didn't bother thinking about why. I knew.

"Okay," I said at once. "Let's go. Marcus, your shield can move with us, right?"

"I didn't mean that we *all* should shuffle forward like a blob," Quinn complained. "At this rate we're going to get stuck between tree trunks or worse, we'll—"

The light rose in the air, as though it had noticed us approaching, then shivered and winked out.

"—scare it."

you're invited!

Please join us to celebrate the love of Cinnabar (aka Red!) and Luca as they speak their vows with a special magical display!

Chapter Eight: Discussion

❦

Marcus

In the end, there was nothing to be done. Sakura asked me to bring the three of them—herself, Quinn, and the goat, Lulu—back to her chosen cabin. In the wake of disappointment, she and Quinn managed to reconcile, if tenuously. Sakura offered us a late meal, and we stood in her small kitchen drinking cocoa and eating toasted sandwiches.

It was not, perhaps, as late as it felt. But Quinn took his leave early. I didn't mind this; there were a number of things weighing on my mind which I thought it better to address with Sakura alone.

Her goatling had curled up on the couch near the hearth. The firelight and several strategically-placed candles provided our only light. As she saw Quinn out, I gathered our cups and plates and placed them in the sink. When she returned to the kitchen, she shooed me away.

I lingered beside the old dining table. "Sakura," I began, "perhaps Quinn is unaware of the particulars, because he does not deal with hauntings, as a general rule. But nevertheless the two of you *did* see something tonight, something with presumed malicious intent."

She kept her gaze on the water running in the sink. "The thing that jumped out at him and Lulu. If you think it means I'll leave—"

"That is not what I think," I said gently when her voice broke off, leaving the threat sharp in the air. "What I *know* is that the haunting of this resort is now classifiable as a category four."

"It's not a resort," she said on impulse. Then she lifted her head to look at me. "What do you mean?"

"A category four haunting indicates danger, whether physical or metaphysical, to the living persons involved. As such, the rules when dealing with such a haunting are more strict. A professional must be involved. If no resolution is found in three days, more assistance must be sought. And no living person is to be left at the site alone."

Her hands wavered over the sink, pale in the reflected glow from the glass windowpanes. "Should I even ask? Are *you* a professional?"

"I do not often serve in that capacity these days, but nonetheless, I am competent enough." I inclined my head. "If it is acceptable to you, I will stay in one of the empty cabins until this matter is resolved."

For a moment, she looked lighter, sweeter—amused. It was a look I loved seeing on her face. Then she shrugged it off and returned to her work. "If that's what you need to do, then it's fine. But I warn you, they're not the most hospitable of places, these cabins."

"You've done well in one night with yours," I observed. I glanced once more at the curtains framing her reflection, the snoring Lulu by the fire. Then I refocused on her face. "Sakura. There is something else. I can see that you have protected this space." Her distinctive black sparkles were in every corner, etched into the floorboards. She must have been frightened indeed last night to imbue her magic so deeply in the place so soon, and my heart ached for her, but there was more work to be done. "Nevertheless, the nature of this haunting means that you must be protected when you are *outside* of this cabin, too. Perhaps—I could offer you—if you wished—"

My words always fail me at the most important moments. She turned off the water and looked up at me.

"Are you going to ask me why?" she said.

"I was only—going to offer an amulet you could wear, if you like," I said, struggling to keep my gaze on her blue eyes. The emotion in them made it hard to think.

"You're not going to ask me why I won't use my magic around people." She turned her face back down to the sink, staring but not seeing.

I almost moved to her then, but stopped myself just in time. "I hope it is not because of me, or what happened over the summer," I confessed, my voice low.

She shook her head. Her eyes, her fingers on the edge of the sink squeezed shut. Her jaw clenched even as she managed to say, "It's not because of you."

"Then I am relieved, but I am still concerned."

Her control broke then. Her head slipped lower, her hair

swinging forward to hide her eyes as she cried over the sink. I could no longer hold myself back either, and I crossed to her at once, only to hesitate. Her back was to me, her hands still clutching the counter.

"Sakura," I said, very softly, "I would comfort you, if I could."

She laughed abruptly, a hiccuping sound, as she shook her hair around her face. One hand lifted up, and I caught it, placing my palm under hers.

"Just being here—that's what I normally would tell you." She still did not look at me. "You don't have to try so hard, Marcus. You're already comforting just by being here. That's what I would say if I was giving you advice. But the truth is I don't think—I don't think you should comfort me. I don't think I deserve it."

I spoke without thinking. "I do."

She straightened in surprise, her head hitting my chest as she looked back at me. "You don't know what I've done."

"True." I held her gaze until her breath caught and she closed her eyes, leaning in to me, understanding that to me, it did not matter. Because to me, there was only that moment, and nothing could change her value.

"You're too steady," she murmured, eyes still closed. In the darkened window, I could hardly read her expression. "It's going to be your downfall. I'll tell you," she added, opening her eyes to meet my gaze, twisting between me and the sink. "Give me your arm—there."

Bracing herself on my forearm, she leveraged herself up, so that she sat on the counter beside the sink. Smoothing her skirts over her knees, looking more directly into my face now. Her gaze was closer, and she held me there, tethered by one hand lingering on the counter.

68

"Do you know very much about Witches?" she asked, her fingertips so light and hot on the back of my hand.

"I know some," I replied. Though she called me steady, my heartbeat felt anything but.

Her lips twisted in her sweet, wry smile, and her gaze on mine was knowing. "You're going to make me tell you every detail."

"I would like that," I confessed. "Please."

Her expression settled, pensive. Half-dried tears lingered on her cheeks, but I dared not touch them, not as she collected herself. Her fingers still traced my hand. "You know I'm not one," she began. "Not a Witch, not a real one, with the capital letters and rules and everything. I couldn't have been, I never wanted to be, really—I didn't realize until just recently that maybe there's something to be said for it, the way their spells are controlled, how they don't have to worry about things going haywire."

She glanced briefly up to me, then let her gaze fall, running over my collar. "Witches, when they go to school, they have this divination ritual that they do. It shows them the person who will be their true love. It's supposed to—solve problems, I guess. Make things easy for them, since they're supposed to go off and be posted in some town who knows where, and live there all their life. And find their true love there, I suppose, is the way it's meant to go.

"I'd only just got to Belville," she said slowly, "when the Witch there told me he'd seen me."

My hand gripped the counter. I hoped she couldn't tell the way I tensed—but if she could, there was nothing for it. She was watching me now. Quietly. Her eyes very, very sad.

"Did you," I said, trying so carefully to choose my words,

but so uncertain what I wanted to ask, "feel—the same?"

Her gaze on mine remained inescapable. "No."

So simple an answer. So many directions to go. "Then did you—did you—"

"No," she said softly, taking pity on me. "What happened was, I used all my savings and I bought an old building, and I built my cafe. I spent two years throwing parties and matchmaking my friends, even my business partner, who you would just adore, by the way. I watched everybody find their happily ever after and—I watched him love me, or—think he was in love with me.

"He's a nice guy," she added, straightening up, pulling her hand away, looking over the counter and into the wall. "The best Witch you could want. He's taken up healing, and he's done real good in town. My friend Red—you remember her—she loves him like a little brother. And she should. He's a good person."

I didn't like the way she was going, the distance in her gaze. "But you didn't make him any promise."

"I did not." She looked back at me, though her eyes were still faraway. "I wanted to. I was thinking about it. It would have been so easy—*should* have been so easy. We were all planning Red's wedding, and there's a lot of love in the air—there always is, in Belville, in our cafe. That's why I loved it there. If we hadn't come here—if I hadn't—"

In that instant her gaze was *not* faraway any more, it was everywhere on me, my burning lips, my flushed face. She whispered the words. "I would have, if I hadn't met you."

But she hadn't made me any promises either, and I had not known.

"I don't understand how the magic got it wrong," she added,

70

her voice falling to a whisper again, our eyes locked. "Even if I'm not a Witch, I know that the divination ritual he did should be right. What *I* am shouldn't have mattered—it should have been right for him. Instead I went back to Belville and I was so miserable until everybody could tell, and finally I had to just say to him—not *someday, maybe*, but—*never*. And it was horrible and sad, and I ran away, because—because sometimes I think that the worst part isn't that it ended in *never*—sometimes I think that the worst part is that it took me so long to know. *He* knew all along how he felt. Why didn't I—why didn't I ever *know*? Why didn't I see it from the start?"

Her eyes fell, and mine followed. But this was a question safe to answer, at last. The answer was in everything she'd already said. "Because you weren't looking at yourself, Sakura."

"Please. That's *all* I do. I'm the most self-absorbed person you could ever meet," she replied at once, dismissive.

I knew this was the shame she felt speaking—I could feel it. And I thought I knew a way to show her that, too. I held my breath as I leaned closer. "Tell me why you came here."

"Because Trent deserves his town back, and Red deserves her happy honeymoon time, and I couldn't—I couldn't take it any more. Not after what I did."

Trent. That was his name, then. I watched her face, the way her lashes curved over her cheek. "Don't you see how you are looking at the effects on others—not at what you are?"

She bit her lower lip. "What I *am* has caused no end of trouble. Completely out of control magic, ruining what's supposed to be a really important divination ritual, not to mention Red's—"

71

I stepped in, I put my hand out to stop her—I brushed her lip just barely with my thumb. The thrill of it raced through me, but I tried to focus. "Your magic and your shadow witchery come from deep within you, I am certain, but you are still speaking of it the way others might see it. What I mean is, the way you *are*, just yourself."

Inevitable—that was how she felt to me. She had kissed me over the summer to undo her own banishing spell, but returned and did not want to speak of the contact. I understood it now, but still, I ached for it.

As my touch lingered, her gaze wavered. "I don't want to hurt you."

"You already did," I said softly. Surprise widened her features, and before pain could rush in, I stepped nearer, raising my hand to her cheek. "For that day last summer, it was agony not to see you, and to know you had banished me because you were afraid and upset. But then you worked so hard to fix it, Sakura, and you succeeded. You are trustworthy. I trust you."

Instead of pain, light filled her eyes, and her open mouth eased into a slow smile. Then she framed my face with her hands, drawing me closer, and her lips closed over mine.

I was so entranced by the touch and thrill of her that I didn't notice the way her magic, before so firmly tamped down, suddenly welled up. For one instant I was lost in joy and desire. In the next instant, I found myself thrown across the room and into the hearth.

Saki,

Are you alright? We're worried about you! I hope you're not worried about what happened. You know Luca and I love you, right?

To Sakura
c/o Minotaur Enterprises

BELVILLE

Chapter Nine: Frying Pan

～⚬⚬⚬～

Sakura

So. Kissing Marcus and then knocking him into a wall with uncontrolled magic is, combined, probably the second-most embarrassing thing I've ever done. The added element of shame brought on by the facts that I'd only *just* told Trent we could never be together a few days ago and that I'd *sworn* to myself I wouldn't get Marcus into any more trouble only made it more prickly.

Look, I know it's probably very hard to believe right now, but I'm actually a pretty powerful witch. Which only makes it worse . . .

Fortunately, it's difficult to damage gods. Marcus was a sweetheart about it, because when is he ever *not* a sweetheart? He remained kind and understanding even as I basically shoved him out the door for fear that it might happen again.

The only other nice upshot of it all was that I had not, apparently, terrified Lulu into chancing the woods on her own rather than continuing to live with a rogue witch. I woke the next morning to find a lump on my bed which turned out to be a small white goat. The *same* small white goat, even, not some interloper who happened not to know that I'd created a magical explosion the previous evening.

I've never had a pet before. Certainly I've never had a creature in my bed! I almost squished Lulu in my surprise, but all she did was roll over and press her little hooves into my back. Her white coat was so pretty against my new blue quilt. She looked peaceful, and I had to admit she was right: this attic bedroom could be nice, if we strung up some string lights—preferably star-shaped ones to match the quilt—and got a nice dresser to replace my half-undone luggage, and . . .

And I wasn't staying there: right. As soon as I figured out how to get Bertram off my back and solve this haunting, I would have to leave to . . . where, again?

Well, I'd have to go back to Belville *eventually*.

Faced with this unpleasant reality, I hopped out of bed and was, for a moment, lost. A lot of my normal routines had been disrupted lately—these days I didn't even bother putting protective wards on myself like I had once done, because now I spent so much time trying to keep the magic *in* that I just didn't have the heart for daily shields and the like. But I could cook. So I proceeded to make an enormous omelet.

Yes; I knew quite well that I was distracting myself from some Big Important Scary Things. But I'll let you in on a secret: dealing in shadow magic and being reasonably self-aware doesn't mean that you *always immediately face the thing*. Sometimes it means that you take a step back, take stock, and realize that you could face the thing a lot better after breakfast.

Sometimes it also means recognizing the fact that you're going to make questionable decisions, and the only real thing you can do about them is be prepared to handle the fallout.

All that to say, I then took the omelet to the cabin next door. Goat in tow.

I owed him an apology, after all. Plus, he probably didn't have any kind of food in his cabin. Also, I realized when I'd knocked several times and gotten no reply, maybe *he'd* been snatched by the monster somehow? Maybe last night as he was leaving my place? He'd said he was fine, but he probably had at *least* had a headache, and maybe that had made him easy prey—

Marcus opened the door, and I almost dropped my frying pan.

He was wet. And naked. Well—except for a towel. How had he gotten a towel? There hadn't been anything but rubbish left in any of these cabins when I went through them with Quinn yesterday. Had he just magicked one into existence? Why hadn't I thought to lend him one of mine?

All of these things were much easier to think about than the fact that his slate gray chest, usually tidily tucked behind a collared shirt, was unreasonably attractive.

"I thought it was an emergency," he said.

"I'm sorry. I knocked. And then I got worried, so I knocked more. I can see how that might seem like there was an emergency, in retrospect," I babbled.

He put one arm across his chest, anchoring his hand on his shoulder, which absolutely did not hide the fact that he was lovely, and that his arms were very nice too. "I was showering."

"Carry on," I said brightly. "Um—not here, obviously—back in the comfort of your bathroom, of course. Which I hope is goat-free. Ah, except for the fact that Lulu followed me over just now." On cue, said goat darted between us, into the cabin. Presumably, straight into the bathroom. She seemed to enjoy gnawing on pipes.

Marcus hesitated. "Do you . . . want to come in also?"

"I could heat up this omelet!" I waved the massive frying pan at him as though he might have missed it up til now. "If you want breakfast. I figured you might not have anything. Maybe?"

His dark eyes found mine. I tried so hard to keep my gaze on his face. After a moment, he smiled slightly. "I'll only be a moment."

"Take your time," I assured him.

He stepped back from the threshold as I stepped in, which was a little bit disappointing, but really, for the best. In another moment he had disappeared into the bathroom, safely behind a closed door. And I was left in a kitchen very much like the one I'd just left, to set my frying pan on the stove and wonder *what in Beyond is wrong with me?*

Potentially, nothing that kissing Marcus again wouldn't fix.

But I waved that thought away as I set about lighting the stove and rummaging in cabinets for dishes. I reminded myself very firmly of what had happened the night before. I've *never* lost control of my magic that way. I hadn't even been feeling that emotional. Aside from, you know . . .

Okay obviously I'd been *very* emotional. But it was still confusing why the magic would have pushed Marcus away when actually, *away* was the last place I wanted him. That was the real problem; if I could get a handle on that . . .

Right, right. There was still the resort and the goat and the ghost and everyone back in Belville to consider. And I mean really, even if everything was fine, what kind of future would I have with Marcus anyway?

I'd found a pot and was contemplating if there were enough cups laying about to try to make tea when the man himself rejoined me.

"Please, let me," he said, his hand brushing mine as he reached for the stove.

I gave it up immediately. And remembered, as I watched him, that Marcus deserved a lot more credit than I'd given him lately.

He *was* conjuring things. He did it without thought. I watched as he stood at the sink, filling the pot, carelessly gesturing with his free hand and making a cabinet appear against the wall to one side. He set the pot on a lit burner behind my omelet, fashioning a lid for it before turning to his cabinet. It was wide and tall, made of dark wood, the kind that has glass doors sheltering the shelves on the top half and drawers on the bottom. He'd probably called it here from his home, I realized, as he opened the doors and began making selections from a variety of glass jars and ceramic cups. He pulled down a small black tea pot and a glittering tea cup painted with butterflies. Quietly, confidently, he began pulling ingredients from individual jars and combining them in a small bowl. He wasn't just making tea—he was creating a specific tea blend for us, in the moment. Knowing him, he was probably even making one for himself and one for me. Lulu was nibbling at his trousers, and even that was not distracting him.

Watching him move so intently, I let my omelet burn.

Almost, that is. Hurriedly, I flipped the thing over. Glacial always did the cooking at the Pomegranate. It was my job to take orders and make drinks. But I wasn't nearly as good at making drinks as Marcus was. I just knew enough to appreciate exactly what he was doing.

I thought it was an emergency, he'd said earlier. I'd been so surprised I hadn't thought about his tone, but it came back to me now, in the cozy silence.

He'd said it apologetically. His dark skin had been flushed. Then the way he covered his chest—like he was *shy*.

I hadn't thought about it before. Because it was a silly thing to be, when he was perfectly competent, and very powerful.

But it was *adorable*.

The water was boiling. He reached over the counter for it, dipping past me, and I was staring at him now with open curiosity. Not to mention appreciation.

If it wasn't for the magic, I would . . .

Maybe even *with* the magic, I could . . .

Well, obviously I still wasn't going to let him get stuck with me, and surely at this point he wouldn't want to: the danger was clear. But we were going to be investigating together—maybe that wasn't such a bad thing.

"I hope you don't mind," he said, passing me the butterfly teacup and saucer with glittering blue tea steeping from a flower-shaped strainer.

I glanced at the tea, then at him, then at the cabinet behind his head. He'd picked out exactly the cup I would have. What was there to mind?

"I'm the one who literally blew things up last night," I said. I'd meant it to be funny, because it *was*; but it came out in a very small voice. "I—I came over here really because I wanted to apologize."

"I told you last night I don't need an apology," he reminded me. He leaned on the counter, and beside his hand, his own black teapot and cup was steeping.

"You're really kind," I said to my tea.

"Hmm." When I looked up, he was gazing at me, his expression thoughtful. Normally he didn't have very much expression, especially in public or mixed company. But then sometimes, he was as easy to read as an old friend. Gently, he repeated my own words back to me. "I don't think you have to work so hard, Sakura."

"Saki," I insisted without thinking.

I knew he was watching my face but this time I didn't dare look. He repeated it so softly. "Saki."

However much he had blushed before, I was definitely blushing more now. But there was something so—nice about it. Something so incredibly *freeing* about the fact that he'd seen me do a banishing spell and an explosion, not to mention heard my sad story and seen a strange monster in the woods, and still he was here. Steady.

"Alright, then," I said, turning back up to him, beaming. "I guess it's about time we finally had breakfast."

The Twelve
Deities of Mount Hallow

Jupiter
Ceres   Juno
Mercury   Vesta
Apollo   Neptune
Diana   Minerva
Venus   Mars
Vulcan

Chapter Ten: Cops

❧

Marcus

She thanked me when I conjured chairs and a small table on the cabin's porch. For a moment, I forgot that I hadn't just spent days carving them each from wood for her.

I'd never encountered somebody who made me so interested in small details.

And it had been a very long time since I'd encountered someone whose problems were beyond my reach. In my many years of dealing with the dead, I'd seen so many patterns repeat. I knew how to help those who didn't want to pass over, and those who hadn't learned the lessons of life. I could reach those who sequestered themselves. But even after a night of searching, I hadn't yet been able to reach any spirit at Hideaway Lake, hadn't been able to solve Sakura's mystery.

When I apologized, she smiled at me. "It's not proving to

be an easy place, is it?"

We sat peacefully, side by side, looking out at the reflecting pool. Gray clouds were amassing in the sky, darkening the water, but her presence was warm and bright.

"But still, it *is* a lovely place," she remarked after a moment. Her saucer cradled in her hand, her teacup at her lips as she considered the ruins and the woods. "What did Bertram and the tourists call it—the edge of the world, I think. Seems kind of fitting."

There was a tremor of sadness in her blue eyes as she glanced at me before focusing on her plate, and I knew she was thinking of herself as exiled. And I—was I only an added punishment, to torment her conscience? Though I knew full well she hadn't meant to harm me the night before, I couldn't help but take heed. Something in her didn't want me near.

I pondered this. It had preoccupied me all night, even as I looked for souls left behind. As often happens, I forgot to say anything. Quinn once reprimanded me for failing to see conversation as a back-and-forth. He said that for me, conversation was an effort, not a game. He was right.

Fortunately, Sakura—*Saki*—did not seem to mind. She gave me time, and then very easily, she asked, "Is it a place you visited often, before?"

Too easily. And she'd named her café the *Pomegranate?* Flustered by the implications, I turned away from the delicious breakfast she'd made, facing the water. "I do not remember much of the early days."

"Don't you?" I could hear the amusement in her voice. And always, that sympathetic tone. Like she already knew what I would prefer not to say.

"You know," I told her. Against my better judgment I looked

back, meeting her gaze. I was curious what I might find there. "You've heard all the stories, the myths. Surely. If you . . ."

"Yes." When I let my words trail away, she picked up their direction. "When I was learning how to lean into my magic, it was Persephone who came to me in dreams. She was the first deity I encountered, and I owe her a lot for what she showed me. So I named my café for one of her symbols, and I embraced her connection with both death and love. But that doesn't mean I have any expectations of *you*," she said, and when I looked back at her, startled, her face went rosy with embarrassment. "I mean—not either way—it's neither here nor there. You don't have to tell me.

"That said," she added, looking down into her tea as she stirred it with a small golden spoon, "I *did* tell you quite a bit last night . . ."

Something in seeing her that way made me smile. "Are you trying to manipulate me?"

She grinned back. "Technically I'm just pressuring you."

"Pressuring a god," I reminded her, amused.

"Like I care what you are. I'll pressure that ghost monster, too, as soon as we find it." Though she spoke lightly, I had no doubt of her words.

And it was a relief I had not realized I wanted. In fact, it made me laugh. She was watching me, interested and bright, then chuckling to herself as if swept along, giving up on understanding.

But she was a person who *would* understand. I settled back into my chair, vaguely excited at the prospect of telling her. "Though I'm sure there are people out there for whom life worked in accordance with the story, I am not one of those people."

She set aside her plate and fork, leaning over the arm of her chair toward me. "Okay, say more."

I did—gladly. "Stories often repeat—legends, myths, fairy tales. You know this. Divinity is the same. It is not quite magic, but a primal force bound up in the stories, in the fabric of existence. The thread of it that I am attuned with represents the world beyond, and the dead; but I am not the only one. There are many other deities associated with death and the dead. Some even have similar stories—tales of marriage to a deity of life or prosperity, brought about through chance or crime."

"For the record, I wasn't accusing you of crime," Saki said, her head tilted, her words like honey.

"I did not think so." She made me smile: she brought out a light in me I did not often see. "The stories repeat for everyone. Gods are only remarkable because they were often players in the very first stories that played out."

"And for their 'attunement,' as you put it," Saki put in.

"Perhaps. Though all power is dependent upon its context," I said, thinking of her own forceful magic and how helpless I often was in the face of it. From the way she bit her lip ruefully, I knew she was reminded of the same. I went on, "I did know the goddess Proserpine, who is very like your Persephone. But for us the story was not a romance. She wanted a refuge, a place to hide, and I provided one. But I knew it would not last forever. Indeed, she was discovered, and . . ."

This time as I let my words trail off, it was in memory. Looking out over the reflecting pool, I could see them all again: the drama, the argument.

"You have a habit of doing that, you know," Saki said.

I glanced back at her, wondering if perhaps she *did* mind me losing the thread of conversation. "What?"

She smiled. "Taking in people or trying to help them and suffering the backlash."

Four days. She'd known me for four days over the summer, and somehow she'd seen so many details of my existence. My wondering became amusement as I thought that maybe I didn't need to tell her any of these things anyway.

But it was strangely addictive. "You might say Proserpine was the first. But she went on to fight her own battles, and had no further need of me. I was never cut out for life with the others. Places like this." I gestured to the reflecting pond, its surface now rippled by a cold wind, the image of the legendary mountain peak always obscured. A fitting image, I thought. These early stories had happened so very long ago. Once I had seemed bound together with those other deities, Proserpine, Jupiter, Ceres. Over the centuries, though, they had gone their own ways, settled into their own temples and empires, or abandoned any thought of power for new lives and anonymity. For many years I had been the only one left in Helenia, and here I was, sitting at the feet of a place that had been so holy to them: and now it was empty and cold.

Except for Sakura.

"Nonsense," she said. Confidently, lightly, matter-of-factly. "There isn't anything *lesser* about you. And there's nothing about you to be simply 'no further needed,' either."

I couldn't look back at her this time. I couldn't. There was a painful tightness in my throat. When I *could* speak, I said quietly, hoarsely, "Less dramatic, perhaps."

"That, maybe," Saki granted me. "Though I'm not so sure all this brooding and keeping to yourself and being so *hard* on yourself isn't its own kind of drama."

"Really?" I couldn't help it—I glanced back at her. She'd let her little goat up into her lap, and she was laughing at me. Even Lulu seemed amused.

Overruled by the two of them, I chuckled softly at myself. Perhaps she was right. Sweet Sakura—she could see me so clearly, and yet had such a tainted view of herself.

"Tell me something else," she said, flushed and cheerful. "Did you at some point have a home in the afterlife? Do you still? Do you know what happens to people when they die?"

I hesitated, busying myself with my own cup of tea. "That is a question that no one asks me, Saki."

Her eyes widened. She liked to hear me say her name. She leaned forward, one arm carefully around Lulu. "I'm sure they want to. Quinn is probably dying to. No pun intended—mostly."

"I do not know." Despite myself, I laughed. "Often I think that they must be. Wanting to ask, I mean. It used to make me very uncomfortable."

"Does it still?"

"I am not made uncomfortable by very much, these days."

"If that's the case," she declared, triumphant, "why are you avoiding the question?"

I shook my head, beaten, and very glad to be. "It is metaphorical, the 'home' or 'domain' you speak of. It is not a place you could visit, the way my house is. And I do not have control over life or death—that is existence itself, and I am only a part of it. I can interact with the dead, adjudicate problems . . . but to do so, I often must let go of this part of me that you see. When I return, I can't always—it's not an experience I can put into words."

87

"I think I get it, though," Saki said, musing. "It's like you're tapping into your power to do it. Something almost higher than yourself."

"Precisely. That is what it is to be divine—to be guardian and caretaker of that small piece of higher power with which you're aligned," I replied. "It is not me, but I embody it. I am one of many faces it may wear."

"So you're also going to tell me you don't remember, or don't see, what the afterlife is really like," Saki guessed.

I shared her little smile. "More the latter. I encounter bits and pieces of it as needed. I know enough to know only that individuals' experiences vary."

She settled back into her chair, one hand absently preventing Lulu from licking at the empty plates on the table. Her gaze was thoughtful, watching the storm roll in. I watched her for just a moment—only as long as I dared. I could have stayed in that moment for an eternity. To feel that she could see me, truly, was something no words could do justice.

The wind picked up, rattling the loose shingles on the roof above us. I thought I could come to like storms in this little haven very much.

"That's the hardest part," Saki said eventually. "Don't you think? Making peace with the fact that sometimes you just won't know the whole picture. I can't stand it sometimes. I know I *should,* but—it's hard."

I thought of everything she'd told me the night before. The way she'd kissed me, and the way something in her fought to keep me away. Had an ancient creature risen from the lake at that moment and offered to exchange my powers for an understanding, I would have made the deal instantly.

"Yes," I said, softly. "It's hard."

Lulu the goat sat up with a bleat. Sakura leaned up too, following her glance, and so did I. High as the resort was, the clouds had settled in around us, making the very air more difficult to see through. But after a moment I noticed it. The wires of the gondola line were straining. As though—

"Oh, curse it," Saki murmured. "I was hoping he wouldn't have the guts to come up here, not if it was going to rain."

"Saki," I said, reminded suddenly of my own dealings with her unfortunate assistant, "I went to see Bertram yesterday. He gave me a copy of the full legal measures surrounding your inheritance and this resort."

"Did he?" Saki looked at me, intrigued.

"I had meant to give it to you to look through, in case he had not been honest with you. But then with the appearance of the unknown lights and apparition—"

"We can talk about it later," Saki agreed, businesslike. "He's already at the station—and not alone, either. Curse him, what's he brought up here?" She stood, setting Lulu down carefully before putting her hands on her hips. "Marcus, let's good-cop bad-cop them."

"What?"

"You'll get the hang of it," she promised. "It's business 101. Glacial and I did it all the time at the Pomegranate. We'll separate them: that'll add to the confusion. You take Bertram, since apparently you can talk to him without bashing his clipboard over his head. I'm going to make short work of whatever construction person he's brought up."

"But . . . which 'cop' am I?"

"Whichever you need to be!" She was already at the porch steps. When she turned and winked at me, my heart skipped a beat and any further protest died. Without another word, she hurried across the lawn to the gondola station, her skirts bouncing.

I looked down at Lulu—but the goat, too, was gone, devotedly following her benefactor.

To myself, I sighed. Then stood, straightened my cuffs and collar, and went to face Bertram.

The Spa Hallow Project

Phase Two

- ☐ glass panes (unbreakable)
- ☐ lumber delivery
- ☐ hardware (assorted)
- ☐ support beams
- ☐ roof tiles (leakproof)
- ☐ pipes (plumbing)
- ☐ floor tiles (mold proof)
- ☐ hardwood floor planks
- ☐ ghost repellent (guaranteed)
- ☐ monster trap (one)

Chapter Eleven: Bots

Sakura

I breezed right past Bertram, which was easy actually, because the wind was at my back and he was already striding down from the station like he owned the place. Ha! Like Bertram could spend a night in a cabin in the woods. Alone. He probably worked best surrounded by secretaries who actually did everything for him.

Without even looking his direction, I went straight for the gondola. The success of this plan depended on Marcus having my back, and distracting Bertram before he could follow me. It must have worked, because I ran up to the gondola without hearing so much as a *wait, don't you want to approve the plans for Phase Two: Complete Destruction?*

The gondola itself was heavily weighed down. Through the open windows, I could see beams and paper-wrapped panes of glass and over sorts of construction supplies, things I thought I'd headed off by telling Bertram to cool it for a few days. The heavy shadow of it had been obvious even from the cabins.

But—there was no crew to unload the cargo, or use it all to change my little bit of forest into a cookie-cutter resort. I peered into a few windows, confused. Had there been no room for the crew? But no: the way the gondola line worked, only one gondola could come up to the station—or down from it—at a time. It would be silly to send up supplies first with no one to use them. And while Bertram had definitely gotten himself on my bad side, I didn't actually think he was *that* silly.

I stopped by the gondola's head, peering into the driver's compartment. There *was* a person there, at last! Somebody bent over, so that all I saw was their canvas overalls and the curve of their back, ending in the back of a head that seemed to be covered in deep green scales.

"Oh!" I said aloud, before I could stop myself. "Are you snakekin?"

"Oh," the person repeated, understandably confused as they turned to face the completely random stranger who'd interrupted their work (me). "Nope, gorgon. Hi, by the way. My name's Gwyn."

"Yes, I see it now," I admitted, blushing. What had looked like scales were in fact many small snakes lying close to Gwyn's head. When she straightened up, the snakes waved in the air around her face like a mane, though their little eyes stayed closed. So I was annoying, but possibly *not* annoying enough to try to turn to stone, as it was rumored gorgon's snakes could do.

Gwyn herself was taller than me—which is saying very little—she was about average height, sturdy, and in her overalls and long-sleeved cotton shirt, she looked exactly like she belonged behind the wheel of a gondola. Or behind the—levers? I wasn't sure how gondolas worked, and I was quickly realizing I'd been incredibly rude to her in more ways than one. "I'm so sorry. You've been driving the gondola this whole time, right? Is that what they call it? I have been far too distracted. And I never should have interrupted you like that and asked—only, my adopted family is snakekin." Maybe I was missing Ryu more than I thought. Well, he and Belville were going to have to wait. I set that aside and added, "I'm Sakura, by the way. You probably knew that, I guess?"

"Yeah, I figured." Gwyn grinned widely at me. Everything about her face was wide and friendly, including her golden eyes, which sparkled against her dark brown skin. "Don't feel bad. Not many people think too hard about how the gondola works. Some're afraid to, you know?"

"I do know," I confirmed, returning her smile. "I'm not a huge fan of air travel myself. But still, I should have introduced myself before. Um, they didn't leave you here to unload all this yourself, did they?"

"Not quite." Gwyn nodded down toward her feet. I balanced up on my toes to look down through the window, and saw that an entire herd of automata crowded around her legs. They were each only as high as her knee, with little clockwork faces and slot-shaped eyes that glowed faintly green in the dim light.

"Oh my." I settled back down onto my feet, feeling a bit unsteady in my surprise.

Gwyn chuckled. "Started off as a hobby of mine, but my

partner got tired of it—said she didn't like all those little eyes watching whenever she had to go to the shed. So they come to work now. Turns out they're useful in the gondola business. And strong. They'll get this unloaded in no time."

"Give me a moment," I replied, shaking my head. "To be honest with you, I ran over here ready to have to argue with a construction manager! But your little workers are adorable, even if watchful, and it's not you I'm mad at. But—do you know what all this is for?"

For a moment Gwyn smiled fondly at her shiny brass robots. Then she looked at me, tilted her head to one side, and came to a decision. With an even more endearing grin—this one rather lopsided and confidential—she leaned forward, setting her arms on her open window, so her head was nearly level with mine. "I'll tell you something. I wasn't too happy about all this either. But if this is your reaction, I think we'll get along fine."

I laughed. Behind me, Lulu bleated curiously, so I picked her up so that she could feel included too. "So, you're another one against the development?"

"Yeah, me and all the 'bots, and this little critter too, I bet." Gwyn's eyes twinkled as she looked at Lulu, who was sniffing curiously at the gondola's wooden beams. "The way I hear it, just about everyone on Helenia is against the development. With the exception of a few business folk," she added, with a pointed look toward the lake.

I glanced that way too, and caught sight of Marcus talking with Bertram and somebody else. That is, the somebody else was talking, and Marcus was looking at me. He looked away after a moment, so it wasn't like he was thinking, *why in Beyond did she leave me here?* It was more like he liked looking.

I flushed, and turned back to Gwyn.

"I knew nothing about it until I got here a few days ago," I confided in her. "And having seen this place, I think it's nonsense. I thought I was very clear about that on the first day. Did they tell you what's with all this stuff?"

"Sounded to me like they'd already paid for it, so it needed to get delivered *somewhere,* and the only place was up here," Gwyn said, clucking sympathetically as she looked back at the laden gondola. Her snakes waved in the wind, which was increasingly wet. "I don't think you have too much to worry about, though. It's only the rest of the materials for the station."

"What do you mean? The station isn't done?" I looked around us. The station seemed perfectly functional to me. There was a roof over the platform, which extended in a U-shape around both sides of the gondola when it was docked. A few simple steps led down to the ground, and most importantly, under the gondola, there was a lowered stage—so that when people stepped on or off the platform, they weren't stepping over a drop along the cliffs. Plus, the wires seemed perfectly well-anchored, and the gondola had been fully functional every time I'd been on it so far.

Gwyn was grinning again at my confusion. "You're not wrong. It's done enough. But the builders had this vision, see, for something that made more of a *statement.* I gather there's supposed to be some kind of receiving hall. There's certainly enough glass back there for all the windows you may want."

"Ugh." The last thing I wanted was more construction work being done, especially when I hadn't made up my mind about what to do and we potentially had a ghost or weird ghostly lights haunting the place. Lulu wriggled, and I let her down so that she could trot over to the steps and stare at what was now, definitely, rain.

"That said," Gwyn began, in a tone which clearly said she was about to propose something she'd do in my situation, but wasn't sure how I'd respond, "you don't have to use all this stuff for *that*."

I wasn't sure yet how to respond either. "What do you mean?"

"Just that, it's all only materials," Gwyn told me, warming to the theme. "You can use them for anything. Just 'cause they were ordered for the station doesn't mean you have to use them that way. You can make anything you want out of wood and glass and nails. Make yourself a nicer house, maybe."

She shrugged one shoulder toward the line of cabins, which was no longer visible through the weather. I pondered this. I didn't especially need a bigger cabin—I liked my cabin—I liked living in *the* cabin for *these few days*, that is. But maybe Gwyn had a point. There was already a gondola line up here. It didn't need to be a resort, but maybe there could be *something*. A little vista-viewing shelter, maybe? People liked to hike to things like that, right?

"Probably not something *small*, though," Gwyn added thoughtfully. "Panes of reinforced glass like that are hard to cut down. They got the good stuff—charmed, you know. It'll do pretty much anything you want it to except break."

I was trying to focus, really I was. But the rain was coming in through the open walls of the station, and I was wondering about Marcus out there in the cold, and what I really *needed* was a cup of tea.

I think I had the idea at the same time Gwyn met my eyes and grinned. "Nice snug restaurant, maybe."

"A cafe," I breathed. "Oh, that's not a terrible idea."

Gwyn laughed. "I'll admit it'd be nice for me if you set up a place for a mid-shift snack. Not sure what kind of business you'd get up here, but then again, there's always people asking about the ruins. And the creature. You could make a killing on the tours."

"I like the way you think," I told her. Though the land had come to me free, there would eventually be taxes to pay, and a little bit of practicality didn't hurt. Of course this was all *if* we did tours and *if* there was enough material for another building entirely and *if* I stayed . . .

But I could also set it up nice and leave it for someone else, couldn't I?

"Yeah, the wheels are turning now," Gwyn said companionably. "So, what's it going to be, boss? Want the 'bots to go ahead and unload?"

"You might as well," I told her. "If it all comes to nothing, we'll just take it all down the mountain again. I'll—" I stopped myself. I'd meant to promise her that *I* would do the work in that case, with my magic. But as soon as the words formed, I saw not only the shocked faces of Belville, but also poor kind Marcus thrown into the hearth.

"You just say the word," Gwyn said with good humor. She had no idea what I'd been about to say. But it didn't seem to matter to her a bit. She turned to organize her automata again, and it was obvious that either way, she was willing to help.

I felt a rush of gratitude and warmth for her. I also felt terribly, desperately homesick for my friend Glacial back at the Pomegranate.

"I really appreciate you doing this," I told Gwyn, as a parade of tiny, toddler-like metal creatures began carrying stack after stack of wood and other things off the gondola. Lulu snorted and kicked at one that got too close. I added, in all seriousness, "I really appreciate you talking to me, too."

"Hey, don't worry about it," Gwyn said easily, leaning out her window once more. Like the wind and rain didn't matter a bit. "After talking to you, I'm starting to look forward to what this might become. Just mind you don't get chased off by a ghost, alright?"

PROPOSAL

FOR OFF-SITE STUDENT
LEARNING EXPERIENCE

UNIVERSITY
OF HELENIA

DOCUMENT
PREPARED BY:
ADRIENNE MYRTLE

DEPARTMENT:
HISTORY

OBJECTIVE:
CONDUCT SURVEY OF GODS'
REFLECTING POOL AND
SURROUNDING AREA

Chapter Twelve: Ancient History

Marcus

Fully aware that Sakura was counting on me, I made my way toward Bertram and his companion, doing my best to appear approachable. As Saki passed them, Bertram turned, his mouth open.

"You must have come on important business," I called, "to make your way here as a storm comes in."

Bertram's head swung back toward me, and Saki made it to the station uninterrupted. I smiled. Perhaps it would be more rewarding to be a "good" or "bad" cop than I thought.

It only remained to be seen which I ought to be. Bertram was already consulting his clipboard. "Only a routine delivery and check-in. And, of course, I was hoping to get Sakura's final opinion on some matters . . ."

I came to a stop in front of the pair as he spoke. We stood

far enough from the station that our conversation was our own, near enough to the reflecting pool that the lapping of waves whipped up by the wind filled the silence. Bertram was in a suit and black rain slicker. His companion wore an old woolen coat and carried a blue umbrella. Not a lawyer, then.

Normally I might have waited for him to reveal what the "matters" might be, but in this case I was aware I'd have to talk to keep him from going to see Saki herself. "You often make a point of visiting the site yourself, then?"

"Oh—well—only right now, to help with the transition, you know." Bertram straightened, holding his clipboard to his chest as though to block out the wind. "Have you met Professor Myrtle?"

"I have not." I turned to his companion. A professor, then—that much made sense.

"Call me Myrtle, and please know I prefer 'they,'" the professor said, extending their hand to me. I shook it: Myrtle had a cool and firm grip. Thick green-brown hair and dry, almost bark-like brown skin around their green eyes made me suspect nymph heritage. The professor was tall and slight like many nymphs, as well, and spoke in quick, high tones. "There, that's the formalities out of the way. I met Bertram when he was in school—I expect you might have been wondering. I'm in the History department, though, not Business! But that's why he asked me to come along today. He seemed to think that the new owner might like a bit of background on the site?"

My gaze had strayed to Saki, still busy at the gondola station. She'd met the driver, it seemed, and was talking animatedly. The wind was blowing her hair in her face. If I was there . . .

"Um," coughed Bertram. "This is Marcus . . . Pluto."

He gave the final name too much emphasis. Inwardly, I sighed, though the reaction was not a surprising one. It was part of the reason I'd taken to using a new first name. "A pleasure to meet you," I said, refocusing on the conversation. "Forgive my distraction. History, you said?"

"Yes, with a specialty in the Classical Ages," Myrtle replied. I noted an eager, speculative gleam in their eyes as they considered me. Another familiar reaction. "I'd go so far as to say I'm the expert on these ruins in particular. Unless, of course, you . . . ?"

All these unspoken questions and half-sentences were vaguely annoying. I wondered if "bad cop" had indeed been the path to take. "I am here to assist Sakura," I said, fully aware it was a non-answer. I turned from Myrtle back to Bertram. "To that end, might I ask what you were hoping to receive her opinion on?"

"We'll need approval to move ahead with Phase Two of the station construction," he admitted. "If we don't get started in the next few days, we'll fall behind."

"Behind what?" I asked.

Bertram seemed baffled. "Behind schedule."

A misty rain had begun. I wondered if that had been accounted for, too. "Who set the schedule?"

"Ah—I did," Bertram said. "On behalf of the company, of course. And with consultations from all the builders. There's the carpenters, then the masonry guild, and of course the gondola system—the town permits—the plumbing—"

"If you set the schedule," said I, "surely you can change it. After all, I doubt anyone anticipated the project changing hands?"

"No one did," Bertram confessed, eyeing Myrtle as though the professor could help him.

"Naturally such a change would create delays," I concluded. "What other problems are there?"

Myrtle chose this moment to jump in. "Bertram, do you know if any of the excavations so far have uncovered any *artifacts*? That would be very important!"

"We've really only excavated to put the station supports in," Bertram said uneasily. "It's set directly into the rock. I don't think they found anything. We don't expect to—not if it could derail the project—"

"I gather it's not the sort of thing one could anticipate," I commented.

"On the contrary, finding artifacts *should* be anticipated at a site like this!" Myrtle now turned to me. "Think of all the centuries of history here! People making pilgrimages, people holding rites. Why, people may have even stayed here, once upon a time, and they would have left trash!"

I paused. Trash sounded like a bad thing to me, but Professor Myrtle was quite excited about it. What would Sakura want me to do?

"The rain is picking up," Bertram said plaintively. "Maybe we should come back another time."

I saw my opportunity. "Perhaps you should wait at your office for Sakura to come to you."

"We could set up a meeting." As he said it, a faint light came into Bertram's eyes. He did seem to enjoy his occupation. "That's if Sakura still feels comfortable staying here?"

I paused. "Why wouldn't she?"

"Only the—the rumors," Bertram said. He glanced at Myrtle, then squinted at me.

I was unmoved. In fact, I was glad *I* had been the one to talk to Bertram Paige. "Sakura is comfortable here, thank you. In fact she mentioned to me that she would appreciate *time* to get to know the site before making her decisions," I told him, feeling inspired.

"That's why I brought Myrtle," said Bertram. His gaze returned to the professor.

The professor, in turn, was already reaching out to me. One hand with knuckles like gnarled wood emerged from under the blue umbrella and brushed my sleeve. "It could take years to get to know this site properly. All the legends—if even *some* of them were true! Would Sakura listen to them, do you think?"

"You'd have to ask her," I said. "Perhaps at a meeting."

"It's not for myself as much as for my students," Professor Myrtle continued, as though I'd said nothing. "If we had access to this site—the surveys we could do!"

I glanced at Bertram, wondering. He had said he only wanted the professor's expertise. It sounded like Myrtle wanted more.

"That's *if* the resort is built and there is a safe place for them all to stay," he reminded Myrtle tightly.

I addressed Myrtle also. "It seemed to me you said that the very building of the resort could endanger artifacts left beneath the surface."

"The site needs to be protected," Myrtle agreed at once.

"And studied, right?" Bertram sounded like he was pleading now. "You said—"

"And studied too!" Myrtle agreed again. "But you must take the proper time, and—"

Bertram. "We don't have *time*—"

Myrtle. "Consider the grand scale of the site—"

Bertram. "It's not grand *yet,* there's nothing *here*—"

Myrtle. "The history! The gods themselves!"

The argument faltered as both looked at me, self-conscious, perhaps expecting me to weigh in somehow. I shifted from foot to foot. It seemed to me I'd done enough.

Bertram sighed, letting his clipboard fall. "We'll have a meeting in a couple of days. Tell Sakura I'll send her a note. And if she runs into any ghosts or monsters—I'd be happy to arrange lodgings for her in town . . ."

I studied him without comment. Was it more pleasant to be treated as a messenger, or as a god? Truthfully, I acted as both. Mildly amused—not to mention surprised at myself—I bowed as the two of them took their leave. The rain was pouring now, but through the dim light I could see that the gondola had been unloaded: stacks of materials took up most of the station. Sakura herself was nowhere to be seen. Bertram and Myrtle departed without further incident, so far as I could tell.

Left to myself in the rain, I turned to contemplate the pool. The chaotic shades of water and shadow comforted me, as they did with every storm. Today, however, was different from so many days in my past. Today, I felt a lightening inside myself. An interest. As I gazed at the mountaintop the clouds obscured, I smiled.

Would she want my report? Should I go see her? Or would that be too much?

Even the uncertainty of it was somehow lovely.

I was surprised, finding this quickening of interest and action within myself. "And how appropriate," I murmured, to myself and the rain, "to see the unseen at Hideaway Lake."

I am not often given to whims, of course, but I had always been partial to the lore of Hideaway Lake. Though I kept myself at a distance—perhaps *because* I kept myself at a distance, in fact, I was taken with the idea of a mirror lake which mirrored nothing.

Because it didn't mirror *nothing*: it simply didn't mirror what people expected to see.

For the briefest moment, the waters parted. I was aware of a presence—a presence I had not looked for in my night of ghost-hunting, a presence which I had been hesitant to seek. The long, smooth lines of a very large creature which moved with complete silence in its legendary home.

Sakura was the very first thing I thought of. My Saki, she would want to know.

And then I thought—*of course. The answer is hidden within our own desire.*

Chapter Thirteen: Dreaming

❧❧❧

Sakura

Meeting Gwyn had been just the inspiration I needed. I had the hang of this whole Helenia interlude now: I would take over the "resort," stop Bertram's silly plans, and create something nice and tasteful and respectful of the ancient site. I would also put the ghost or apparition or whatever it was to rest. Then, having done a good deed and recovered some of my confidence, I would sail off into the sunset . . . which in this case *did*, unfortunately, mean returning to Belville. Once I knew that I was still capable of solving problems, I could go back there and solve my biggest problem of all.

I wasn't ignoring my magic problem, not exactly—more like hoping that focusing on another problem would give it time to sort itself out.

And for the first time in a long time, I was truly excited. I had a new project, and it really had *potential*. It just might work!

Lest you wonder, I wasn't ignoring my Marcus problem, either. But deciding to throw myself into the resort—temporarily—had its benefits there too. I wasn't in Helenia to stay, which meant I didn't have to worry about bringing Marcus down. And without that worry, I could just enjoy how fun and interesting he was—so long as I was careful to manage expectations. Mostly mine.

Lulu and I took refuge in our cabin without once having to talk to Bertram, which was an added plus. I dried Lulu off with a tea towel and left her in the kitchen snacking on vegetable remains while I went to warm up with a shower. Knowing Bertram—and having learned that Marcus preferred doing his ghost-hunting alone—I figured I had some time on my hands.

Strange that hot water is the antidote to cold water, isn't it? I sang to myself in the shower, wondering cheerfully what Marcus's report on Bertram would be. Would he come over to share it? Would he knock at just the wrong time, as I had done to him earlier?

I was perfectly comfortable with Marcus, comfortable enough to know he'd never do such a thing, at least not on purpose. I risked using magic to dry myself and my hair, even more pleased when it worked like normal.

Isn't it fun though, sometimes, to think of sharing these tiny pieces of ourselves, our daily life, with someone who might like us? Pulling on shorts and my fuzzy travel sweater, settling my headband in my hair, I amused myself by picturing Marcus looking on. Obviously he'd be admiring my singing voice and thinking I was unbearably cute. We'd just omit the parts where I burped or tripped or had to adjust my waistband, alright?

Still humming, I returned to the kitchen to make something warm—and perhaps something lunchish. Hot herbal tea, strong and warming, and possibly some cheese on toast. Lulu hopped up on one of the kitchen chairs to watch and, most likely, in hopes of snatching any further leftovers. It didn't seem like goats ever got *full.*

I gave her a piece of the tomato I was slicing for my toast, still a little thrilled that she would eat things from my hand. Not only had she never seemed wild, she seemed like she'd known me and been here forever. Maybe goats were simply brave in that regard.

I pulled out my favorite cup and stirrer for the tea, setting them on the counter. I'd spent so much time this morning watching Marcus in the kitchen; what might he think if he got to watch *me?* It was fun to think about, mixed in with thoughts about what we could do with the resort. A cafe, a tea house, a restaurant? Or keep it simple with a viewing shelter, possibly some picnic tables? I rifled through my purse and pulled out an old order pad—the sort of thing I'd always meant to take out but always forgotten to follow up on—and set it on the table to make some notes on.

Lost in my own little worlds, I didn't notice Lulu hoist herself onto the counter. But when she stole my stirring stick and it *clink*ed against the mug, I was all attention.

"Lulu! Drop that, it's glass," I told her firmly, as though she'd understand. She did not. Instead she saw me coming for her and hopped back down to the chair, and from there to the ground.

"Don't you dare eat that," I tried again, diving after her.

"Lulu! Bad! Dangerous!"

In goat language, I suspect that "dangerous" means "fun game!". Lulu darted out of the kitchen and over the sofa. I followed as best as I could, but despite my impulsive nature, I like to be careful on my feet—especially when I'm not actively using magic to keep my prosthetics steady. Where the tiny goat leapt, I scrambled. There was really no hope of catching her. I did magic the bathroom door closed—at least I was *that* on top of things—but then she veered right, ducking under my outstretched hand and making a beeline for the front door, which at first I thought was the perfect chance to catch her—until I heard the polite knock.

"Don't open it!" I yelled, while simultaneously throwing myself on top of my goat. I managed to both catch her and roll over so that my back ended up against the door, which I felt was pretty slick. "Ha! Got you, you little thief. That'll teach you to steal my favorite accessory!"

"Saki?" On the other side of the wall, Marcus's voice was muffled and worried.

"One moment." I hauled myself and Lulu upright, far less than graceful—more like winded but triumphant. Then I opened the door without thinking about it. "Hi!"

Marcus's dark gaze drifted over my hair—probably mussed—and my cheeks—most likely bright red—to my hanging-out-at-home outfit. Darn. Even though I'd had fun *imagining* him seeing that, I'd meant to actually change into something presentable before he *did* see me. Then his gaze wandered back up to the goat I now held under one arm. One end of my glass stirring stick was still sticking out of her mouth. I hadn't thought to retrieve it yet. I was really going to have to get better at pet care.

Instead, Marcus lifted his hand, and Lulu deposited her spoils into it like this had been her plan all along and really, why hadn't I just *asked* her to give it back?

On seeing *what*, in particular, Lulu had stolen, Marcus smiled. There was a familiarity to that smile that made me heat up all over again, head to toe. He could have bottled that smile and sold it as a cure for hypothermia. Slowly his eyes met mine as he held the little glass stick up between his fingers. "This is your favorite?"

It was the same butterfly stirring stick he'd given me months ago. If it had been at all possible, I would have melted there on the spot. Turns out that wasn't possible though. I licked my lips. "Maybe?"

His smile deepened. "I suggest you put down the goat. And come outside."

"Why?" Even though I asked, I did as he suggested. Even closed Lulu in, like she shouldn't see what we were about to do on the porch. Not that we were going to do anything. Not when I might make something explode—or perhaps explode myself.

But Marcus, as usual, was taking his own time. In the darkness of the storm and the low-hanging roof, I could see him, but really *only* him. It helped that he was so close. He seemed to have forgotten that in coming outside, I would have to move past him. He was still holding that dratted stick. It glowed in his hand.

"Take it," he said softly, offering it to me. My hand met his as I did, and I did appreciate that it was no longer covered in goat drool, but I was more preoccupied with what his *other* hand was doing. He'd reached up, his fingertips delicate on my chin, like I was made of enchanted glass too, or maybe something even more special.

"Marcus—" I finally stopped looking at the butterfly stirring stick, ready to remind him, to warn him. But when I met his gaze, he was already leaning into me, his dark eyes warm too, just like his touch and his smile.

"It's going to be alright, Saki," he murmured, right before lowering his head the rest of the way and kissing me.

I bounced back immediately. Cushioned against his palm, my hand was clutching at the stirring stick. I was definitely trembling. I'm not sure I was even coherent. But there was only one thing on my mind. "Don't get hurt."

"I won't." His thumb stroked over my hand, and I glanced at it. The glass butterfly was still glowing—almost alive in the gloom.

"You—did something to it? Some sort of protection?" I glanced back up at him.

"Mmm." He smiled down at me, and that was more answer than the rumble in his chest—all the answer I needed, really. Relief mingled with the heat in my veins—for a moment.

"I'm leaving," I added. Just so that he would know. "After I get the resort set up, I mean. Not today. But—soon. Ish."

"Hmm," he said again, his voice lower this time. Still gazing at me. Not moving. But he obviously wanted to—didn't he? "You've made up your mind?"

"Yes." I leaned up into him, setting my free hand on his chest. To see what he would do. But I didn't have the patience. "Would you like to kiss me again anyway?"

He did, his lips coming back onto mine, warm and gentle and all of a sudden I was so aware of the storm around us, and the heat from the glass butterfly. With one hand, he cradled my head, his fingers slipping through my hair, pulling all my concentration back to him. My heart was free-falling through space. Under his wet shirt, I could feel his doing the same. But he stayed right where he was. Whatever he had done, it had worked.

Too soon, he pulled back, though he didn't make it very far. His nose brushed mine as he asked, "Would you like to know what I did?"

"I think it's better right now if I don't," I confessed, still breathless.

"Sweet Sakura." He was amused—he was teasing me, curse him. As if he could get any hotter. "But you know everything, don't you?"

My fingers twisted in his shirt. "All I know is—"

There was a scrambling, and then a small crash, from inside my cabin.

Marcus and I both leaned back, watching each other like teenagers uncertain if they were about to get away with a heist. From the corner of my eye, I noticed Lulu's white face appear in the window, and through the storm I could faintly hear her bleating. The answer was no—we weren't getting away with a thing.

When I met Marcus's gaze again, he was wearing the most adorable lopsided grin I'd ever seen. And when I burst out laughing, he joined in.

I took my new and improved butterfly from him, and led the way inside. At the door I turned and smiled at him over my shoulder. "Trust me, she's fine. The little criminal."

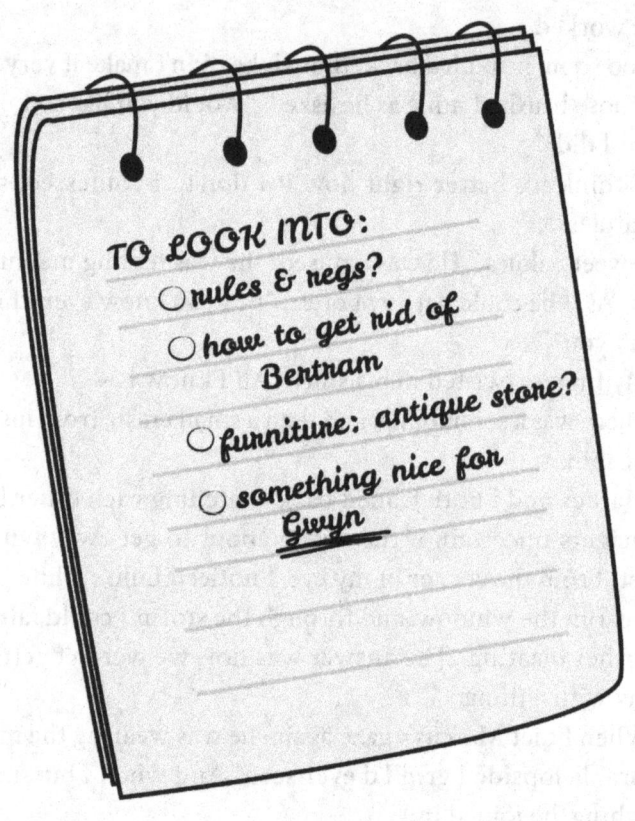

TO LOOK INTO:
- rules & regs?
- how to get rid of Bertram
- furniture: antique store?
- something nice for Gwyn

Chapter Fourteen: Business

∽◦◦◦∽

Marcus

I followed Sakura into her cabin. I would have followed her anywhere.

And she said she was planning to return to Belville . . . Well, I was glad to hear her sound more confident about it. Anything but the grief and uncertainty that had been in her voice the night before. Nevertheless, I no longer believed that that would be an end to whatever was between us. She herself had not said as much, and her return to Belville last time had not been enough to take her off my mind, either.

She could return again: that was all very well. But I was determined that I would act differently this time.

The goatling was, indeed, fine. It was soon clear that she had overturned a chair in her effort to get at Saki's uneaten lunch. I was put on goat-watching duty while Saki resumed her meal preparations, this time making food and tea for both of us. She kept talking all the while, explaining her encounter with Gwyndolen. It was marvelous.

". . . And then she pointed out, it's only a bunch of wood and glass and things. Really, we could make whatever we wanted."

My gaze had dropped to her mouth. It *was* marvelous, the way she could speak her mind so freely. But it was also so very tempting to try kissing her again.

"So, don't you—don't you have any thoughts about that?" Saki joined me on the couch, gracefully shooing Lulu away with one hand and managing a tray with mugs and plates in the other. The firelight from her hearth was casting soft light over her skin. I'd never known her to wear shorts—not even in the summer. It was *extremely* hard not to think about kissing her again.

She nudged my arm with the corner of the tray. "Thoughts?"

I looked at the ceiling and did my best. "What should I think?"

"Usually at this point in a conversation, you say something like, 'oh no, it's a category seven haunting,' or 'I can't allow it!' or 'banish her from the island before she does something dangerous!'"

"I've never said *any* of those things," I protested, distracted from the ceiling. Her eyes twinkled as she passed me a mug and plate. "There's no such thing as a 'category seven' haunting. The scale was only designed to go to five, to account for—"

"Marcus," Saki interrupted. "I thought you might have thoughts because you might have noticed I said 'we.'"

"Oh." I watched her sip her cocoa, her mug held in both hands. The sleeves of her sweater came nearly to her fingertips. It took me another moment to untangle what she had said. "Meaning yourself and—Gwyndolen? Or—?"

"Gwyn is lovely, and she has an army of robots, so that's useful," Saki remarked. "But she has her own work to do, not to mention a partner already. No, I meant 'we' as in me and—*you*. Not that I meant anything official, or anything dramatic, this is something I had been thinking *before* you showed up on my porch and—"

Saki blushed, which made me smile. It was good to know I wasn't the only one having some difficulty. I turned to my open-faced sandwich at last.

Only for Saki to tap me over the head with her plate. "Don't make fun of me, and don't be smug," she demanded, laughing. "What I meant is, you're the one who knows how things work around here. If I'm going to build a business up here, I need a local contact. Also, a sounding board. And probably more money. Also someone who can make sure the local ghosts or whatever don't get mad. So, want to go in halves with me?"

I kept my gaze riveted on the cheese and tomato sandwich she'd made. "I believe Bertram's primary purpose is to be a local contact, is it not?"

"Bertram? Have I not fired him yet?" Saki swallowed, then went on more seriously, "You can't honestly expect me to work with him. He's just a lackey. What did he want, by the way, other than to be annoying?"

"To convince you to either leave, or continue the development, with the aid of a local professor," I replied. "However it soon became clear that he and the professor differ on a number of important points."

119

"See, this is why you'd be an excellent business partner." Saki shifted on the sofa so she faced me, beaming over her sandwich.

Now seemed as good a time as any to let her know what else I'd done. "I visited Bertram's office yesterday. He was kind enough to provide me with a list of everyone who was working at the site and reported a ghostly encounter. I took the liberty of giving the list to Quinn last night."

"Also perfect." Saki's smile widened. "And don't you dare say next, 'why not work with Quinn?' because that man is *also* insufferable, just for different reasons. Also, isn't he leaving? And are you really sure you want me to look around for someone else to partner with?"

This last question was delivered with a knowing smirk. All I knew was, had it not been for the lunch plates and tea, Saki would have found herself in my lap at that point. I let my gaze linger on her just long enough that she realized it, and then I said, "I have never gone into business with anyone, Sakura."

"Good thing I'm not just anyone," she replied. "We can always sell it after we get things set up. But I *would* like to know I'm leaving this place in good shape, with someone who'll look after it properly. We can be all official and sign a contract and everything if you like."

She was making it so difficult to be civil. With an effort I finished my sandwich and set the plate on the floor. "I would *like* to know that the grounds aren't haunted and that you are safe."

She smiled at me angelically over her mug. "That's why you're here. So let's make it official."

The fact that she had honey on her lip only made her harder to resist.

But I had one more reservation. It would never do to go into business under false pretenses—particularly on such holy ground. I had no claim to this kind of site. "Sakura . . . you do realize that the only reason I am interested in this property is that you are here, don't you?"

Over the rim of her mug, her eyes glinted, her eyebrows arched. "Did I ever say it wasn't the same for me?"

So this was why she wanted me for a business partner? Very well—but I wasn't planning on being professional about the matter. Particularly not when the look on her face sent a thrill down my spine.

I leaned toward her at last, slowly, carefully. I took her mug from her and conjured an end table to place it on, reaching past her before settling my arm on the couch arm at her back. She was leaning under me now, and knew full well what my intent was, but she was watching me. Smiling softly. Biting her lip. It was possible she didn't fully trust herself and her magic, even still. But I did.

I kissed her deliberately, running my tongue over her bitten lip. Her quiet moan made me need more. I shifted one arm under her folded knees and the other around her shoulders, pulling her back into my lap. She came willingly, though she laid her hand on my chest, pausing to laugh at me.

"I didn't think you were so pushy," she murmured.

"Only with shadow witches who tease and flirt while looking so sweet," I replied, kissing her nose.

She laughed again. "You know . . . I don't really like a lot of people looking at me, like this."

Her legs, still draped over my arm, kicked nervously through the air. I had noticed, of course, that she didn't have any kind of glamour over her feet, but had thought no more of it. Clearly it was something she had thought of, though. I leaned back to look at her properly.

She was in a fuzzy sweater of some kind, and black shorts that ended midway up her thighs. Certainly not her usual attire when going outside, but it looked very comfortable, which was no doubt why she'd chosen it. This, then, was a look she considered private. And for her own sake, clearly no glamour was necessary. Just under her knees, her pale skin ended and her calves and feet were shaped in a smooth, pearlescent white, doubtless some kind of charmed substitute. The effect wasn't startling; I had known she used a glamour, and in my experience, when people went to such effort to conceal part of themselves, this was often the reason why.

When I met her gaze, she was biting her lip again. Worried.

"I don't mind not a lot of people looking at you like this," I told her contentedly. She was, after all, extremely cute.

As I'd hoped, her demeanor changed at once. She sighed with exaggerated exasperation and rolled her eyes, smiling nonetheless. "Really? That's all you have to say?"

"You keep asking me to say things," I told her, amused. "You seem to have forgotten who I am."

"Believe me, I haven't forgotten." Her eyes lingered on my lips—the effect was very pleasing. "But I don't know, this is another thing where I thought you would have—thoughts. Or questions. And let's not go through the whole routine again, okay? Let's just get it out of the way. Only people I consider family really see me this way. I was just feeling lazy earlier—I would have changed before letting you in if I had realized—if my magic wasn't being so—so—and if Lulu hadn't been such a little demon—"

As one, we glanced at the goatling, now curled up on the

rug by the blazing hearth. Lulu opened one eye to assess our attention. I smiled at her.

"Sakura," I said, taking advantage of the break in the conversation. I shifted back to her before she was quite done staring Lulu down, and because she was clearly more distressed than she was letting on, I couldn't help myself. I kissed her hair before going on, "I see that you are worried. But I do not see that you have anything to worry about. Why do you think I would mind?"

Once more her face turned up to mine, her blue eyes wide, bouncing from my face to her legs. "You don't find it—odd? Or distracting? Or—off-putting?"

"I am not surprised, if that's what you mean." It was difficult not to touch her, but judging by her uneasiness, I suspected that was not the right question to ask. "You didn't want to show me?"

"Well, it's not really the kind of thing I enjoy springing on people. Though it has to happen eventually—the way it all happened, they were made magically and bonded to me, so I can't remove them now," she said. "It was—a choice I made a long time ago. For better or worse. Anyway, I mean, I *was* hoping you would stop by. I was just expecting that I'd have made myself more presentable by then. I don't know, it's nothing to do with you, yourself, I know you're a perfectly kind person. But it's not exactly . . . a sexy look."

At that, I let myself start to smile at her. "You wanted to look sexy before seeing me?"

"Don't you even give me that," she retorted, grinning once more. "Don't you dare! You're the one who pulled me into his lap and went all smouldery at the thought of me working with someone else on this inn!"

"An inn, is it?" Though it was tempting to stay on topic, and to continue teasing her, I had a feeling she would be more comfortable if we let it rest. After all, she still hadn't started using her magic again. And I was curious what she had in mind.

"Well—I hadn't decided. We hadn't decided," she corrected herself, looking up. "This whole conversation started because I want your input, which I still do, by the way. But I was thinking—that might be good, mightn't it? This was already going to be some kind of super-resort, so there's already some interest in that. I did think of doing a tea house or bar instead, but I've spent the last several years running a cafe, and, I don't know, if I could maybe spend the next phase of my life washing fewer tea cups, that'd be nice—"

"A bar?" I was just catching on. She was, after all, still in my lap. But—a bar? Had she come up with that idea for me?

"I just thought, I know you like mixing drinks," she said, smiling as she confirmed my suspicions. She had no idea how close she came to not finishing her sentence. "So it seemed like something that might fit. I find that it really helps with a business if it's something you're passionate about, you know? Like with the Pomegranate—obviously I am really into tea—but for me it was always about helping people, giving them a place to come in from their busy lives and whatever was going on in the world, maybe even giving advice if they need it." She hesitated, and shuddered. "Okay, I'm done with that part of things. But—with an inn—it's a way to be even more helpful, you know?"

I considered her. "I thought you weren't going to be the one running the place?"

"Maybe not, but I'd still be involved, especially at the beginning," she replied. "And—I want to feel like it's something that will make this place better. Or—not that this site needs improving, but—something that would honor what the site is. Does that make sense?"

"It makes perfect sense," I told her. "And I believe it would be very much in keeping with the spirit of this place. To appreciate its history and importance, more than an evening or an afternoon is required. Giving visitors somewhere to stay is creating a refuge, an opportunity to reflect."

"Exactly." Saki beamed up at me. "See? You definitely have a lot to contribute. We can still have the inn have a bar if you want."

I chuckled. "I appreciate the thought, Sakura, but if you are not staying to run it, I do not expect to stay and tend bar. I will go as you go."

"Well—alright, if you don't mind." Her brow furrowed for a moment as she thought, her eyes fixed on my face. One hand still leaned against my chest.

I wondered what she could possibly be thinking. I wondered if she knew that the only thing I could think of in that moment was her.

Chapter Fifteen: Keys

❦

Sakura

I sat there in Marcus's lap trying for the life of me to think of businessy things and practicalities, and it was next to impossible. Sure, I could have moved. But he was so comfortable.

And that was how I wanted people to feel in this place. Comfortable . . . Safe . . . Accepted . . .

. . . Like they might kiss the face off the next person they saw?

Yep, definitely time to move on. I hopped up, gathering our empty plates as I went. "So, that's decided. Sort of. Obviously we're not committed yet, but I think it's a good idea, and you—?"

When I finally got the courage to turn round and glance

127

at Marcus, he was wearing that knowing smile again. Curse him. And judging by the way his gaze flicked up, he'd most likely been checking out my butt.

Well . . . This was definitely the most of me he'd ever seen. And I wasn't too unhappy about that . . .

Before my blush threatened to take over my entire face, I turned away again, headed for the kitchen. Marcus spoke to my back. "I believe it will be a good thing, Saki."

"So you're in, then?"

"I'm in."

"Good." I settled the dishes in the sink. I could have run cold water over them and simply heated it up over my wrists, probably. I was probably pink all over. Where in Beyond had this man come from??

I mean, the underworld, obviously, but aside from that.

I guess when you think about it, it's no surprise I've always been a little macabre.

"Anyway," I said loudly, apropos of nothing, "so, before we go making too many plans, I guess we should talk to Quinn again, right? See if he hunted down the haunting victims and all?"

"Something like that." Marcus's voice, when it came, came from entirely too close. Rather than opting to remain on the sofa like a good and polite house guest, the terrible god had snuck up on me, standing behind me at the sink. I jumped about a foot—he was lucky I didn't take out his chin. The fact that he was chuckling softly at me made it clear that he was fine. "Will you change first?"

"Oh, *now* all of a sudden you're interested in my clothing," I retorted, twisting to look up at him.

"I never said I wasn't interested before." His smile was very much cat-that-got-the-cream. Or goat-that-got-the-tomato-sandwich, actually.

"It's like pulling teeth to get you to say anything," I reminded him.

"I'll tell you something now." Marcus bent low, bringing his lips to my ear. "I think you're very lovely, Sakura. All of you. In all my life you're the person I've found hardest to resist. So if you want me to behave, you will have to tell me so. Otherwise I am liable to become distracted."

"Me, tell a god to behave?" I twisted to frown at him again, but was met halfway by his mouth, which wasn't such a bad thing. The way his hand slid slowly over my waist made me want to melt. He obviously wasn't kidding about his troubles with resistance. But I wasn't having such an easy time in that department either . . .

"The answer is no," he whispered, his breath tickling my cheek. "Your question earlier. No. I don't want you to partner with anyone else."

"But we're still remembering that I'm leaving, right?" I'll admit it—I was out of breath. Trying to remember why in Beyond I was standing at a sink in a tiny cabin beside the woods.

"Mmm. Yes. You will go wherever you please," he said thoughtfully, still leaning over me, so technically, I couldn't go anywhere. "But right now, you are here."

"Right. But we should be in town," I reminded him. "To see your friend. Remember?"

Marcus gave me a crooked smile, as if to say, *why is that important again?* but he did step back for just a moment. I took advantage and pressed him farther back, giving myself enough room to escape before I also forgot why.

Racing up to my room, I had to admit, I had my own silly grin plastered all over my face. Because it felt so good! Marcus was so good and passionate and apparently very determined and—well, let's just say, having him see me at very much less than my best and still having proof that he was into me was . . . freeing. A relief. More than that, it was wonderful.

But you still have to go back to Belville, a little voice in my head said.

That helped dim the rosy glow. Not just because I'd be leaving—after all, I could come back. Conceivably. But—because of what I'd done. Marcus was awfully good, but I sure wasn't. We could be into each other for now, sure, but—even with the charm, I had to make sure that he didn't get hurt.

I tucked that little butterfly into my headband, so that it perched just behind my ear. The sweater and shorts I exchanged for a plaid dress and several warm petticoats—after all, it was still raining. I could hear the sound thrumming against the roof. For the first time, I understood what people meant when they said that rain sounded comforting or homey.

Once the outfit was complete with stockings and rain boots—a change I had to make magically, and which I did with my eyes squeezed shut, but ended up being just fine—*thank you, butterfly*—I ran back down the stairs. Lulu looked up sleepily from the hearth, but didn't bother moving. Marcus stood at the sink. He'd just finished washing our dishes.

See? Too good.

"Thank you for that," I said, bouncing slightly on my toes.

"You are welcome. Thank you for lunch," he replied, his

dark eyes warm on mine.

"Yes, well, thank you for the end table also, by the way. I'm keeping that, if you don't mind," I said airily. What a show-off, conjuring furniture left and right! But it had served a very useful purpose, so I couldn't mind. "I just have to check that everything is goat-proof, and then we can leave . . ."

"Is there such a thing?" Marcus mused mildly from the kitchen.

"I suspect not," I confessed. "But I don't want to be a total failure as a goat-keeper, so I try to at least hide the knives and other sharp things."

"She loves you," he said simply.

That pulled me up short. I glanced at the curled white form on the rug. "It's only been a day. But—I really am glad she settled in."

"Animals have a way of choosing their people," Marcus replied.

"Not unlike some gods I know," I retorted. The moment I said it, I couldn't believe I'd let it escape. But from the look on his face, it delighted Marcus. Before he could take that as license to do anything else, I added hastily, "Okay, good to go? Good. We're going now. Should we try to . . . reach Gwyn?"

That hesitation was me looking out the window and noticing that the path to the station was more like a small but mighty river.

"Saki," Marcus said, in his you're-overlooking-something-and-I'm-sympathetic voice. "I can take you with me. We could travel straight to his building."

"Oh. Right." I steadied myself, realizing just how much it had taken a toll on me, this trying-not-to-use-magic thing.

Even with the charm, even with someone else wielding the power, I felt briefly nervous. "You don't want to go straight for his rooms?"

Marcus smiled—he knew I was kidding. I knew very well that when given an option, Marcus would appear outside whatever door he wanted to enter, and would knock politely as if he was somebody's grandparent waiting for tea, not an actual deity with business to perform.

Not as though he was moving through space—and probably, to some extent, time—by use of a divine key. I knew some of the mythology about it, of course, from my research into Persephone. That's the thing about death: it can show up anywhere. I found it endlessly fascinating that Marcus could have these powers and still be so present and sweet. It was probably something I needed to learn from, to be honest.

"Okay, fine, let's go," I sighed, unable to put it off. "Um—how do you—"

Marcus crossed the small cabin floor and his arm slid around my waist, and I turned naturally with him, as if we were dance partners who had been practicing this kind of thing all our lives. He stepped and I stepped with him. And just like that, we were in a dimly lit, carpeted hallway.

"Oof." I wasn't at all uncomfortable: not even remotely so, actually. But that was what was surprising about it. Marcus was really good at that kind of magic, apparently. But, I reminded myself, he'd had time to perfect his technique. "Never thought I'd be in this hallway again," I added lightly.

"Come along," he said, his arm still around me. "Let's see if he's in."

"Of course he will be," I muttered rebelliously as we climbed the stairs. "Does he even have any actual clients aside from you?"

Marcus grinned at me but didn't deign to answer. He didn't have to, because in that moment, Quinn opened one of the doors on the landing above.

"Marcus, I was just going to ring for you when I heard your step," the insufferable man said, grinning broadly. He must have ears like a cat's. But to me he added very nicely, "Good to see you again, Saki. How is Miss Lulu?" so I decided we were on friendly terms again for now.

"Guarding the castle," I replied. "Marcus said you were going to interview people about the site?"

"Already done. I've had a busy morning," Quinn said smugly as he ushered us into his living room. He probably did have a right to the smugness, so I let it slide. "Take a seat anywhere. You can just toss those newspapers off the armchair. Unless you two would like the loveseat . . . ?"

Okay, that, I couldn't let that slide. I disengaged from Marcus to turn and stare at Quinn, hands on my hips. "Could you be more obvious, please?"

"I could say the same to you," Quinn replied, his impossible grin widening. "So, ghosts and orbs are what pass for romantic atmosphere these days, eh?"

"You heard confirmed sightings, then?" Marcus sat primly on a stool by the fireplace, effectively ending our squabble. I gave him a suspicious glare too for good measure, and he smiled faintly in response. At that point, I decided my best course of action was to shove all Quinn's papers onto the floor and occupy the armchair.

"I heard all that and more." Quinn actually rubbed his hands together as he paced before us. Apparently, whatever news he had was too good for sitting down. His living room was totally unlike anything else in Helenia, which tended to be balmy, tiled, and sunlit. Meanwhile Quinn's quarters were stuffy, overcrowded with notes and pictures, and strewn with strange-smelling cups and bottles. The curtains were drawn, leaving only slits of gray light and the glow from the fireplace to see by. As he paced, he ran his hand over the back of the loveseat, leaving dust in his wake. I was now glad I'd avoided it.

"You have incredible luck, Saki," Quinn continued. "As it turns out, you've not only managed to inherit the most ancient and revered site on the island—but also the most cursed."

"... it was after the dawn broke, after we'd kept watch all night, that we finally saw the back of an enormous creature breach the surface. But in an inkling it was gone ..."

from "An Expedition to Summit Mount Hollow"

FOR MARKUS

and Sakura

... but really Lulu

Chapter Sixteen: Curses

Marcus

My friend Quinn is keen-eyed and likely to notice when someone is not listening to him. So I focused on him. But from the seat I'd chosen, Saki was visible in my periphery.

She startled when Quinn said *cursed*. I was surprised myself.

"You'd be *less* surprised if you paid attention to anything half as much as you did each other," Quinn said, correctly interpreting our blank faces. He pointed at me. "You in particular should have seen this coming. You would have, if you hadn't spent the past six months pining."

Saki glanced in my direction. "You were pining?"

"Again, not the point," Quinn declared. "Talk about it later. Do you want to hear my reports or not?"

Saki swung back to look at him, her eyes narrowing. "Has anyone told you today that you're insufferable?"

"This morning when I went to get my daily coffee," Quinn replied cheerfully. "I then went to see Vera, the *former* project manager for the grand spa. Care to guess why she is 'former'?"

"She wasn't a ghost, was she?" Saki asked, more sober now than teasing.

She looked at me, and I shook my head. "As far as I know, no one has died at the site. Lately." If anyone had, I would have sensed them during my time there. And I would have been far more determined to get Saki to abandon the property. Not that it would have done much good. But Quinn was right: I should have been paying more attention.

Quinn eyed us, one then the other, and seemed mollified to see that we were taking the matter more seriously. He sat on the loveseat across from me, elbows on his knees, fingers beneath his chin. His eyes had the glow which I had learned inevitably accompanied an investigation.

"Vera is the premier construction manager in Helenia," Quinn informed us. "In order to see her without an appointment, I had to employ strategy number three, which involved dropping *your* name," he told me meaningfully. I nodded, appreciating the warning. Usually I was more circumspect in making my business public, but this was an exception. Quinn went on, "I figured it wasn't too far from the truth. And with the right prompting, she was very helpful.

"Mind you, this isn't the kind of thing she talks about," he added, glancing at Saki. "Vera is known in Helenia for being no-nonsense and down-to-earth. That's how she's gotten where she is. Only the biggest and most complicated development projects get her attention these days. Her schedule is booked out years in advance. Even so, Spa Hallow would have been a feather in her cap."

"Okay, enough preamble, I get it," Saki said. "Tough construction lady, didn't want to tell anyone about ghosts. Except you."

"Not ghosts," Quinn said. "Curses. She's been on site since last fall, when 'Phase One' began, and she said they started having trouble almost immediately. She's *convinced* that your property is cursed. That orb we saw in the forest? She says it's a magical spirit of chaos bent on destruction."

At that, I was puzzled. I hadn't sensed a destructive force at work on the mountain. But then again, as Quinn had pointed out, I had been distracted. I had overlooked the presence in the lake, even. Had my lack of focus endangered everyone?

Saki's nose wrinkled as she thought. "It didn't seem all that destructive in the woods. It was just . . . watching us."

"It was frightening enough that we ran," Quinn pointed out.

"But that could have been something else," Saki argued.

"Either way. Maybe it's a destructive spirit of chaos that likes goats. Maybe it decided to leave us alone because we had Lulu."

Sakura's obvious disbelief morphed into disdain. "*That's* your answer?"

"Let me remind you that *you* two are the magical experts here," Quinn replied. "I'm merely the *investigative* expert, and I'm reporting what I learned. After talking to Vera, I tracked down her second-in-command, one Catfight McGee. And that was no small matter, let me tell you. I found him on a fishing boat in the harbor under an assumed name. He corroborated all the tales of stolen materials, broken equipment, and terrorizing howls, but *he* attributed it all to a vengeful spell that took the form of a giant monster bent on freeing the land from whoever tried to own it."

"If that was the case, it was targeting the wrong people," Saki said. "Why didn't anything try to track down the owner herself?"

"Would you like me to bring the witnesses straight to you next time, so that you can argue with them?" Quinn asked.

I decided to wade in. "Saki has a point. Magic of this variety, curses and spells, tend to be very specific. A curse targeted at an owner shouldn't bother a construction foreperson."

Quinn glanced once more from me to Saki, his expression mild. "The two of you are conveniently forgetting that something *did* happen to the previous owner. Nothing so dramatic as being chased through the woods with a goat in arms, perhaps, but nonetheless, she: became embroiled in crime and unsavory characters, was accused and convicted of multiple serious offenses, lost her entire financial empire, and was forced to give up her dream of a mountaintop spa." To emphasize his point, he counted the events off on his fingers as he spoke. "Doesn't that sound a bit like destructive vengeance to you?"

"It sounds like justice." Saki was more thoughtful, but her brows were still creased. "*I* haven't committed any crime."

My gaze lingered on her. While true, this was perhaps the most positive thing she'd said about herself since she'd arrived in Helenia. I wondered if she realized that.

When she caught my gaze she blushed, and *I* realized that I might have reminded her of her troubles.

As I cursed myself, Quinn continued talking. "Maybe that was just the curse going for the path of least resistance," he suggested. "It could look different for you."

Saki now looked torn. I did my best to rectify the situation. "You are speaking as though you, yourself, believe in a curse.

Can you be so certain?"

"Honestly, I'm just trying to make sure you two understand the possible danger," Quinn said. As he turned to me, he ran his hand through his hair. For a moment I could see real worry on his face. "And I know you knew it from the start, Marcus, but still, I can't help but feel responsible for sending you up there. I don't want you to carry on unprepared. You still haven't heard about my third visit—to one Hetty de Saumon, confirmed victim of the floating lights."

Saki wavered on her perch. "But *she* also wasn't—"

"Not a victim in that she died," Quinn said, correcting himself. He leaned forward, now ticking off points against his palm. "She was in charge of the team building the workers' cabins. One evening after hearing reports of rustling and unease among her employees, she decided to investigate. The lights led her into the woods behind the lake, and at that point, the monster appeared. Scared her stiff, she said. And mind you, this woman is a proud troll. She wasn't found until next morning, and when she could talk, she gave her notice immediately. Hasn't said a word about it since."

"Except to you," Saki pointed out. But the mischief had left her.

Quinn inclined his head. "At the risk of immodesty, this *is* why Marcus hired me."

"So the lights and the monster *are* separate, but—might be working together?" Saki puzzled. "And neither is necessarily a lake monster or an old deity . . ."

"Unless you know better?" Quinn asked me.

"At this moment, I do not." I shifted, unwilling to admit what I did know—and what I did not. I had not been so uncomfortable in centuries.

As though she could sense it—perhaps she could—Saki provided me with a respite, turning to Quinn. "You've spoken to people involved directly in the project, but still, all people who sound as unfamiliar with magic as you are. Do you know anyone else—some scholar, maybe—someone who might understand the theory involved?"

"For the record, I'm not *unfamiliar* with magic. I just know my weaknesses." Quinn's smile flashed briefly before he became thoughtful. "That was the second reason I wanted to reach out to you. As I see it, that's the next step. I was thinking of going to my contact at the Department."

I understood the thought. It was logical, and Quinn would of course suggest it. Nevertheless I glanced at Saki, uncertain.

She met my gaze. "The 'Department'?"

"A special branch, of sorts, of the local university," Quinn explained. "A collaboration with Witches, aimed at dealing with the ancient, *magical* artifacts that crop up from time to time. With Helenia's history, they're more common than in other parts of Beyond. And with tourists running amok, it's proved a lot simpler to have someone with expertise track such things down rather than letting them be randomly discovered."

Saki glanced at me again, one eyebrow raised. I knew precisely what she was thinking of: my own collection of arcane artifacts, safe at home. But no one, not even one as long-lived as I, could possibly track down *everything*. I shrugged and bowed my head in acknowledgment of that fact. Sakura smiled, amused.

". . . And while I reach out to my contact, you two could start your own department on nonverbal communication," Quinn added. "If you get tired of chasing down orbs. One hesitates to ask, but what *have* you been doing up there? Any more sightings?"

"Just Bertram so far, unfortunately," Saki said, turning back to Quinn. "And some professor he was hoping to intimidate me with. That wasn't—?"

She turned to me, and I obliged. "The professor in question was from the History department, and harbored some hopes of conducting digs at the site. Professor Myrtle," I said, for Quinn's benefit. "They were unconnected with the Department."

"You both make it sound like a spy organization." Saki chuckled at me, and I smiled back.

"More spy than professor," Quinn agreed briskly. "They don't run classes at all—it's more of a public service. And a service to the university's considerable museum, of course. Saki, Bertram hasn't mentioned anything about a curse to you?"

"He went on about monsters and ghosts, but that was it, I think. Oh, and the lake monster being able to sense your darkest fears, or something." Saki scrunched her nose as she tried to remember. I was surprised to hear Bertram's version of the lake monster story. I had never heard any such thing myself—nor had I sensed it earlier. As I thought, Saki went on, "But he didn't come over yesterday, and he didn't get to talk to me this morning. I was busy meeting Gwyn. I wonder what *she* would say about all this? She must have some expertise—after all, she's the one carting everyone to and from the site."

"She says her bots sometimes go haywire if she lets them out around the lake, but she's never thought it was anything evil," Quinn supplied. At Saki's look of surprise, he grinned and went on, "What do you take me for? As a reliably chatty and outside perspective, not to mention someone who works conveniently close to my favorite cafe, she was naturally the person I went to first. She was of the opinion, though, that the haywire bots were due to some kind of leftover divine energy, not any curse or haunting."

As one, Saki and Quinn turned to look at me. Still thinking of this morning's events, I stumbled a little on my words. "Well—I wouldn't have said—there *is* energy present at the site, particularly the lake," I said. Though I looked at Saki particularly, it did not seem that she caught my meaning. "But nothing that would explain the hauntings or 'bots'."

"Unless the hauntings and orbs *want* the divine energy," Saki pointed out.

"That's not a terrible thought, actually," Quinn mused.

"Oh, *thank you*," said Saki, with exaggerated sweetness.

Sensing more than bickering might ensue, I cleared my throat. "Perhaps we should focus on the lead we have. Quinn, why don't Sakura and I accompany you to meet your friend. We can explain the matter and determine our next steps."

Quinn, who had been pondering the matter with his elbows on his knees, sat up. "Now?"

Rain lashed at the curtained windows.

"Now," I said.

I was aware of Saki's gaze on me, and slightly embarrassed by it. It was *her* site, after all, and she might not like me making decisions. But—she *had* asked me to be her business partner. And I felt strongly that we needed to resolve this. The fact that my own endeavors had uncovered so little worried me . .
.

I caught her glance. There was an appreciative quality to it that made me wish that, instead, I had suggested Quinn go on his own so that I could sweep her up and kiss her again.

"Sounds like a perfectly good idea to me," she announced, her words warming me further. "What's the matter, Quinn? Haven't you got an umbrella in all this mess?"

Trent,

I'm so sorry you're going through this. I can't believe the True Love ritual lied to you, and how awful she turned out to be! None of this is your fault. If you need anything, just let me know.

Your friend forever

Chapter Seventeen: 2.0

Sakura

It turned out that the University of Helenia was one of those places that's so old, it's aged into its own sort of magic. Not unlike Hideaway Lake, really, but in this case it was a much more ivy-covered, academic sort of magic. The U of H was the kind of place that had been around so long, the city had had to fill in around it. We walked off of a perfectly normal, bustling street and into a tranquil park full of old white buildings, statue-dotted lawns, and students wrapped up in scarves carrying too many books.

Students, and professors too, it turned out. We'd only made it partway through the campus before a person under a blue umbrella accosted us—accosted Marcus, in fact.

Quinn and I were deep in a conversation about the scale of hauntings at the time, but I noticed the moment it happened.

We were sharing a very large umbrella that might have been as old as the university itself, after all. Marcus's presence beside me was a constant comfort (and source of interest, particularly after his conduct at my cabin). When he stopped politely, I jerked to a halt.

"Pluto, what a pleasant surprise," the stranger was enthusing.

"Professor Myrtle," said Marcus. I took a hint from his intentional tone. This, then, had been Bertram's partner-in-attempted-intimidation earlier!

I took a closer look. Myrtle had more of an absent-professor air than a persuasive-accomplice one, I thought.

"Are you here to research Mount Hallow, and the Gods' Reflecting Pool? I have records of all the past expeditions—not that they ever came to much. Is this Sakura? What a pleasure to meet you. Please call me Myrtle. And Quinn Doyle? I've heard of you, of course—are you investigating the legends too?"

Myrtle's handshake was wet, cold, and just as insistent as their conversation. Despite my surprise, I had to admire the professor's commitment to purpose. "Hi, Myrtle," I said, taking over for Quinn and Marcus. "Sorry I missed you earlier. Bertram and I are having a difference of opinion, which he doesn't seem to realize yet. I hope he didn't make you any promises?"

Myrtle blinked, but refocused on me without missing a beat. Their eyes were deep and foresty green, almost mesmerizing. "Bertram! The boy is all at loose ends, has been since it became clear which direction the trial was headed. He just needs a little patience."

That was a new take on Bertram. I caught Marcus's eye,

amused, softening a little despite my better judgment.

"But in the meantime we can *absolutely* help each other. I'm so glad you've come to see me," Myrtle carried on, like a magitech train loaded down with optimism.

"I'm afraid we're actually here on some business with Quinn, and don't have much time," I said, bright and apologetic but very firm. It was raining buckets, after all, and I wasn't about to get drawn into *another* investigation.

"Let me just give you my business card, then," said the indefatigable Myrtle. Neither Quinn nor Marcus had managed to get in a word. "The students would *so* benefit from an expedition. You know what they're like these days—no practical experience, none at all, the lot of them. It'd do them real good to get their hands dirty. And I have the ear of Town Hall, too, don't forget that! If you'd like a historic marker, or any kind of designation, just you let me know. Of course, the land is yours, but the city does recognize some shared responsibility for ancient sites—or they *should*—such a *good* thing," said Myrtle, smiling at me in a rather ferocious fashion, "that you put a stop to the development and—and *all that!*"

"Thanks?" I glanced at the business card that had been pressed into my hand, my head spinning. Myrtle and their blue umbrella were already gone.

"Word on the street had it that Minotaur Enterprises paid Town Hall to look the other way as they built the resort on an ancient site," Quinn told me helpfully. "Professor Myrtle might have somebody's ear, but I doubt they had deep enough pockets to fight construction."

"Ah. That explains it, then." I tucked the green-and-gold business card into my purse as we began walking again, almost cautiously, as though we might get stopped again at any moment. Despite the whirlwind of it all—or maybe even because of it—I had to admit that I kind of liked the professor. "Was that pretty much what they had to say this morning, too, Marcus?"

"This meeting was rather less restrained," he reported. There was a strain in his voice that indicated he had found it to be a bit *much*. I caught his eye again, and he smiled at me, acknowledging his conversational limitations. The warmth of his camaraderie almost made me forget the weather.

Fortunately, we didn't have to linger in it much longer. Quinn led the way to the corner of campus, where a particularly decrepit building lurked behind a row of cypress trees. From the outside it looked like it might cave in on us. However, the moment we made it in through the double glass doors, my impression changed.

The lobby was wide and long, and absolutely *crammed* with art. Pictures on the walls, so many you couldn't see a paint color, and statues everywhere—to the detriment of any sofas. Marcus and I loitered in the midst of it, trying not to drip on anything too ancient, while Quinn signed a few chummy words with a receptionist behind an enormous desk. He had to *open a new case*, apparently, *and get us assigned an agent*, which all seemed far too spy-like to be happening in what was basically an art gallery. Even when he'd rejoined us and was explaining things, in his non-explanation sort of way, I found myself a bit overwhelmed.

And into this strange limbo, *she* came.

Listen, I was never the kind of girl who "just doesn't have girl friends, and I don't know why!" (gag me). I know I can be competitive and jealous and that deep down I still believe I'd be prettier if only I was taller and more willowy. But I

149

also know that my first impulse is not always right, and after years of practice, I can usually check a bad impulse with the best of them.

(Plus, I got very lucky with Glacial, Red, and Mel back in Belville. Home.)

So. The Witch who'd apparently been assigned to our case entered the lobby. She led with her hips, that super confident, swaying kind of walk that's hands-down impossible as far as I'm concerned. Her complexion was creamy and her lips and lashes were curling all over the place. Her hair was so black it was iridescent and it rippled behind her, falling straight to her waist in thick layers. Witches don't have a "uniform," unless they're students in school, but nonetheless her clothing screamed *I'm a Witch and I'm here to take charge*: a black silk top with bell sleeves and a neckline that revealed almost too much perfect cleavage, a black miniskirt and silver belt over fishnet tights and, yes, thigh-high black boots. Teenage Saki would have died to wear that outfit.

But teenage Saki had been neither tall nor willowy, nor especially confident. This Witch, obviously, was all three.

She batted her eyelashes at Quinn but went immediately to Marcus. We'd all turned toward her, standing at attention— though my jaw was probably on the floor—and she was only an inch or two shorter than him. Perfect height for tipping her head up into his face as she shook his hand.

"It's a pleasure to see you again," she told him, her voice as gorgeous as the rest of her.

Meanwhile I made an awkward, clumsy noise, along the lines of, *eep!*

Everyone turned to me, and all of a sudden she was coming over to shake *my* hand too. "Quinn I know, of course, and

Marcus I've had the honor of doing business with. Which just leaves you. You *must* be Sakura of the Black Wings, yes? You can call me Scarlet Onyx."

Scarlet Onyx? Her eyes were ruby red, and so were her nails. Her hand made mine look like a blob. I know everybody is their own person and we all have our own journeys and whatnot, but in that moment, my first thought was, *It's like she's me, 2.0. The impossibly improved version.*

But like I said, we don't always cling to those first impulses, right? So I gave myself a mental shake and tried to be normal. And reminded myself to focus on what she'd done, which was *to say my full, true name.*

Who *did* that, out in public? No one, that's who. No magical practitioner, anyway. I wasn't even sure Mel or Red *knew* my actual name, that's how private it was. And come on—Scarlet Onyx? No way had she just given me her real name. But she pulled out mine? Was she trying to make some kind of point, or to threaten me? It wouldn't be a shock, coming from a Witch to a shadow witch. But most people were more . . . *covert* about it.

"You've met?" Quinn asked, in his annoyingly offhand and, in that moment, truly wonderful way. Because my words were all dying in my throat.

"Don't be silly, Quinn." Scarlet turned her catlike smile on him and finally let go of my hand. After a beat, though, just long enough to prove everyone here was waiting for an explanation, she glanced back down at me. "I've heard *all* about you, honey."

For a moment my heart leapt. Had Marcus already said something? If he had, then—

"Some of the other Witches in my year and I are still *very*

151

close," Scarlet continued. Squishing my hopes like a bug full of pus. I knew where this was going. My first impulse was sheer terror, and I don't think I managed to control it. "I've had so many letters about you . . . from Trent."

My name, when did I tell him my name? How many people did he tell? Visions of a circle of avenging Witches in black surrounding me, casting spells impossible to escape, closed in. The lump in my throat was huge. Any moment now, I'd—

Get a grip, Saki. Cry later. Focus now. Just get through. One breath. Then another, said the wiser voice in my head.

Infinitely grateful, I clung to that idea. I squeezed my eyes shut for just a second. When I reopened them, I was ready to return Scarlet's smile.

"In that case," I said, firmly stamping the quaver out of my voice, "I completely understand if you'd rather not work with someone like me."

Scarlet's eyes widened, like she was surprised—but only for a flash, and then it was gone. "Are you kidding? I've always thought I might have gone into shadow magic, myself. Something about it is so seductive, don't you think?" She smiled lazily at Marcus.

My blood was boiling. "How very *brave* of you," I said. "To hide behind your fake name and your comfortable job and think about how attractive you could be if only everyone approved of you less."

This time her eyes definitely widened. Her nostrils, perfect as they were, flared. "Trust me, honey, dealing with a curse at Hideaway Lake, a site running over with divine energy, will be *anything* but comfortable. Still, I'm surprised that you needed to call in help . . ."

"That was my idea," said Quinn. We all ignored him. I

ignored Marcus, too. I couldn't bear looking at him.

"Meaning what? That because I'm a shadow witch, I must deal only in curses? Spit it out," I said, focused on Scarlet. "You've got no problem spilling secrets, it seems."

"Meaning I thought you were supposed to be powerful," she retorted.

Oh—my magic. My magic! I could have cried all over again. Oh, to let it out, to do anything! Instead I was fighting tooth and nail to keep it *in.*

"Many a powerful force is notable for its ability to cloak itself," Marcus said quietly. "It becomes a survival skill."

Scarlet clearly made note of that. She looked at me suspiciously this time, like I might throw a snake in her face or flap my petticoats and turn into a ginormous harpy. But she knew a good exit when she heard one—I had to give her that. She turned her back on me, to face Marcus instead.

"I'm happy to be of assistance," she told him, her voice all smooth and perfect again. "I'll have to start by investigating the site. *Very* thoroughly. To be of any real use, I'll need to be there all night long."

Everyone turned to me. Because I'd scoffed. Very loudly.

"Have fun with that. Knock yourself out," I said. "And in case you were wondering, no. That wasn't a curse."

the Department
hereby recognizes

Scarlet Onyx

for exemplary service to
town, comrades, and posterity
in her efforts to contain
ancient magic.

Chapter Eighteen: Witches

~∞~

Marcus

Scarlet left us to ourselves for a moment, to gather whatever supplies she felt she needed. I had indeed crossed paths with her before, but I had never known her to be so performative.

What I was truly worried about, though, was Saki and her obvious vulnerability. Though I wanted nothing more than to pull her into my arms, she stopped me, her hand on mine. Her eyes not meeting my face.

"Just let me have the umbrella for a moment?" she said quietly.

I glanced around us, at Quinn, who demurely looked away. "Saki . . ."

"I'll be fine. You know I will," she said, a challenge in her voice.

It seemed to me that the best thing I could do was show

my faith in her. "Of course." I let her take the umbrella, and though my gaze trailed her out the door, I stayed put.

When we were alone in the lobby, Quinn moved closer to me. He let out a low whistle. "Sorry, Marcus. It didn't occur to me that Saki might *know* some Witches here. I thought we'd find a neutral third party."

"It is not something you could have foreseen," I said. Through the glass doors, I could see Saki pacing. My heart ached. She must be hurt, yes, but also frightened. To have someone speak her full name so easily . . . I had not minded it when she had done it to me, because I trusted her, and she already was such a force in my life. But for a powerful stranger to do so, and with obvious dislike, spelled danger.

And while *I* was afforded a great deal of calm by the fact that I was protected by my own divine power, what must Saki think now, given that she was still loath to use her magic?

"Hey." Quinn nudged me back to the present. "You've seen it too, right?"

I turned to him. "Seen what?"

Quinn glanced around, lowering his voice, speaking quickly. "I don't make guesses, you know that, but I'd put money on the fact that there's a living person behind this cursing and haunting at Hideaway Lake. The timing is too convenient for it to be *just* ancient magic, and the stakes are too high."

"But you told Saki the curse might act on her, too." I frowned.

"And I stand by that. It might—or something very *like* a curse might, also," Quinn said. "Now that the Department is involved, we're going to find out, one way or another. But in the meantime I think it's best if you two stuck together."

My frown faltered as my heart shuddered.

"You and Saki," Quinn added, an unnecessary clarification to make his point. "You need to be looking out for each other. I know it seems like this is a remote site up the mountain and no one can get you, but it should be obvious now that nothing is farther from the truth."

I swallowed. "You really suspect someone of meddling?"

"Let's just say I see plenty of people with motive." Quinn checked them off on his fingers, his body angled toward me as though even the gesture was a secret. "Bertram, the assistant, who according to your paperwork, gets ownership of the property if Saki leaves. Catfight admitted to a fling with Bertram, and who's to say he wouldn't act on his behalf? Then there's Hetty, even Vera, the former employees with axes to grind and no love lost for Minotaur Enterprises— or Spa Hallow. Gwyndolen and her bevvy of convenient accomplices don't like the construction, either, and her partner is a leader of the local parks movement. Professor Myrtle's just odd enough, and determined enough. For a committed academic like that, there's nothing in the world as important as their research. She might even *want* Bertram to take over, if she considers him more malleable than Saki. And now Scarlet—"

"That's a different matter," I said, startled.

"Is it?" Quinn gave me a hard look. "Or is it the mythology of a 'curse' catching up with us?"

I shook my head. "It was your idea to come here—"

"It was, and I stand by that too. Sometimes you have to poke the bear to find out what's in the cave." Quinn turned, and in a moment, I too heard Scarlet's approaching footsteps. In our last moment alone, he added, "I'm just saying. I know

I'll be careful: I need *you* two to be careful, too."

In thinking it over, I understood that this sentiment was a reasonable one. It was, however, foiled when we left the Department with Scarlet and soon realized that Saki was nowhere in sight.

After making me swear to stay put, Quinn conducted a few quick inquiries. They served only to confirm what I already felt sure of: that Saki had headed toward the gondola—toward her cabin, and her goat. In the meantime, I was watching Scarlet—and Scarlet was watching me. It was a new development. She had always before been one of those people who was a little *too* interested in my role, and inclined to be overly friendly. Now, her demeanor was decidedly prickly.

As was my own. I needed no warnings from Quinn, whispered in lobbies, to understand that Scarlet had been rude to Saki and therefore had caused much of this distress.

"So," she said, as we waited for Quinn under the Department's awning, "I'm sure you did your research, before you got mixed up in this affair?"

I did not dignify this with a response.

She tried again. "I'm surprised to see you involved in something like this."

I continued to feel no need to comment.

Scarlet turned away. "I thought you had better taste."

At that, my anger broke. *Angry*—I had not been angry with anyone in a very, very long time. Not like this. It filled my chest, distorting my power, distorting my mask. When Scarlet glanced back at me, I saw fear cross her face.

That was the point at which Quinn returned, and I immediately snapped back to normal. Because with Quinn present, I was able to take action. The moment he offered his findings, I offered to take them both to the lake. Though he might have had thoughts of his comfortable home and a private dinner, my friend was steadfastly loyal. He made no complaint, and I whisked them both along with me.

We got to the lake before Saki could, of course. Her travel was far from instant. I wished I could have gone straight to her, but the idea was irresponsible with Scarlet in tow. Instead I hoped to set Scarlet and Quinn up with their investigations as quickly as possible, and then . . .

And then?

Quinn had told me he wanted both myself and Saki to be careful, and I agreed. But what would Saki want?

Worry for her consumed my thoughts. It made it difficult to deal with Scarlet's careful preparations. To her credit, she prepared for her work thoroughly, but it soon became clear that she didn't prefer to work without an audience. She kept us with her at the edge of the lake, under a little canopy she'd constructed with a spell. Her initial survey, she explained, would be done via divination.

"That's *if* the bones can tell me anything, given all the shadow magic around," she added. "Reading the bones works well with ancient and divine energies, but *loose magic* can sometimes interfere."

I thought the comment superfluous. I turned to watch the station behind us, where Saki was just arriving. Though she must have seen us, she lingered on the platform, talking to Gwyn.

"We went to the Department because you're supposed to be the best," Quinn told Scarlet, a coolness in his voice.

"And we are. I am. It takes a strong power to deal with

disruptions like the ones around here," Scarlet replied.

I ignored them. Saki was hurrying to her cabin. The umbrella, caught in the wind, was carrying her along. She didn't glance our way, not once.

"I'll take a few readings here generally, then you can tell me the details of everything going on. Then I'll move around the site, do some specific readings, and see what comes up," Scarlet was saying.

"If *something* doesn't interrupt you," Quinn remarked dryly.

"Yes, I'm sure you'd love to have something to chase down. But that isn't usually how these manifestations work," Scarlet said. "The power involved is much more subtle. Especially at a place like this—Mount Hallow has *always* been a home to gods and a pathway to divinity. Right?"

Though I was watching the lit windows of Saki's cabin, I could feel that this question was directed at me. It sent a shiver down my spine. Saki had asked me about death and my powers this morning. But this question was far more common. Inevitably it filled me with a sense of dread, not for myself, but for the ill-fated seekers who asked it.

"Right?" Scarlet stood, and asked the question directly. "Isn't it true that any mortal who gets past the Gods' Reflection Pool, climbs the stairs, and makes it to the top of the mountain is rewarded with the nectar of immortality?"

"I have heard of a legend to that effect," I said.

"Refresh my memory," said Quinn to Scarlet—a welcome interruption. "Why was it supposed to be difficult to get past Hideaway Lake?"

"The *Reflection Pool* is a test of a hero's self-awareness." Irritation colored Scarlet's voice. Her work at the Department required her to be an expert on all local legends, and it was clear she expected us to be more familiar with them. "It shows you what you keep hidden in your heart. According to the legend."

"Ah. So naturally, those filled with envy, greed, or violent intentions get eaten up by the monster?" Quinn suggested. "Do your legends say what the monster *is*, by the way?"

"It is whatever it needs to be," Scarlet said.

"But always *in* the lake?" Quinn.

"It doesn't need to be out of the lake. The lake is the test."

"But if it wanted to chase down an unworthy soul who had strayed from the shoreline?"

"Why should it care? Your questions don't make sense. Just let me do my work, and you'll understand later," said Scarlet impatiently. "Gods above, Quinn Doyle, you could argue with a fence post."

"On the contrary. I never argue with facts, only with people," Quinn said, grinning.

"Just be quiet while I do my first cast," Scarlet told him.

While she knelt before a velvet cloth she'd laid over the stones lining the lake, I caught Quinn's eye and inclined my head. I was grateful in this case that he had argued, because I had not wanted to speak with Scarlet on the matter. However, it seemed that he had something else on his mind. In the dim light of Scarlet's magic lanterns, he raised an eyebrow at me. With my mind full of worry and Saki, I didn't see his point, though—not then—not until much later.

Scarlet's chosen tools rattled as she focused on the ground before her. I was aware of what she was doing, but not interested. A "cast," she had called it—like throwing dice. She would read the symbols that landed face-up and make her proclamations. I wished she was done already. The kitchen light in Saki's cabin had gone off.

"Yes . . . I see . . . How interesting," said Scarlet, before looking back up. "This is going to be a very complicated case."

SAKI,
I KNOW YOU LIKE
GOING OFF ALONE,
AND YOU'RE MOST
LIKELY FINE, BUT MEL
IS WORRIED AND SO IS
RYU. ALSO RED
KEEPS ASKING IF
WE'VE HEARD FROM
YOU. AT LEAST MAIL
SOMEBODY
SOMETHING, WON'T
YOU?
GLACIAL

SAKURA
RHEA MIN—
ENTE—

UNDELIVERED

—ALLOW

163

Chapter Nineteen: Fears

Sakura

"Well, then," Gwyn had said. Like everything was totally normal. "What will you call your inn?"

I sighed. It was hours later, and I was sitting atop my bed, arms around my knees. Lulu was snoring. *She*'d gotten herself under the covers, like a rational person. But me, I was up brooding.

I wasn't staring at them from my living room window, though. Or cackling or actually cursing them. So there was that.

All evening, I'd tried to focus on Gwyn instead, on her question. On the inn. Forget hot Witches. I had an inn! Or— I was going to. If I could survive the process of securing the land and building the darn thing . . .

Maybe Scarlet was right, a small part of me worried on repeat.

Maybe it was a bad idea to get help, and there's no point un-cursing the property anyway. Since I am cursed.

What was the use in removing wayward magic from the site if the owner herself was nothing better than a magical time bomb?

Now, I recognized these thoughts as depressed and anxious and self-blaming. And I knew I was entertaining them because deep down I was scared. Terrified. Scarlet knew Trent and they both knew my name and plenty of other Witches . . . and maybe I *was* powerful, under normal circumstances, but if they had the right friends . . .

. . . It didn't bear thinking about. I shivered, pulled my knees closer, and went back to obsessive melancholy about my dreams of an inn instead.

When somebody knocked at the door, I swore and hit my head on the sloped ceiling, convinced that a gang of holier-than-thou magic wielders was here to take me away for toying with people's hearts.

Lulu didn't even bother waking up.

I scooted under the covers with her, head first, the better to pretend I couldn't hear more knocking. It was probably just Scarlet, I told myself. I'd just pretend like I was a really deep sleeper the next morning when she said something mean about how I hadn't let her in. Best case, it was Marcus, but he'd no doubt have Scarlet with him, so really—

The knocking was now a tapping. Like, on glass. And very nearby.

I jerked my head up, pulling the blanket down around my shoulders to peer through the dark. Could they see me?

After a moment my eye caught the movement at the back window. Without magic, all I could see was a dark shape

165

against a background of more dark shapes. But it was Marcus-shaped, vaguely, and knowing him, he could *definitely* see me. A god of the Underworld would definitely be able to see in the dark. And—there didn't seem to be any other shapes present. How would there be, at a second-floor window?

I slithered clumsily until I was upright, taking the blanket with me. Lulu bleated at that. But I clutched it around my shoulders self-consciously as I stumbled across the room.

The proceedings hit a snag when I realized there wasn't actually a way to open the window. It was literally some glass built into a wood frame. It wasn't going anywhere. That is—not until Marcus intervened. Suddenly, there wasn't a window. There was an open doorway, and he stepped through it and then there was a wall and a window again, like nothing had happened. But now he was standing there, in my room, his arms crossed over his chest.

My first impulse was to lean into him. But this, I had discovered, was not an evening for first impulses. I kept my gaze on the floor. In the scattered moonlight, it was all I could see anyway. "Is there, um—did something happen—out there? Did you need me for something?"

"Saki," he said.

I couldn't stand it. Couldn't bear that I hadn't bothered telling him my whole name, and instead some fancy Witch told him. "It's half your property too, you know. I know we didn't sign anything yet, but you can just do whatever you want," I said. "I've been thinking, maybe I should just—maybe it's better if I just—I mean, how good is it really to have me just—"

"Sakura," Marcus interrupted. "Why won't you look at me?"

I bit my lip so that my words wouldn't tremble. It didn't

work. So I whispered. "Because I can't see in the dark without magic."

At that, Marcus shifted. I waited to see what he would say. Was he tired of this, of my self-imposed punishment? Surely he must be. He could say I ought to just let go already, and he'd probably be right. And it'd probably be fine. I still had my butterfly—I'd never taken my headband off . . .

He lifted one hand, and there was a string of star-shaped fairy lights hanging from the ceiling, looped around the room. It gave off the warmest, gentlest glow, enough to see his dark face but not enough that Lulu woke up fully. It was exactly what I would have wanted to match my quilt. This man truly had some kind of luck. Or—

That was the point at which I broke down and cried.

To his credit he tried to say my name again, and ask what was going on, but I just didn't have the breath for words. Everything came out as more sobs. He probably warned me what he was going to do, but I didn't pay attention. When he picked me up I just gave in and curled into his chest. Until I realized that he'd sat on the bed and I was all swaddled in quilt, and Lulu was nudging at my legs, draped over his arm.

"You have to stop doing that," I whispered, watery.

He seemed surprised. "Do you not like it?"

"No, I just—I must be heavy, and—I don't know." I wiped my eyes with the quilt, still not brave enough to look up at him. "It confuses Lulu."

Marcus chuckled softly. "I suspect she wants her blanket back."

As if to prove his point, she chose that moment to clamber over us both and end up in my lap, where she tucked herself under the wayward edges of blanket and settled in. Like nothing could be cozier. At that, even *I* laughed a little.

"Sakura." Marcus leaned his head against mine, since I still wasn't brave enough to meet his gaze. He pulled his arm from under my knees and wrapped it around me and Lulu instead. Though he'd been amused a moment ago, he did everything so deliberately that I knew he had something on his mind. The wonderful thing about Marcus was that I did not have to wonder what it was: he brought it up directly. "Why didn't you tell me what danger you are in?"

"I didn't know," I protested. "I didn't know Trent knew. I don't remember how it could have happened. And I certainly didn't know he had friends like *that*! I mean of course I know all about Witch school—and how they all keep in touch—it's all a big *community* for them—!"

When I started crying again, I stuck my nose into his collar, as though that might help. It sort of did. He was so warm, and always smelled the same. But thinking about the snot I was probably getting all over his very nice shirt did not make me feel better about myself. "The worst part is she's right to be mean."

Marcus's arms tightened. "I do not think so."

"Well, but—but what if the curse on the property is actually on *me*?" I asked, as the thought finally occurred to me. "What if that's why you didn't find anything? What if they already did something, and that's it?"

"If that were the case, it would not have affected the construction crew. Quinn's stories dated back from last fall, when the building began." Marcus shifted his head up and then paused for a moment—waiting? Thinking? Then he kissed my hair. If you had asked me any time before that day, I would have said hair kisses were kind of silly or even patronizing, but the way he did it was so sincere. "I know I can not tell you what to do. But I think you need to keep shields up, Saki."

"But I am!" My hand shook as I pressed tears away from my cheeks.

"You are shielding everyone else from your magic, keeping it in," Marcus said gently. "When I first met you, you were also adept at keeping influences *out*. I think, to keep yourself safe, it is time to resume that."

"I *can't*, I—it was hard enough today just to stand there and keep it all in. Unless—" Another terrible thought hit me. "Do you think *that's* how she knew? You think she just—picked it up by reading me?"

"Such magic is forbidden for Witches," he reminded me, his voice drifting down over my ear. Lulu looked up and yawned. I traced her little nose with one finger, half trying to think, half trying not to.

Invasive magic was rare. It was aggressive. It wasn't part of Witchery, and it wasn't part of shadow witchery, either. Sometimes you'd come across a sorcerer who just didn't care, and did it because they thought they were already better than everyone else. But most magic users saw it as exploitative and simply unnecessary. Why focus a lot of power on trying to *maybe* read someone's mind and most likely end up making an enemy of them, when instead you could ask what they thought, and judge for yourself if the answer they gave you was true? It was a matter of getting to know people. Of course, Witches weren't always adept at that—that was more of a shadow thing. Still—if Scarlet was going around surreptitiously mining people's auras for information, or something—*it could explain why she's so attractive*, I thought,

169

rather maliciously.

Which brought up an unrelated point. Did Marcus find her attractive? I felt so ridiculous over it. It wasn't remotely important. But . . .

I wriggled against Marcus's arm, leaning my head back so I could look up at him. Finally.

The impassive mask which often covered his face was down, and I saw worry in his eyes, so much worry it was like pain. Here I was thinking I could sail in and out of Helenia and maybe he was into Scarlet and there he was, *invested*. The realization that hit me then was trite but deeply, undeniably true. There's a reason things become trite, you know.

"Oh," I said quietly. "Oh, Marcus, I'm sorry. You're right, I haven't been shielding myself from others—I guess I kind of thought I deserved whatever might come. But I *have* been shielding my heart, not with magic, but just by—keeping you out."

Chapter Twenty: Charmed

❧

Marcus

Sweet Sakura, so accustomed to looking through masks. I told her the truth. "I do not care where you keep me. Only let me help you, if I am able to. If you want me to."

Her eyes were red-rimmed and weary, but for the first time that night some life flashed in them. She pressed herself up, nearly dislodging her goatling. "No, Marcus, you deserve better than that. You deserve consideration. All this time, since Scarlet said my name, is this what you've been doing? You've been worrying for me, while all I could do was feel sorry for myself?"

I did not understand her point. "What else could I do?"

"You could—I mean, for starters, you could—you ought to be mad at me—didn't you even wonder why I didn't—" She looked at me, exasperated, at a loss for words. An unusual predicament. The moment I thought of smiling, she smiled too, and she threw her arms around my neck. This time Lulu was dislodged, but I did not have a moment to feel sorry. Saki kissed me deeply, impetuously, her cheeks still damp with tears. "You're nonsensical," she informed me when at last she stopped to take a breath. She could not go far: I'd pulled her close against me, her heart beating over mine. As she leaned her forehead on mine, I could feel her words. "You're one of the most powerful beings in Beyond, and you won't stand up for yourself."

"I could say the same to you," I whispered.

"Yes, but I already knew *I* am nonsensical." Her chuckle became more soft kisses, each one easing more of the weight on my shoulders, weight I hadn't realized I was carrying.

"Sakura," I confessed, giving in, "I can protect you, but only if you want me to. And as much as I might want to, I can not undo anything done by others."

"I know." Though I myself was not certain I'd made sense, Saki did seem to understand. She leaned back, her arms slipping free until she framed my face with her delicate hands. "We can't undo anything. That's not how it works. If there was a way, I'd've found it, believe me." Though she bit her lip, her fingertips skated over my cheek, reassuring. "I kept saying no when you were offering protection because I didn't want to get you involved," she explained. "But you're already involved. I see it now. Okay. So—I'm not really sure what we should do, but—I do know I don't want you to get hurt. And if you hurt when I'm hurting, then—"

"Just let me help," I offered softly.

She was smiling her wry smile at me. "I was going to say, I should probably stop hurting *myself*, huh?"

173

I returned her smile, crookedly, for I knew it was something easier said than done.

"I know," she said, amusement threaded through her voice. "Could we get any more sappy? I thought you were supposed to be god of the dead, not of self-help."

I could have pointed out that I wasn't being of very concrete help in that moment, and that I had no more idea what to do than she did. It was difficult even to admit what I wanted. Her hands drifted down, my shoulder, my chest, and her eyes followed almost thoughtfully, as though she was deciding for herself if I was solid. Watching her make the decision was terrifying. Had she decided I wasn't, I felt she'd probably be right.

When her voice came again it was different, gentle but resolute. "Alright," she said, meeting my gaze once more. "This all could be nothing, I know that. We have no idea what Scarlet or Trent or any of them is thinking, and frankly, I doubt they're actually thinking worse things than I've been imagining. But—nevertheless—I've made mistakes and I've gotten myself in trouble, and I need time to trust myself again. Marcus, will you help me, please? If you could make me a protective charm, I promise I will wear it. At least until I'm steady enough to keep up my own wards again."

Her promise had the echo of prayer to it, and it woke something in me, something most often forgotten and hidden away. The power of it surged in me, and I knew she could see it by the way her eyes lightened as her gaze remained on mine.

But she didn't know the way it filled my heart. The way I wished this promise could also reflect something between us. Did she?

Even if she did not. I had offered her protection with no conditions, no further promises necessary. That, I decided, is what I should enact.

She was still watching me, patient. The words were more difficult than I'd expected them to be, but they did come. "Yes, of course, Sakura. It would be my honor to help you."

I wouldn't realize what I'd done wrong until she pointed it out to me much, much later.

But in that moment, neither of us saw it. Her smile was beatific, and she shifted gracefully to sit by my side as I focused. Conjuring furniture was simply recalling matter from somewhere else, but to create something and give it power was another matter. I had not had reason to do so in a long time. I brought my hands together, concentrating on the small space between them. I thought of Sakura, of her smile and her tears, and of my own desperate determination that she should be safe. It was not difficult.

When I handed her the charm, however, she looked at me as though I'd summited mountains.

It had manifested as a large teardrop of polished black. Sakura was delighted. "Thank you, Marcus. It's perfect. I have a chain in my jewelry box—"

I put my hand on her arm. She'd been about to rise to her feet, to go and get it. I do not know what made me act; I shouldn't have interfered in her choice. She faltered into uncertainty as she glanced at me, but before I could take my hand away, she nodded.

She lifted one hand, and black sparkles swirled around her fingers, shivering down her arm. It was far more power than needed to pull such a small object across the room. It made me shiver, too, realizing how much she was holding back.

What would happen with all of that magic? I did not know for certain the way magic worked. The power I drew on as a deity was different, just different enough that I'd never had to think about these nuances. But now I could take comfort in the fact that, no matter what happened, her amulet should keep her safe from harm.

From the old table across the room, the chain rose, surrounded by magic. It flew into Saki's hand, and she glanced up at me sideways, as though embarrassed. I knew she had no reason to be, though. The important thing was only that she'd let herself try.

She strung the chain through a small hole at the top of the teardrop, and then paused. I did not understand why until Lulu butted her small horns into my arm, and Saki laughed.

"She wants to know what you were waiting for," she offered.

"I was thinking, you might want to do the honors?"

She held up the ends of the chain, and at last I understood. Gingerly I took the halves of the clasp from her, and shifted to close it round her neck. Her white hair brushed over my hands as I did so, reminding me that there was more to think of than magic and charms. Before she moved, I leaned down and kissed her shoulder, where the collar of her pajama shirt had slipped down to reveal pale skin.

"Stop that," Saki said playfully. Her eyes met mine as she looked over her shoulder and I straightened. "That tickles, and you have no idea how—how tired I am."

As if to prove her point, she yawned.

"You have been awake all night?" I guessed. Though she had been moved by my worry, it was clear that she had been more preoccupied than I had.

She nodded. "As have you. Lulu is the only smart one of us.

176

Not that I suppose it matters for gods."

I was almost hurt by it, by the reminder that I was so different. But she was teasing me, even going so far as to stick her tongue out at me. The rush of warmth I felt buoyed my spirits. "*Everyone* needs to rest at times, sweet butterfly."

For a moment she simply held my gaze, smiling. Behind her, Lulu curled up on the discarded quilt.

"It doesn't seem very nice to ask you for a favor and then send you away," Saki admitted, her voice low.

"On the contrary," I assured her. "It is only now that we have spoken—now that I know you will be safe—that I can rest."

"In that case, I suppose I won't feel bad." Saki smiled at me once more as we both rose, reluctant, tender. "I'll make you breakfast again, though, if you like. Unless there are more investigation plans for the morning?"

"That strikes me as the most important plan I could possibly have." And as I leaned down to give her one last goodnight kiss, there was nothing I could have meant more.

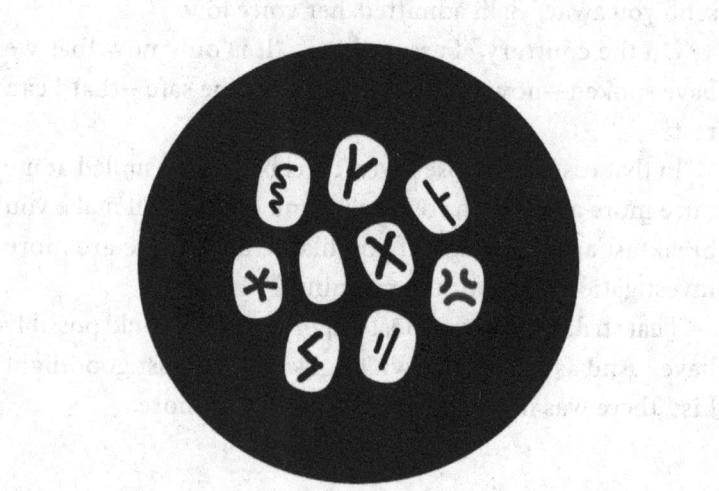

Chapter Twenty-One: Divination

❦

Sakura

Not even being glared at could pierce my happy bubble.

When Lulu and I set out the next morning—*late* the next morning—with a basket full of bread pudding and scrambled eggs, we were met with sunny skies and a pristine lake. And Scarlet and Quinn, unfortunately.

Quinn came over first, almost as though something ghostly was chasing him. Lulu ran over to him and he picked her up. "I see you haven't bothered with a leash yet, Saki."

"*You* try leashing a goat," I suggested cheerfully. "Good morning, Quinn. Scarlet."

Scarlet, trailing behind the annoying detective, gave me another of her suspicious stares. It resolved into a catlike smile. "Out to make a delivery in your little traveling cloak? How very Red Riding Hood of you."

I did twitch my cloak over my shoulders a little further, I'll admit. It was embroidered with flowers all over and *definitely* not the sort of thing a hot Witch would wear. But it was warm against the chilly morning air, and I could feel the weight of my new pendant around my neck, and my bread pudding smelled delicious—even Glacial would have been proud of it. So I answered breezily, "I learned from the best. Maybe you've heard of *her*, too," before continuing on my way to the cabin next door.

If Scarlet knew I was talking about an alchemist who liked to solve mysteries, so much the better. It was her turn to worry a little about who else in the world might find themselves pitted against her.

Hopefully she didn't also know that I'd ruined said alchemist's wedding.

Quinn marched along with me, with Lulu draped over his shoulder now, like they were some kind of two-headed beast. I looked at him askance.

"Fire me for pet endangerment," he suggested. *"Please."*

I grinned as we climbed the steps of Marcus's porch. "I know Lulu too well. She endangers herself. Besides, where's your detectively pride in seeing a case through?"

"I shouldn't have seen the case at all," he replied. "This is what I get for playing matchmaker. Never again!"

"Sakura." Marcus opened the door before we got to it— fully dressed this time, which was maybe for the best, seeing as we had company. The way his eyes lingered on me made me regret the cloak after all. Just as my blush heated up, he turned to acknowledge the others. "Lulu, Quinn. Scarlet. We could sit here on the porch, if—?"

He looked back at me, and I nodded, hefting my basket.

However complicated my feelings about Scarlet and Quinn were, I *had* made food for them too. Being in the café business for several years had taught me plenty.

With all the polite murmurings and sorting things out, as if we were about to have a tea party rather than an impromptu meeting about a cursed holy site, the four of us got ourselves settled around the rustic table. It was too little to really sit around, so instead we sat in a horseshoe shape, looking out over the lake. Almost as though nobody wanted to block the view. Or no one wanted to get too close?

Except Lulu. She hopped down from Quinn's shoulder and, deciding she wasn't hungry for once in her life, investigated the muddy grass nearby.

Marcus caught my eye and smiled gently as we passed around plates and utensils. Once everyone had heaping servings of gooey bread and fluffy eggs, there was a moment of silence at last.

In that moment of peace, while everyone was eating and not even Scarlet looked mean, I glanced out over the lake and I thought, *yes. We could have a sanctuary here.*

And then, of course, Quinn ruined it. He swallowed a massive bite of eggs and peppers and looked up. "Not bad, Saki. I'm starved. We were up all night. Want to guess how many curses are on your property?"

I frowned at him. "Are you going to actually tell us, or just tease us about it?"

"I think I'm going to start not telling anyone anything until I've got it all figured out and am ready for the big reveal at the end," he said. "I'd get a lot less grief that way."

I considered flicking some bread pudding at him, but it was too good to waste. Instead I got halfway through saying, "If

181

you wanted less grief, maybe you could try not being so—"

"Two," Scarlet interrupted. "There's two. *You* are taking this seriously, aren't you?"

She looked at Marcus. I couldn't quite read the look in her eyes, but I didn't like it.

"I consider the matter very serious," he agreed gravely. "And I am certain Saki and Quinn do, as well. Please elaborate."

Scarlet glanced at us again, and this time the look was clear. It was a little smug but mostly contemptuous. I got that she had a problem with me, obviously, but it seemed like her night with Quinn hadn't exactly been a picnic either. She was sitting at one end of our horseshoe, not even really across from Marcus, because Marcus had pulled up his chair close to mine. Instead she was sort of off on her own, as much as the porch railing would let her be. Like she thought whatever we had was contagious.

It did make a good position for giving a presentation from, though. Just like she had yesterday, she paused just long enough to make sure we were all staring at her.

"There are two things going on here. At least," she said, with a significant look at me. I wasn't sure if she was speaking metaphorically, or insinuating that I was a curse too, or what. I still wasn't even sure I disagreed with her. I let it pass, and she went on, "I was able to do some deeper divination work at the witching hour."

"Throwing bones," Quinn added helpfully.

She glared at him. I was in knots. Scarlet Onyx did her work by interpreting symbols inscribed on pieces of bone? Seriously, this Witch was exactly who teenage Saki would have dreamed of being.

"The particulars aren't important, since apparently it's

beyond shadow witchery anyway," she said.

And she was awful.

I *could* have argued that actually I did use divination, but I liked tarot, which was much more introspective and focused on internal answers and intuition rather than reflecting outside sources—but why bother?

The real reason I hadn't done my own divination at my own site was because I wasn't doing magic at all. But we didn't need to get into that with Scarlet.

Gods, I realized suddenly, my stomach plummeting into a pit. *What is she writing back to Trent about* me?

"There is definite disturbance here," Scarlet went on, while I tried to remind myself that it didn't matter what people thought of me—except maybe for when I had done a terrible wrong to said people and then run away. Maybe? "It muddied up my reading. *That* disturbance is present but short-lived, according to the bones. It is merely a mortal affair."

"'Merely'?" Marcus was using his *I'm upset by what you've said but too genteel to be loud about it* voice.

"Good luck. That's what I've been trying to tell her all night, but she won't believe it's important," Quinn said, clearly picking up on his friend's alarm.

"Wait," I added. "Are we talking, 'mortal' as in people are doing it? Or 'mortal' as in causing death? Aren't both of those things exactly what we were worried about, anyway? What could be *more* of a problem?"

"An immortal matter." Scarlet was smirking; I'd obviously asked exactly the question she *wanted* to be asked, so she could show off how much power she was working with. Not to mention cozy up to my boyfriend. She turned her full attention on Marcus. "Maybe *you* remember something about it?"

Wait. Boyfriend? Did I just say that?

Gods. No wonder Scarlet, friend of Trent, hated me.

Beside me, Marcus was as steady as a rock. "What in particular do you wish me to remember?"

"It's woven into the very fabric of the site," Scarlet told us loftily. "No doubt it was a spell cast by the very first temple to be present here. There is *divine* power behind it. I'm sure you've sensed something?"

While she tried her hardest to collude with Marcus, *again,* Quinn elbowed me. We both knew Marcus would take his time and weigh his answer.

"Ow!" I hissed at Quinn.

"Stop whining," he retorted quietly. "Did you notice she said 'spell'? She didn't say curse. She hasn't said 'curse' all night."

Scarlet was ignoring us. Marcus was too, but his inattention was much more nice.

"So what? Maybe it's just super-correct Witch speak," I whispered, because I knew that even though she was ignoring us, she was listening.

Her nose crinkled. *Victory.*

"It matters," Quinn informed me. "You may not like me, but I know you'll be on my side about this when you think it over."

I set down my empty plate. "I don't *not like—*"

It wasn't a sound that interrupted me. I think that was what worried me about it. Marcus didn't clear his throat or murmur something sensible and neutral, as he so often had when Quinn and I argued. Instead, Marcus twitched. His hand came up, toward me, almost like we were driving in a

184

cart and the cart was headed too fast for something large and hard, and he was hoping to shield me. Then just as suddenly it was back in his lap. His plate was tilted, forgotten, and a fork clattered to the floor.

I turned more toward him, to look at his face. For an instant I thought maybe he'd become so annoyed by our side conversation that he'd made the gesture to get us to stop. But he didn't look annoyed. His mask was up, but behind it, he was very clearly biting his cheek.

What in Beyond, I wondered, *is this man trying not to say?*

He was inscrutable enough that it could be anything. He could be recalling the founding of the first temple and disturbed by some ancient clue, for all I knew. But it wasn't the first time I'd wondered that. Last night, before he gave me my pendant, I'd wondered too.

"Marcus?" I asked, curious.

He opened his eyes, though it took them a moment to focus on me. "Sakura. Please forgive me, I—I do not remember anything that would help you," he said, glancing at Scarlet before fixing his gaze on the floor.

"I only wanted to be sure," Scarlet told us. "The truth is I'm perfectly confident in what I've found out. It isn't a relic that's causing you trouble—at least, it's not an item. It's a place. *That* place."

She was pointing, very dramatically, at the mountain peak behind the lake.

"So, what? You're saying we go there next?" Quinn rubbed his hands together.

"I'm saying it would be wise, if you want to understand the energy that's disrupting your *retreat,*" Scarlet corrected.

She said the last word with just the right amount of venom,

and I knew it was directed at me, and I knew exactly what she meant. But I didn't care. I was watching Marcus.

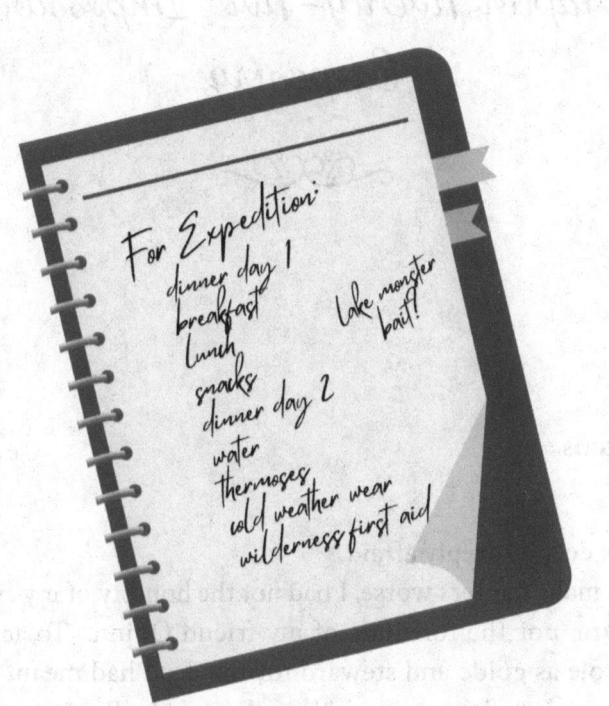

For Expedition:
dinner day 1
breakfast
lunch
snacks
dinner day 2
water
thermoses
cold weather wear
wilderness first aid

Lake monster bait?

Chapter Twenty-Two: Impossible Carpentry

Marcus

I was deeply, deeply afraid.

To make matters worse, I had not the honesty of my sweet Sakura, nor the fortitude of my friend Quinn. To accept my role as guide and steward for the dead had meant that long ago I made peace with the unknowable. But to face the unbearable—that, I had not prepared myself for.

I should have.

"Marcus," she said again.

I returned to the present to find that Quinn and Scarlet had left. I remained seated on the porch, and Sakura stood beside me, her eyes looking down into mine. Her goatling was in her arms, several strands of long grass dangling from its lips as it chewed contentedly.

"They've gone to the station to hail Gwyn, and head into town," Saki told me, as though sensing my uncertainty. As ever, her patience was a relief. "Quinn swears he knows all the supplies we'll need. Scarlet said we can't just ask you to take us straight to the top of the mountain since using magic to get there might just make things *more* disturbed, but—but I think—well, I'm just not certain it's a good idea for you to go there at all. Is it? What's going on, Marcus?"

I looked at her carefully, not only to think, but to ground myself. Her cloak was thrown over the chair she'd abandoned. Today's sweater was rose pink and it had a wide neckline, a neckline that made me remember kissing her shoulder. Her rose-patterned skirts brushed my knee. The thin chain around her neck disappeared below her outfit, but I knew the pendant hung there. I knew she was safe. Upon that, I could rely. And she still wore her glass butterfly above her ear, nestled against a pink silk scarf. It looked as though it might slip away easily, freeing her hair . . .

Lulu bleated, and Saki set the goat down with a firm reminder to stay away from the dishes. Then she rose once more and set her hands on her hips.

I cleared my throat. "I—I am not certain."

"You remembered something," she prompted, not unkindly, but with the same firmness she'd used on Lulu.

"I didn't remember it. It wasn't something I'd forgotten." I drew a deep breath, knowing her eyes narrowed, and that she waited. "I'm sorry, Saki, I am not trying to be obtuse. Nevertheless I—I did tell you that this site was never mine, that I never had any right to it?"

"Yes, you told me that." The look in her eyes eased,

becoming thoughtful as she set one hand on the chair behind my arm. "And I still think you're being too hard on yourself. Is that what this is?"

Slowly, I nodded. "More or less."

"And the top of the mountain, that's supposedly the most holy part of this site, isn't it," Saki continued, not so much asking a question as taking my measure while she spoke. "And probably all tied up in this first temple business Scarlet's going on about. So you don't want to go up there . . . Out of respect for who was there before?"

"If you are going, then I will go too," I told her.

She was not distracted. "But you will be worried?"

"I'm not worried." I drew another very deep breath. "I know you are safe."

"Marcus. I need more words, please." Saki smiled wryly at me as she moved closer, setting her arm over my shoulder, running her free hand through my hair. "You're being nonsensical again. Can't you see that anything that worries *you* this much must also be worrisome for me and the others? Anyone who can make someone with your ability worry wouldn't bat an eye at Quinn or Scarlet. Or Lulu and me."

"It isn't a 'who' that worries me." Laying my hand along her waist made it easier to stay present, to focus on her rather than the words. "It's an old promise I made, Saki. It's nothing to do with any of you."

"Do you want to tell me what the promise was?"

I knew exactly what she would say if she knew.

"Okay, you don't have to spill all the details." One blue eye crinkled as she smiled at me lopsidedly, her fingertips still in my hair. "As long as you think we know enough to really be prepared for whatever is up there, Marcus. Do you think that?"

"I think you know much better than I do, sweet one." I meant it whole-heartedly. She saw more clearly than ever I did, with only the one possible exception. "I do not know what is at the top of the mountain. I do not know the source of the disturbances Scarlet has found. I do not know what the dangers might be . . . I only know that, a long time ago, I was not welcome there."

Saki frowned. "If 'not welcome' means 'might be attacked by magical forces'—"

"I do not think so. The time I am thinking of is too long ago; everyone else has moved on. Whatever curse or magic is here now, I do not think it has anything to do with either you or me."

She lingered for a moment, watching me, waiting to see if there was anything else I had to say. There wasn't. Her face had drifted close enough I could almost touch her nose with mine.

"Well," she said softly, her breath laced with the honey she'd used to sweeten her baking. "Don't the two of us just make a fine example of how to dwell on the past, then?"

"Be it recent or not," I agreed faintly, smiling up at her.

"Scarlet thinks we're running away from things, up here at the edge of the world," she went on, not knowing just how much I wished to kiss her. "But it seems to me now that this is the place where those things catch up with you."

"As long as you are safe," I said softly. "As long as you are safe, they do not matter."

"Of course we're safe here. We'll make this a place where people are safe." Saki tilted her head just so, so that I could see her smile, and I thought that perhaps she *did* know how

191

much I wanted to kiss her. "What do you say to that, darling? Any more worries?"

None. There was nothing to say. I kissed her at last.

When she lifted her head, she was beaming. Just watching her, I knew that I was too. "Now," she declared, touching her nose affectionately to mine, "did I tell you yet that I promised the others we'd get cabins ready for them by the time they returned? We have some work to do."

I would have preferred not to do it. Surely, between myself and Saki, if she were to release her full power, we could straighten a few cabins in only a moment. We could build the entire inn, whatever she wanted. We could wait until Quinn and Scarlet were stepping off of the gondola. We could give ourselves time.

But she laughed at me like she knew what I was thinking, and then she pulled me to my feet.

"Come along," she said cheerfully. "It isn't just a chore, I promise. It's a chance to talk things through. I want to plan what we will build."

Could she read my mind? At that, I had to smile.

She told me about Gwyn's thoughts and suggestions as we gathered up the breakfast things and took them inside to clean. Apparently, the gondola driver was nearly as excited as Saki for this inn, in her own way. In talking about it, Saki also did something which I expect she did not notice: she admitted, in little, unthinking ways, how she had lived her life in Belville. *Gwyn's a lot like Glacial, she has a good sense for practical things,* she mentioned as the tap water ran; then, *I always wanted the Pomegranate to help people, this is what I'd like here too I think. It doesn't get old,* as she took the dish towel from me and hung it up to dry. Moments where she reflected her past self without the guilt that so often colored her words of late. Though she'd accused me of being too hard on myself, I was positive that she was the one doing so.

There was hardly time to mention it, though. I followed as she led the way out the door and down the line of cabins, collecting Lulu on the way.

"At first, these were really just a way to get away from Bertram. And you," she told me, her eyes twinkling as she glanced back over her shoulder. "But they're growing on me. What do you think?"

I considered the cabins. The rainstorm the day before had given them a thorough washing, and now their shingle roofs glinted in the sun. Their construction was haphazard and uneven at best. But having seen the way Saki had transformed her own, I was certain she could turn these into cozy, charming homes.

"Well, and there's not too many, and they're nice and private," she said modestly, once I had told her my thoughts. "Plus, they all have a lovely view. I think it'd be a nice place to start."

"The materials, then, would go to building a central meeting place and restaurant?" I guessed.

Saki paused on the stairs of the first cabin, looking back toward the station. I stopped behind her, one hand on the railing, and followed her gaze. There was just enough space cleared beside the station to build such a structure.

"I think that's a perfect idea. It could be the main lodge. Though you just want your bar, don't you?" She smiled up at me.

My heart skipped, but it had nothing to do with eating establishments. "I would be happy to be of service."

"Oh, you wouldn't be stuck back there all the time, trust me," Saki said as she continued across the porch. "There'd be a lot of work to do. Not just greeting people and checking them in or out, but also maintenance and—housekeeping."

This last she said as she tugged the cabin door open. It was stiff, waterlogged: this porch roof was not complete. Inside, we glimpsed piles of abandoned wood and rusty tools.

"Well, now to prove why *we* are the ones who can do this," Saki decided, winking over her shoulder. "You take the roof and the porch, and I'll see what I can do inside?"

She would use her magic? I smiled. "Gladly."

"It's a race, then!"

I won.

But in fairness, my task was the easier of the two—and even so it took time and concentration. Conjuring items was simple when the item already existed: Saki's end table had come from a rarely-used office in my own house. That was just a question of moving matter—something which, if I may say so with modesty, was intricately related to my work, helping souls move between worlds. Rearranging items already present was also possible, but required me to know where they were needed. Sensing the broken parts of the roof, feeling my way along and finding the places that leaked, then pulling loose tiles over to fix the holes and securing them, turned out to be a methodical, almost meditative practice. It was a helpful thing which I could do quietly and independently. In short, I enjoyed it very much.

I crossed the newly steadfast porch and entered the cabin to find Saki amid a chaotic, sparkling whirlwind of lumber and mops. I stopped dead—but then she turned and grinned. "Watch this!"

She lifted her hands, and in a synchronized dance, the old materials and tools took themselves into the attic. The mops flourished and winked out, and each corner of the cabin gleamed. As black sparkles drifted down through the air, Saki's butterfly glowed.

"Seriously," she said breathlessly. "Thank you."

I met her gaze, smiling. "You've no need to thank me, Saki. You have done all of this yourself."

Goat Ownership Q&A!

Q. What behaviors should I look out for?

A. Goats are well-known escape artists, and very curious. They will climb, headbutt, and nibble whenever possible.

Q. How long will my goats live?

A. An average of 12 - 15 years, depending on breed.

Q. Where should my goats live?

A. A small barn with a sturdily fenced yard is best.

Q. Does my goat have magic?

A. It really shouldn't. If you suspect it does, seek help!

Chapter Twenty-Three: A Wall

～～♡♡～～

Sakura

I grinned unsteadily at Marcus. After so much time spent trying to repress my magic, my cleaning efforts left me feeling a bit drunk. Actually, in my rush of affection and exhilaration, I inadvertently sent several brooms hurtling toward him.

Fortunately, Marcus was *very* good at shielding himself.

The brooms clattered to the floor and I immediately dropped all my other magical tasks. Good thing the lumber and all had already found a safe spot in the attic. Quinn was going to have to sleep on the first floor beside the hearth—if he slept at all, that was. (Because obviously *Quinn* was getting the cabin next to Marcus's, and Scarlet was not.)

"Sorry about that," I told Marcus. "I suppose getting launched into a fireplace taught you a lesson?"

He smiled about it, good-humored as usual. For a moment

I thought about asking him about the butterfly charm. Did it only protect him when we were touching? Or more specifically—kissing? Did it protect everyone? Not that I wanted to kiss anyone else. But apparently it didn't protect from errant brooms . . .

In my moment of weakness, contemplating my wayward magic, a vision of poor Red's shocked face flashed in my mind. My stomach hurt.

Isn't it *horrible,* the way we hurt the people we love most?

"Are you done with this cabin?" Marcus asked gently.

"Yes, I think I've done enough damage for now," I said faintly. Giving myself a shake, I added more brightly, "Quinn can do the rest himself. I wonder if he's remembering to get himself food and dishes, or if he expects us to keep feeding him?"

Marcus remained mild as we left the cabin. "You don't give him very much credit."

"He gives himself plenty. He doesn't need help." I smiled up at Marcus, happy to have something else to talk about.

"If it would help us, or this proposed expedition, I am certain he would." Marcus smiled back.

Lulu pranced around the corner of the cabin to join us. Where she had been and what she had been up to, I decided not to wonder. Instead, as the three of us made our way to the next little house in the row, I realized Marcus had missed a few extra details about the new plan, since he was in his own world while we were talking earlier. "Well, he did mention a camp stove for tea, but it was hard to tell if he meant it," I relayed. "According to his expert calculations—never mind that no one's been up to the mountain peak in living memory, so no one could possibly be an expert on it—it should only take us one day. Up and back. No need for tents and things, but that's why I said they could stay here tonight, so we could leave early tomorrow."

I wasn't sure if Marcus noticed, but I didn't sound quite as confident as Quinn had while talking about it. Not camping was nice. But scaling a mountain and then trying not to fall down said mountain on the return trip, all in one day and on top of possibly dealing with some sort of ancient curse, wasn't a task I normally would volunteer for.

"In which case, I am confident he would bring food to contribute for dinner and breakfast." Marcus's level of trust in his capricious friend was endearing. And, since I was known to be a bit capricious myself, I couldn't complain about it anyway. He added, "Are you comfortable with making the trip so quickly?"

So, he *had* noticed.

"Ugh," I said, descriptively. We'd reached the next cabin, which had a caved-in staircase and a very rough little bench on its porch. I struggled my way up and sat heavily—turned out the bench was rough *and* a bit unsteady—but when Marcus joined me, his knees folding practically up to his chin, we managed to even it out. "I'm not big on hiking, unlike just about everyone else in Helenia, it seems," I went on. "How I keep moving to places where everyone's wild about the outdoors, I'll never know."

Marcus just stared at me. A tender but also half amused, maybe even half hopeful look.

I took his meaning, blushed, and stuck my tongue out at him.

"Not that I am *moving* here," I hastened to add. "But you know what I mean. Anyway. Quinn and Scarlet don't know, about me, my legs, I mean. I mean, Scarlet probably knows everything about me down to my underwear size, given the way she acts, and Quinn probably could guess since he thinks he's so smart, but I didn't *tell* them. It's not a big deal."

Marcus continued staring. This time his gaze was more thoughtful. It was definitely saying, *are you so sure it's not, Saki?*

Well, okay, it was literally the way I navigated the world. But still.

"I don't want it to be a thing," I warned him. He smiled faintly, but there was now an undercurrent of worry in his expression. I sighed. "Just, we need to deal with this magic, whatever it is, and if this is the way to do it, then so be it. Right? If I need to hike up a mountain, then that's what I have to do. I'm not sending them up there by themselves, not when it's technically *my* property and my problem. And no, I do not want to extend it into some sort of group camping trip that takes multiple days. You and I both know I'd probably murder Quinn, or worse, Scarlet, and then we'd have a mad ghost on our hands as *well* as a curse. Or two. However many she said it was."

"Sakura," he said, his voice meaningful. He looked out over the lake, but now I felt even *more* in the spotlight. I looked around for Lulu, as a distraction, but she was busy trying to headbutt her way through the wall at the other end of the porch. Marcus went on, "Do you always joke about what worries you most?"

"Obviously." But then I looked at him, his profile against the ratty porch roof. "Except you. You're too nice to joke about."

He turned back to me. "Do I worry you?"

Yes. I'd blown up a party when I encountered a breaking

point with Trent, and I hadn't ever loved him. Who knew *what* would happen when I left Helenia? My worry and dread of that moment grew exponentially each time I looked at Marcus. Each time he spoke. Each time he kissed me. Each time I kissed him.

Not that I *loved* him. Not exactly. I mean, okay, I did. But even so . . .

"You're worth it," I confessed. This was news to me too. But I knew as I said it that it was right. "You do worry me, but you're worth it. Nonsensical death god."

Marcus was smiling.

"This is the part where you say how I am worrisome but very much worth it too," I told him, even though I knew that the amount of worry a powerful but out-of-control and way-too-independent shadow witch could cause was far too much for a relationship to bear.

"Would you believe it?" Curse him, he had that teasing look again, which was impossibly irresistible. Also, when did he start reading my mind?

I tossed my hair, affecting my best haughty look. "That depends on how trustworthy your word is!"

"Why not let me show you instead?" His voice was low now, that pitch that absolutely melted me. But I was determined not to give in so easily.

It really didn't help when, before I could come up with a response, he spun so that he was kneeling on the deck in front of me, his hands on either side of my hips, resting on the bench. "Do you want to know what you are to me?" he asked.

"I'm your business partner," I reminded him, not at all in a tone which one uses in business.

"You are the sweet reality in front of me, and worry is only shadows," he breathed, completely overriding my attempt at sense.

"I happen to deal in shadows, thank you very much," I whispered. Despite my better judgment, I was leaning into him.

"Not to me. To me, you are light."

Lulu bleated.

Marcus and I were so ridiculously close that as we both spun our heads, we nearly bumped into each other. What had we even been talking about? Why in Beyond was this man so magnetic, and how had no one ever noticed it before me?

And *why* was my goat up to her tail in a wall *right now*, of all possible times?

"I have an idea," I gurgled, doing my best to regain some measure of control over the situation. *"You,"* I turned and pressed Marcus away with one hand on his chest, which just made him grin lopsidedly like this was all an adorable and hilarious joke, "are going to stay outside and fix the walls, and keep your nonsense to yourself for a few minutes. *I* am going to go rescue a goat and tidy up a cabin for someone I don't even like. And then—"

"And then?" Marcus was still grinning.

"*And then* we are going to do some paperwork or whatever we need to, to make you an actual partner in this property. Like actual responsible adults," I informed him. "*Not* like sappy teenagers."

"And when will you tell me why you're only reluctant to kiss me when I'm trying to tell you how I feel?" he asked, like a full-grown imp.

"Preferably never," I retorted as I hopped to my feet. "Which

202

is probably not fair of me, I know, but that's how it is. You knew I was like this before we started. Don't worry, Lulu, I'm coming!"

I scurried off, into the cabin. What I was planning to do, I have no idea. Had no idea. What was I going to do, grab her by her little hooves and tug?

The important thing was to get a breather.

Though . . . the air in the cabin was very musty and unpleasant, whereas with Marcus . . .

I knew exactly what had scared me. It was realizing the way my own feelings were growing. Kissing and teasing and being kind was one thing, but getting in over our heads wasn't an option.

(As if I'd ever had a choice?)

But for the moment at least I knew I hadn't hurt him. His tone had remained light and amused, and he'd still had that smile on his face as I left. He'd be fine. Lulu, on the other hand . . .

I found her little head poking through the wall in a damp corner of the kitchen. The hole from the porch was obvious damage, of course, but now that I was inside, I could see that the whole corner, floor to ceiling, was soft and damp with rainwater. A casualty of hurried (terrified? haunted?) builders and heavy storms.

"Okay, don't worry," I told Lulu soothingly. Pushing my sleeves back, I added under my breath, "Maybe it *is* good that we both have strong magic, after all."

I knew I had to be super careful. I wanted to push the wood away with magic, to make sure I didn't poke her, but that meant using only the exact right amount of force. I was so worried I didn't even realize how clenched my jaw was until

203

Lulu made me laugh—by bopping a black spark of magic with her pink nose. It dissipated immediately, and she remained stuck, and looking at me as if to say, *do another! Is this a new game?*

I grinned. There was something so fun about being seen by someone else—even a four-legged, furry someone else. Somehow in all my worry I'd forgotten that lately. "Okay, then. Here goes!"

Legends of CERBERUS

A three-headed dog monster originally fought by Hercules as his twelfth trial, Cerberus is most famous as the guard dog of the Underworld. He prevented dead souls from escaping, and living souls from entering. But as long as a soul was where it was supposed to be, he was rumored to be very friendly!

Chapter Twenty-Four: Flora

⚜

Marcus

Sweet Sakura. She wanted to move carefully, and that was fine. I was so cheered by the fact that she thought me worth the worry that I didn't feel guilty about getting carried away, either. She knew how to handle me and hold her own, and that was perfectly fine too.

Fixing a rain-soaked wall turned out to be an even more meditative challenge than restructuring a roof. Instead of shifting materials in place, I found I had to draw the water out of the wood, and then encourage the wood to regenerate. That last bit *was* drawing on my divine powers specifically, I'll admit. Though I could never restore life to something, I *could* affect the processes of death and deconstruction. I'd never thought it particularly useful in the world of the living before.

This time, Saki beat me. She must have kept her magic more controlled, because I did not notice wayward patterns as I had before; but nonetheless she was on the porch, goat in her arms, when at last I felt that the cabin's exterior was weather-proof once more.

I turned to find her smiling as she watched me. "Did you know you glow a little when you do that?"

I was surprised, and confessed as much. "I did not."

"Because you haven't done magic in front of anyone for centuries, because you think it's impolite to act like you have power," she surmised, her smile growing.

"I do try not to startle others. Unless it is helpful," I said, a mild protest. "But I never said—"

"I know." She grinned at me now, her head tipping back as I came closer. Her goatling was asleep, horned head tucked into the crook of her elbow. "It's my turn to give you a hard time, I guess. I'm only teasing you. But that said, Mister 'I don't partner with anyone,' I did mean it when I said I want to give you an official stake in this site. Today."

There was no mistaking the look of intention in her eyes, and the tone in her voice. I considered it. "You think it will be somehow helpful in resolving the curse."

"It's more like I want to cover all possibilities," she said. "If we go on this awful hike and something *does* happen to me, I just want to be sure—"

Panic flared, brief but hot. "Sakura, nothing will happen to you. I won't let it."

"You can't stop *life* from happening, darling." For a moment she held my gaze, affectionate and sympathetic. When I had calmed, she went on, "I didn't mean that I think I'll die or something. Just, I don't know, if I get trapped in a magical bubble or sent to some other dimension or something. Temporarily." She was watching me keenly: she had chosen her examples to distract me. I inclined my head. "I want you to be able to make decisions for the site, too," she concluded. "Gods forbid it should end up in *Bertram's* hands again. Speaking of, do you think we have to involve him?"

"The place is wholly yours," I reminded her. I found it sweet that she had not become wrapped up in her ownership of the entire mountain peak, and instead distrusted it, with simple humility which belied the picture she painted of herself. "You can enter whatever agreement you like. You're certain now is the time?"

"Positive." Her eyes twinkled. "I do happen to trust your word when it comes to business."

Not a sentiment I had often heard, dealing in Helenia's underground markets as often as I had. Warmth flooded my chest, but I remained focused, nodding in answer to her decision.

Nonetheless she looked as though she knew how she'd affected me—as usual. Lightly, she added, "Can you take us somewhere to work on it? I was actually thinking of doing this yesterday, but then I realized I don't have any proper witnessing wax. Or paper, except for an old order pad from the cafe, which I plan to use to leave Quinn and Scarlet a message, should they happen to return before us. And on that note, somewhere with lunch might be good."

"We can go to my office," I offered, though I didn't mind the idea of writing out an agreement on an order pad. What could it matter? It wouldn't change the substance of our arrangement. She made a compelling point about the witnessing wax, though. Such magic was commonplace in completing deals.

"Perfect." Saki smiled. "Just let me drop Lulu off at home, and then we can leave."

At home. She was saying things like this more and more. Perhaps she realized it, and that was why she was more prone to shyness?

I followed as she escorted Lulu back to their cabin. I'd been neglecting my own home, but that wasn't far from the norm. Sometimes I would stay in for days; at other times, I would be gone for days. It depended on business and if I was needed in my official capacity. It depended, I realized now, wholly on others. I did not have that sense of grounding that Saki had, not even though I had lived in one place for countless years, and she had grown accustomed to moving in her own relatively short life.

She came down her porch steps flushed, and it occurred to me that she was excited. The idea was charming. I lifted my hand to her, and as soon as she took it, we were in my garden.

"You are *such* a show-off," she told me, chuckling.

"I thought I was at fault for hiding too much, for propriety's sake," I replied.

"You're both. Typical nonsense from you." The way she looked at me then made my heart skip. But then she slipped her hand from mine, and skipped ahead. "Is Flora still guarding your door?"

She would find out the answer in a moment. The answer was yes, and I already knew that Flora would be overjoyed to see her. I'd never known my guard dog to take to anyone the way she'd taken to Sakura.

I followed again more slowly, now thinking of the first time I'd seen Saki. She and her friend Red had come to my house

209

to buy artifacts—so Saki had said: but of course, Saki had set up the entire thing so that she and Red could help a friend solve a mystery. They'd found my hidden house, made their way past the high walls and the garden I'd so carefully crafted, made their way over the little stream which Saki had accused me of crafting simply to remind me of the river of the dead. She had been right.

Now, Saki was almost exactly as she had been then: bent over at the waist, making a fuss of the three-headed stone dog at my front door. Flora was licking her hands ecstatically, wagging her three tails.

I paused to watch her, and I wondered. I did not know the alchemist Red very well. But I could not believe that anyone, least of all a friend such as that, could be as upset with Saki as Saki believed.

I wondered if, perhaps, I ought to find Red and ask.

But it was Saki's affair, I reminded myself. She would solve it herself in time.

"Flora says you've been neglecting her," Saki informed me.

The very word I'd so recently thought. I was struck with guilt. "She is used to my comings and goings, I'm afraid."

"Well, you'd better watch out. One of these days, someone will come and steal her." Saki said the words for my benefit but she was looking at Flora, rubbing her ears, much to the dog's delight.

"Is that why you brought up making an agreement?" I asked as I drew even with them. "So that you could come to my house and make off with my guardian?"

"Of course." Saki straightened, beaming. "I've been waiting for you to ask me over. What are you going to make me for lunch?"

I chuckled as I patted Flora and then led the way inside. After several days atop the mountain with Saki, it struck me how dark and close my house was. I'd never had reason to reflect on it before.

I took Saki straight back to the kitchen, and listened to her exploring as I made us a platter of cheese, vegetables, hummus, and soft bread. And tea—always tea, with a special thought to what Saki might like these days. She poked her head into every cabinet and exclaimed over every vase and mug, it seemed, and I answered her questions with a growing lightness. Her enthusiasm was a great gift.

The day was fine, and it was considerably warmer now that we were farther down the mountain, so I suggested eating in the back garden. Saki agreed at once, taking the platter away from me and leading the way herself. I trailed behind with our drinks, feeling as though I was the guest in her much livelier world.

She chose a small table beneath a trellis of grape vines, their leaves curled against the winter cold. Tender spring shoots were just starting to come up around us. A small snake watched us from a low stone wall nearby, lazy with cold. If Saki knew that it was uncommon to see such creatures out in the winter, she made no notice—nor did she seem frightened of it. Instead she leaned on her elbows across the table toward me, her mug of tea clasped between her hands.

"White tea with rose and a hint of pomegranate syrup," she guessed, correctly. "Not bad."

"Your favorite?" I asked, tilting my smile to one side.

"Possibly," she teased. "And the mug, of course, is lovely. Though nothing could top the butterfly." For a moment her smile flickered into a hesitant frown. Said butterfly glinted in the sun, just above her ear. I wondered if she might ask about the charm on it, but instead she remarked, "You never asked about the name. My name, I mean."

I watched her, curious. "There have been more pressing matters at hand."

"True, I suppose." Saki met my gaze once more, her expression softening. "I had a mentor for a while, when I was first learning magic. They gave me that title, Black Wings. The color of my magic was always black. At first I was worried that for some reason I wasn't doing it properly. Every other sort of magic I'd seen was so colorful and bright. But . . .

"When I was in recovery," she said quietly, kicking her legs under the table, her feet scuffing over the stone patio, "I didn't know it then, but they weren't sure if I would make it. I got better, so—I don't think about it any more, not very much at least, but I was very close to—death. It's funny how intertwined things turn out to be. Anyway I woke up one night and everything was so quiet in the recovery ward. There wasn't anyone else around, but something had made me wake up. Then—it was right in front of me, going through the hall. This stream of butterflies, huge ones, with black wings that glittered as they flew. They just floated by, and—right through a wall. They didn't notice me, and I didn't go with them, just watched them.

"I still don't really know what it was. It could even have been a dream, I guess. But one day I told my mentor and she told me that there had been a night, one night in particular when no one was sure if I'd get up. But the next day, I was sitting. Like magic had picked me up and set me back down upright. Magic I wasn't even sure I wanted, but I needed, back then.

"I don't mean to say it's an affinity, or anything. I've never had any kind of experience like that since. But I accepted the title because—because I wanted the reminder. Deep inside. Something in me struggled so hard to get here, so hard that I wasn't always sure I wanted to keep going. It's a struggle that's mine, but—there are so many creatures and spirits and beings in the world, doing the same. Just floating by.

"So that's why, and next time Scarlet brings it up, just know that you *do* know a lot more about it than she ever will. Now, weren't we going to eat lunch?"

Chapter Twenty-Five: Clarity

~~~oɔ৩oɔ~~~

Sakura

Yikes. At this rate, I'd have to give Marcus some kind of award. *Has heard more of Saki's sob stories and whims than anyone else in Beyond,* that sort of thing.

But as was his wont, he was a total sweetheart about it. He seemed to like it, the silly man. Well, *I* liked that he knew better than Scarlet and possibly Trent, at least, so that was something. To be honest—I did like telling him.

And the lunch he prepared was delicious. Simple, but sometimes simple things are best. Not that I'm good at keeping things simple—but, that's where Marcus shines.

He told me about his garden and his plants as we ate, and I even got Flora's origin story out of him. His adorable three-headed stone dog was clearly a reference to the mythical Cerberus, though smaller and much more stationary. She was, he admitted, a guardian he'd created after his run-in with Proserpine, which he was still a bit cagey about. But it obviously had affected him, because he admitted that Flora was one of the most powerful creations he'd ever attempted: an animated stone creature capable of keeping his home safe. He admitted, too, that he'd thought of making her into a serpent instead, but had changed his mind at the last minute. Somehow, this little bit of indecision just made me like him more.

We'd been sitting for a while, the hummus and cheese all gone, just chatting. Marcus's garden felt like more of a retreat than my site on the mountain possibly could. When I told him as much, though, he just smiled.

"That is only because of the drama connected to the site at present," he said, very reasonably. "It will pass. And once it does, you will make it into a place even more restful than this."

"Would you like to do the gardening?" I asked hopefully.

He glanced around us modestly, at curving stone paths and trellises that overflowed even in winter. "This was merely an effort to make myself feel at home. As you yourself noted once."

I heard that note in his voice, that note indicating a story behind a single word. I leaned over the table. "You didn't feel at home?"

"No." Marcus considered me steadily, reclining against the back of his chair. "I have not the talent for creating warmth that you do."

"You don't think so?" I found it hard to believe. I mean, sure, not everyone's an interior designer, but he'd lived in his magical moving house for centuries now, as far as I knew.

Surely in *that* time he'd sorted it out.

His mouth twitched, as though he could see my thoughts on my face. "My line of work does not have much to do with living spaces."

"Well, you did just fine with living plants," I told him, grinning at his wry joke. "And I don't think you're giving yourself credit, as usual. So, shall we put it in writing? You're going to be the site's new half-owner, bartender, gardener, carpenter . . . Right?" I ticked them off on my fingers, waiting for him to protest. He did, with a faint chuckle.

"I will do whatever you need, but I can not promise to do it well."

"That's the secret about starting a new venture," I told him, with a *great* deal of confidence and quite a bit of joy, too. The Pomegranate had taught me one lesson above all else, and I shared it with him now. "You never *begin* as an expert. And the wonderful thing is, you're not supposed to. It's better if you're learning as you go, because then you see things that you'd miss otherwise, if you were only looking at what you already knew."

"I will trust your wisdom in the matter," Marcus told me gently. His eyes, usually dark and vaguely hidden, shimmered.

The unspoken joke about him dealing with death and therefore only being good with *endings* rather than beginnings hung in the air between us. I knew he was thinking it, and I knew he could see my amusement. Because nothing about Marcus seemed like an ending to me.

With a little teasing, I got him up and back into the house. Once we'd finished cleaning up—another lesson the Pomegranate had taught me: washing up is endless, so you'd better do it whenever you get a chance—he led the way to his study. He had to, because I had no clue where it might be, despite having visited his house before. It was basically one big maze of darkened rooms. I was half convinced it changed to suit Marcus's mood. Its location could change, so why not its insides?

In any case, it turned out that his office was typically humble. And shadowy. The rug on the floor was probably some sort of Helenic antique, and he walked over it without a second thought. There were bookshelves up to the ceiling, which was shadowy above us. As Marcus approached the old desk, the room lightened a little—not from any lamp, just in general ambiance. The only actual light fixture that I could distinguish was a large stained glass window behind the desk.

Which sported a very beautiful and very obvious pattern of a snake among *cherry blossoms.*

Marcus rounded his desk and began fiddling about with paper and quills, but I was distracted. I crossed my arms and waited until he noticed. Because he had to *know* I'd noticed.

"It, ah, changes," he said, half to his desk, barely looking up. "I change it according to the seasons. Usually."

"Uh huh," I said. "And when was the last time you changed it?"

His voice was pure, casual innocence. Even though his look was anything but. "I believe it was . . . over the summer. I've been . . . preoccupied."

"With all the business Quinn says you haven't been doing?" I asked, biting my lip to hide my grin.

"Sometimes I simply forget time is passing," he said, making excuses for himself. Finally, he looked up. "Which makes me all the more determined to appreciate my time with you. I know full well you mean to tease me, Sakura, but can you say you are surprised? You already know I am . . . sentimental."

Curse him. I *was* having fun teasing him, and he'd gone and totally turned it on me. *He* wasn't blushing, but now I was. "Maybe I was just admiring it," I informed him archly, though I knew my smile gave me away. "For the record. It's very pretty."

"Thank you. Though it pales in comparison to its inspiration." Marcus turned back to shuffling his piles of paper, like he hadn't just thrown out an immaculately smooth line. For an instant I lost all track of my words. Mercifully, he glanced up and smiled his little lopsided smile at me. "So, what are you insisting I swear to?"

"Um, I just want to write out something simple," I said, gathering my wits again and joining him at the desk. "It needs to say that you and I will be equally responsible for the site, and that if one or the other of us forfeits, then the other assumes all responsibility. It doesn't actually have to get into roles—I was just teasing you about that earlier."

"How unusual," he murmured wryly, his shoulder just above mine. "Tell me, Saki, is this something you also learned from your efforts with the Pomegranate?"

"Glacial and I did do something like this," I admitted. "And then we added Mel later. I know, it's not everyone's favorite thing to think of, most people are just excited to try something with their—friends." Acting like my voice hadn't done a very strange thing over a totally normal word, I added, now rambling, "Maybe it seems like overkill, especially since we'll be selling it soon, probably. But there's this whole curse thing, like I said earlier, and honestly I—it's not something I learned from business. It's something I learned from magic, actually."

Marcus looked interested. He tilted his head, maybe just

relieved that I'd gotten around to answering his question.

I leaned on the desk as I looked up at him. "Yeah, um, that probably seems weird too. Shadow magic doesn't have any spells or contracts or anything usually, right? But—that's why I know. It's really important to be very clear about your intentions and not only that, your potential consequences. Normally if I'm just working magic, just within myself, I just have to think it through internally but with other people, when I started doing business with them, I knew that in order to be clear we'd have to—to write things down.

"I swear I'm normally a practical person," I added, barely relevantly, in a whisper. "I've really tried to be clear with you."

"I know," Marcus said lightly.

I risked glancing up to squint at him. "Do you?"

"Yes," he replied, affectionately. "But the playing field is uneven, you might say. My situation is very simple and therefore it is easy to be clear. Your situation at present is not simple."

I shifted, full on frowning at him now. Not mad, but a little suspicious, and mostly thoughtful. When he said it like that—well, it made me question myself. *Were* things really so complicated after all?

"Business," I told him firmly. "We focus on business first. One piece at a time."

"Very well," he said, sounding awfully pleased with himself.

"And by that I don't mean kisses or anything I was trying to warn you *off* of when I first showed up," I added, just in case he was remembering that conversation and *that* was why he was so happy to talk about 'business.'"

"The thought didn't cross my mind," he assured me.

I had my doubts. But, maybe that was my own hopes and

very un-complicated bodily urges messing with me. He was standing right next to me, after all. And his office smelled like him.

Regardless, I did my best to focus. *One piece at a time.* My mentor used to say that. Funny how little bits from the past cropped up and stuck around when they were least expected.

At least that particular piece of the past was relatively pleasant.

Carefully, precisely, I wrote out an agreement for us, for the site. The inn didn't have a name yet, I realized. So I didn't mention that quite yet, but kept it very simple, as I'd promised. With great solemnity and a dignity I could never hope to match, Marcus signed his name beneath mine. Then I watched as, at the bottom of the paper, he added an enchanted wax seal.

The magic of it curled around us. That part was normal—it was part of solidifying the agreement. What *wasn't* usual was the way the magic flared briefly before drawing back down into the wax, the spell completed.

"Er," I said, waiting almost as if to see if it was going to do something else strange. "Did you see that too? Have you seen that before?"

Marcus shrugged. "I told you: I do not often enter agreements. I buy and sell, nothing more."

"Hmmm. So you don't know if that was your fault, or mine?" I watched him carefully. It occurred to me now that making a deal with a deity might be a rare thing to do *for a reason.* But this was Marcus. He'd have told me if there was a reason not to.

"Perhaps it was the fault of the spell," he said blandly. "I am sure I purchased it long ago."

"Well, it did complete itself," I mused. "And I don't sense anything else off. So I guess we can consider that done."

"Perfect. One piece settled." Marcus beamed at me as he rolled up the paper. "What shall we do now, business partner?"

Briefly I considered elbowing him for being so impish, or perhaps tugging him down by the collar and kissing him silly. But that was hardly keeping things simple. Besides, I'd tried so hard to be responsible so far this afternoon, and it seemed a pity to ruin that. Besides, we'd have to go back and face Quinn and Scarlet eventually.

"Would you like me to take you back to Lulu?" Marcus suggested, wholly making up for his teasing.

I smiled up at him. "You'd better. If anyone can make a mess of something as simple as an afternoon alone, it'd be her!"

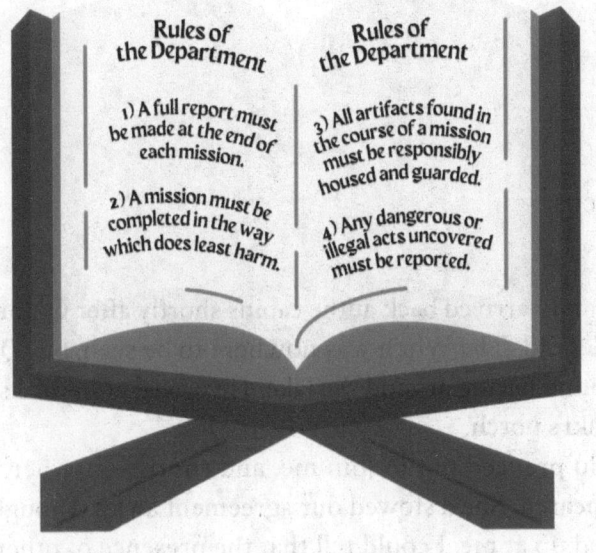

Rules of the Department

1) A full report must be made at the end of each mission.

2) A mission must be completed in the way which does least harm.

3) All artifacts found in the course of a mission must be responsibly housed and guarded.

4) Any dangerous or illegal acts uncovered must be reported.

Chapter Twenty-Six: A Warning

~ஒஃ~

Marcus

Saki and I arrived back at the cabins shortly after Quinn and Scarlet did. The Witch was nowhere to be seen, but Quinn we found pacing around the lake. He waved at me as I stood on Saki's porch.

Lulu pranced out to join me, and shortly after her, Saki reappeared. She'd stowed our agreement away. Though she smiled up at me, I could tell that the presence of others on the site was preoccupying her mind.

We stood in companionable silence until Quinn came within shouting distance. I savored that moment, drawing from it strength for the evening ahead.

"Had you taken any longer to come back, I would've started searching myself," Quinn called to us as he approached.

Saki leaned on the porch railing, frowning. "Didn't you get

my note?"

"Yes. I wouldn't search out of worry for *you*." Quinn's eyes drifted down the line of cabins. "More for the sake of giving myself something to do."

Every so often, my friend Quinn reminded me how young he was, inadvertently. It amused me, this insistence on being busy—and on avoiding someone who was already avoiding us.

"I suppose I can't blame you for that," Saki admitted. "Want to come up and have tea, and tell us what all you bought on our dime?"

"You will, of course, be billed." Quinn hopped up onto the porch, his gray eyes bright. Though he complained, it was clear that he was enjoying the exercise. "And I think you'll be very pleased. Just wait until you see what I got for dinner tonight."

I caught Saki's eye and smiled.

She rolled her eyes good-humoredly and retreated to her cabin, presumably to prepare tea.

"The two of you should give serious thought to writing a book. Or perhaps a monograph," Quinn said, collapsing into a rather dubious rocking chair at the far corner of the porch. "Just what *are* you planning on doing, once you've solved this haunting case?"

Saki's voice drifted out through the window, which she'd left cracked open. "Aren't you going to be gone? What do you care?"

Quinn chuckled. I joined him, leaning against the railing near his seat. The construction groaned under my weight, and I reminded myself to fix up Saki's cabin as I had the others—and soon.

225

"Gwyndolen says it's going to be an inn," Quinn continued, his eyes searching my face, betraying his amusement. "I think it's a capital idea. Scarlet wasn't impressed, but then, she never is. Once you get it up and running, I'll come back and be your first customer. Harley's always telling me I ought to take a vacation."

I had met Quinn's sister briefly, and well believed she was holding her older brother to account. It was good: he needed someone to do so, from time to time. Just as I often did. "Sakura has proposed using the existing cabins," I explained. "And we will build a central meeting-house for the office and dining."

"A lodge. I like it," Quinn said, ignoring the loud creak in his chair as he leaned back and placed his hands behind his head. "A hearth and home at Hideaway Lake."

"I like it also," I confessed. Saki came back out carrying a tea tray, and I hoped that in my expression she could read admiration and support. Her magic sparkled around the tray's edges as Lulu twined around her feet. To see her using it while we were so close—even for so instinctual a purpose—made my heart swell.

"I'll admit you have a way with words," she told Quinn. "So, what else? What's your report?"

"Can't a person even have tea before being put to work?" Quinn teased as he sat up, prompting another ghastly squeak from the rocking chair. As he took a steaming cup from the tray, he went on, "The expedition is set. Some of it is my own gear, for which I won't charge you. I did however have to purchase suitable food, water bottles, hats and gloves, and poles. And a few other sundries. You're on your own for footwear."

"Keep your eyes on your own feet," Saki retorted smartly as Quinn glanced at her glamoured pumps. She handed me a fragrant cup and joined me at the rail. With one hand behind my back, hoping not to be too obvious, I strengthened the construction. She was still talking to Quinn: "What do you mean, you bought us gloves and hats?"

"Have you looked at the mountain lately?" Quinn raised an eyebrow.

"It's covered in snow. I know," Saki replied. "Still, I do have my own clothes. We get snow in Belville too, you know."

"These ones are charmed. Wear them or not, but if you do, you'll be glad." Quinn paused meaningfully. "Saki . . ."

"Not you, too," she protested.

Quinn's gray eyes met mine, and he nodded. "If you and Marcus already spoke about it, fine. I just wanted to offer. If you want me to make any adjustments, all you have to do is say the word. No explanations necessary. I'll say it's my own whim."

Saki obscured her face with her own cup. "Wouldn't Scarlet give you a hard time?"

"Seems like there's a lot of that going around." Quinn glanced at me again. I was so accustomed to him inferring details on his own that it was a surprise to realize that he still most likely knew nothing of Trent. "I'm willing to throw my hat in the ring."

"Well, I appreciate it." Saki sounded like she truly meant it, and I could not help putting my arm at her back. She smiled up at me for a brief moment before adding to Quinn, "But it's not necessary. It'll be fine. I'll be fine. And I'll wear your hats and gloves, even though I'm sure they're hideous."

"If there's a monster up there who eats people based on

what they look like, I'll be sure to apologize," Quinn said dryly. "Speaking of, we'd better start behaving ourselves again."

I was slow to follow this, but Saki glanced toward the other cabins, and I understood. Scarlet had emerged and was making her way toward us.

Saki's teeth were gritted. "I'll go and make more tea."

"Don't bother," Quinn told her. "She doesn't drink it."

"All the better." Saki pushed off the railing and went inside.

The change left me feeling bereft. The atmosphere was, indeed, chilly—both as the sun slowly set, and as Scarlet took over our discussion of the site. When Saki joined us, Scarlet became even more cold, even more determined. I wished I could stop it, but I had a feeling that intervening would only make things worse.

Instead, I focused my thoughts on the pendant I'd made for Saki. Though it would work all the time to protect her— much like Flora watching over my door, even when I was gone—I could strengthen it momentarily, channeling some power into it. From the surprise on Saki's face, the way her hand went to her chest, I saw she could feel the pendant grow warm. She glanced up at me and smiled, acknowledging the reminder.

Still, as the evening wore on, to see Saki so obviously hurt was painful. Normally she did not seem affected by mere words in this way. I doubt Scarlet saw the hurt she was causing, but I could see it, in the flash in Saki's eyes, in the tone of her voice.

Awkwardly, we set our plan for the next morning. Quinn then tried to lighten the mood by revealing his dinner plan, a local favorite—skewers of vegetables, buttered bread, and firm cheese meant to be roasted over an open fire. I myself did not see the reason for this, but Saki did: she teased Quinn about wanting to eat outside and keep watch for monsters. The two of them were quite pleased with it, recovered from their initial encounter with the unexplained apparition, it seemed. Perhaps it helped that Lulu was safely locked in Saki's cabin before night fell.

We set up a bonfire by the corner of the lake nearest the row of cabins. Quinn carried a table and some benches over, and set out the skewers, all wrapped in brown paper, with the air of a chef. Though I was familiar with the dish it was not something I had bothered with before. Saki, laughing for the first time since Scarlet had joined us, had to show me how to achieve the desired effect: warmth and charring without burning.

"It's simple, really," she assured me, her smile reflecting the firelight. "And even more fun when you get to make the skewers yourself. I'd thought about trying it at the Pomegranate, but Glacial said we shouldn't be setting fires inside, even if we *do* have protection charms."

"Thank goodness for sensible business partners," Quinn commented. His wry glance at me spoke of knowledge, but I did not know if he knew about my agreement with Saki—or if perhaps he was making fun of me for obviously hanging on her every word. I couldn't help it: it was so nice to hear her speak lightly of her past. Quinn went on, "Speaking of, Saki, Marcus, we ran into Bertram at the market, buying cupcakes for all the secretaries who have to put up with him. He didn't know us, of course, but I took the liberty of telling him I was a reporter working on a story about Spa Hallow. He seemed to believe the construction would proceed as planned."

"Because he is the *opposite* of sensible, cupcakes aside." Saki made a face as she evaluated the char marks on a bit of cheese.

"I'll agree there's nothing sensible about ignoring some facts and choosing others," Quinn said from his corner of the fire. "He wasn't too keen on admitting that you'd taken up residence. And he insisted that the stories of hauntings were only malicious rumors."

"Maybe because you're an outsider," Saki said thoughtfully. "He did admit it to me, though not at first. Actually, Gwyn was the one who really warned me, aside from you two. *Marcus*," she added affectionately. In mentioning myself and Quinn, she'd glanced my way and noticed that I was having trouble eating a piece of roasted potato. "You can slide everything off onto a plate once it's cooked, and eat it with a fork. Have you got one?"

Easily done. Sheepishly, I held up my hand and summoned a plate from my cabin for her to see.

"Enough. If no one else has thought it yet, I'll be the one to say it," Scarlet announced. She threw away an empty skewer and stood, nearest the lake, in shadow. "All this talk about who knows what and supposed 'hauntings' is cute, but none of it is the *real* problem. You're all avoiding it, which I expected of a failed shadow witch, but not the rest of you. This would be so much easier if *you* helped," she concluded. She was looking at me.

I was baffled. I'd never done divination work of any kind. "Me?"

"Naturally." Scarlet smiled, but the effect was eerie. "Because of your connection with death."

Saki interrupted. "Technically he's a god of the *dead*, not of death. Leave him alone."

"Oh, I'm sorry. Is he not here so that you can use his power for your little plans?" Scarlet glared at Saki, then at me. "I'd watch out if I were you. She seems like your protector now, but she'll just use you up and then walk away."

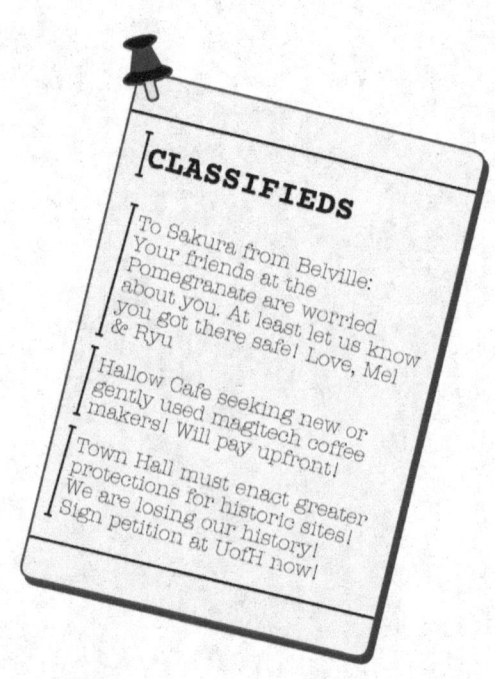

CLASSIFIEDS

To Sakura from Belville:
Your friends at the
Pomegranate are worried
about you. At least let us know
you got there safe! Love, Mel
& Ryu

Hallow Cafe seeking new or
gently used magitech coffee
makers! Will pay upfront!

Town Hall must enact greater
protections for historic sites!
We are losing our history!
Sign petition at UofH now!

Chapter Twenty-Seven: Demands

༺◦◦◦◦◦༻

Sakura

My blood was boiling. Who *says* that to someone about someone else?

Quinn mumbled something in the background but I really didn't care any more. It was hard enough just paying attention to myself, to every stray strand of magic that might possibly get free and then get Scarlet by the throat.

Which is definitely what part of me wanted to do.

"If you were *half* as good as he is, you'd know that your opinion is neither necessary nor informed," I snapped.

"But *yours* is, I'm *so* sure," Scarlet drawled. "Never mind the fact that you're not even using your magic any more, are you, honey. What use are you at all?"

"At least I know how to treat my friends," I retorted, all the angrier because I knew my recent actions hadn't proved this to be true.

Quinn mumbled again but Scarlet pounced. "Tell me, then, what story *have* you told Marcus to account for your sudden reappearance?"

She was leaning toward me now. She was way too loud. My hands clenched as I yelled back. "That's between the two of us!"

"Oh, kind of like the divination I was trying to do to *work on my case!*" She shouted back.

"Please, both of you," Marcus said faintly from somewhere behind me.

"I agree," said Quinn, more loudly. "Saki, Marcus can fight his own battles. And in the meantime—"

"Fine!" I was so incensed I was trembling. Magic was escaping in wisps and whirls around my hands. It was dark, and for once, I was so glad my magic was black. Maybe no one noticed. But I had to get out of there before they did. If they wanted to take over in my absence, more power to them. They'd surely do better than I had. "Fine! I'll leave you to it. I'm sure I'm only making things harder anyway!"

Not my most mature exit line. Future Saki knows that. But obviously, in-the-moment Saki didn't care.

I stomped off toward my cabin alone. This would have been very difficult to do normally, as I was immediately engulfed in shadow upon leaving the fire. But again, I didn't care in the least. I also did not care when Marcus loomed up out of the darkness in front of me.

"Sakura," he began, but he didn't get any further.

"Just leave me be, and if you're going to hold your own, do it," I ordered, not so much as looking at him as I stomped stubbornly on.

234

He appeared in front of me again. "But Saki . . ."

I did stop this time, just for a minute. Because he was trying, and even in my frustration, I could see that. But magic was still pushing and pulling behind my skin and tears were pricking my eyes and I just didn't have time to sit out and wait. The last thing I needed was for Scarlet to witness another explosion. The last thing I *wanted* was to lose control again.

I could still hear Quinn and Scarlet talking behind us. It just made me mad all over again.

"Go and stand up for yourself," I told Marcus as I began to trudge off again.

"But—"

"Marcus!" I whirled for just a moment, exasperated. "When something is important to you, you sometimes have to stop being so *polite!*"

At least in that one particular way, my actions and words went together. I left him behind once more.

I was still seething as I walked but the farther away I was, the quieter it became around me, bit by bit the magic eased. I could breathe again. Then I could even take deep breaths, and not hate it. I was still angry, not least because I knew how poorly I'd behaved. But I'd have a night to sleep on it. They could do their work, which really did matter. And maybe in the morning I'd try setting a spell that made it so that whenever Scarlet spoke I only heard the chirping of birds . . .

That wouldn't change the fact that I'd let myself down, though.

And Marcus, too.

I had to pause at the bottom of my porch steps and wipe furiously at my eyes. The tears were those terrible stinging kind that only made things worse. I couldn't see a thing. I could have risked magic to illuminate the porch or even just lift myself up—the idea did occur to me. Surely the others were far enough away. Even if the tendrils went a little wild, surely they'd be fine. But even so, at the last moment I decided against it and hauled myself up by the railing rather than by sight.

I could hear Lulu bleating inside. I'd left her in the cabin, not willing to let her out so close to dark, especially not when I'd known most of my attention would be on Scarlet. If only I'd known *how* much! If I had, I'd probably have just stayed home.

Feeling quite disappointed and upset and sorry for myself, ready to curl up on the sofa by the fire and cry, I opened the door.

But instead of a small white form waiting for me, there was a very tall gray one.

"Sakura." This time, instead of staying at a respectful distance, Marcus crossed the room toward me in about two steps. In one motion, too fast for me to follow, he'd picked me up by the waist and I was pinned between him and the closed door at my back. And then he was kissing me so hard I forgot about everything else.

The rest of the world and everything I'd done just fell away. I twined my arms around his neck—my legs were already around his waist. He'd picked me up before but I'd never felt so close to him, so surrounded. Between him and the door I could barely breathe, and I wanted it that way.

I did my best to kiss him back, but honestly, it was hard to keep up. His tongue was hot on mine, his lips demanding. He certainly didn't need more encouragement. He didn't need any arguing or any words, either. He was making it very clear that all he needed was that moment, and me.

He kissed me until I was panting against him, and only then did he slow, kissing the corner of my mouth, then my cheek. "Please," he murmured softly, "forgive me."

I could have laughed aloud if I wasn't so breathless. "You're ridiculous."

"So I've been told." He did chuckle, though he sounded pretty breathless himself. "Sakura, my sweet soul, I am grateful. I am very grateful for your impulse to protect me. It is true I can fight my own battles, but as you said, I am slow to, too slow sometimes. The dead—perhaps you already know—the dead do not speak with words, not in the place where I meet them. I do not always need words. And so I am prone to forgetting them."

"I didn't know that, silly." His face was still next to mine, his body keeping me up. I turned to kiss his jaw, overwhelmed by affection for this strange, dear person who could be so open and sweet. "Why would I know that?"

"I just assume you know everything. Don't you?" He chuckled again, gently, kissing the tip of my nose as I had done to him so much earlier in the day.

"If I did, I'd clean up my act," I confessed. "I'm so sorry, Marcus. Of course I know you can look after yourself. It wasn't at all about you, not really. I mean, I really couldn't stand her being mean to you. But I should have checked in with you instead. She just got under my skin."

"Sweet one," he said, for the second time, making my heart thrill. "Everything gets under your skin lately."

"Yes," I admitted, finally laughing at myself—if a bit pathetically. The admission brought up the tears that Marcus's

237

kisses had swept away. "Yes, you're right. Everything gets under my skin, because—because under my skin's not a place I want to be, myself, not any more. I'm so disappointed in myself, Marcus." Tucked against him, his cheek against mine, I was safe. I could admit it. "She's right. And there I was listening to her all evening, listening to her being mean, and thinking about what you said. That she shouldn't be, even if she *is* friends with Trent. And that made me start to think differently about things a little. It seems to me now like the worst part of it all is actually the fact that I didn't mean to. I never meant to. I wasn't trying to do anything that would hurt anyone or make anyone so mad. I was trying to do the opposite. And that's the worst, because if I could hurt him that way, then—it could happen again, and—"

Marcus spoke gently when my voice became choked. "You have said that before, Saki. I know it is something you are afraid of, and I don't mind."

"Yes I know, and you are the sweetest, even though you call *me* sweet." I lifted my head for just a moment to smile at him, despite my tears. "But the fact is I'm just so mad at myself. Because the whole point of all my training and all my efforts at self-awareness is to inform my behavior. But if I'm going to mess up so badly anyway—and I have no idea what to do instead or how to fix things—then Scarlet's right—it's a failure—I've *failed*."

Marcus waited a moment, his head hanging beside mine as I snuffled. "Is that all?"

"Of course it's all," I replied, rather petulantly. "It's everything."

"It's nothing," he returned. "I see that it hurts you, Saki, and that does matter. But this confusion, from my perspective it is nothing compared to what you are. You say you do not know right now, but I am certain that you will. As long as you keep going—and I know that you will do that. You will sort this out and be better for it. I believe in you. I have faith in you."

My breath had caught somewhere in the middle, and by the end of that speech I might as well have been floating. "M-Marcus? *You* have faith in *me*?"

"The deepest faith," he assured me, that little glimmer in his eye like he guessed how affected I felt.

"Carry me to the couch," I demanded, faintly. "Sit down."

He probably had no idea why, but he did as I asked. He crossed the room, a bemused Lulu wandering past to look at us. I paid her no mind for the moment. Marcus had to be dealt with first. As he sat, carefully, I shifted so that I was straddling his lap—sitting above him. And from there, *I* was the one looking down. I could, and did, very purposefully kiss just about every inch of his face. I just wanted to be certain he knew how much he'd affected me, and I didn't have words at first.

"You're a miracle," I told him finally. "I don't even understand it."

"Maybe it doesn't need to be understood," he suggested. Looking up at me so serenely, smiling.

And then, with impeccable timing, someone outside screamed.

GUIDELINES FOR
GHOST MEDIATORS

WHEN A HAUNTING
GOES CAT 5

AS SOON AS A
HAUNTING RESULTS IN
REAL INJURY, CALL IN
THE HIGHEST POWER
POSSIBLE. UNLESS
YOU HAPPEN TO
KNOW A DEITY,
THAT'LL BE THE
POLICE. DON'T WAIT
FOR ANOTHER INJURY
TO HAPPEN!

Chapter Twenty-Eight: Haunting

❧

Marcus

The screamer wasn't Quinn. I watched Sakura above me and I knew she hesitated. Then she made a face of reluctance at me.

Sweet Saki.

We were out on the porch in a moment, careful to leave Lulu trapped inside. The campfire was still blazing beside the lake, and figures were visible in front of it—running from it. Not from the fire itself, but from another lumbering shadow it illuminated.

"You go to them and do your bubble," Saki said at once.

I could see what the other half of her plan must entail, and it was to that I responded. "No."

"Yes," she insisted, pushing her sleeves back. "I have your pendant. This might be exactly what I need."

I put my hand on her arm, and she glanced up for a moment. What I felt was nerves, nothing more: I could see her determination. The apparition behind Quinn and Scarlet roared. I'd wasted time.

I nodded, and Saki smiled briefly at me before she raced away.

Meanwhile I carried out her suggestion. I met Quinn and Scarlet in front of my own cabin, my arms out to stop them. As the shield came up, Scarlet collapsed. Quinn came to a halt beside me, breathing hard.

"My magic, my magic," Scarlet was moaning to herself.

"Yes, so," Quinn panted, "turns out the thing that likes—or doesn't like—goats can also affect magic."

I thought instantly of Saki. "What do you mean?"

"I was trying to tell you earlier—something was moving in the woods—it came out from between the cabins—" Quinn began.

Ah. This explained why Quinn had been sitting with his back to the lake at the fire. He'd expected something to come. I should have known—he always sat facing the direction from which he expected a threat.

Scarlet wailed. *"It took my magic!"*

I looked down at her for a moment, focusing. If I drew on my own power, I could see her soul, the forces that made her self. I knew Scarlet's magic to be a deep red-tinged violet color. I could still see it within her, though not so near the surface as it might normally be. She had not lost it. But she had suffered a shock.

And a terrible premonition had come over me. I refocused up, in the direction of the bonfire.

The *apparition,* as Quinn so rightly put it, had stopped some distance away from us. It was not casting any light, which made it difficult to focus on, and my Saki—

She was casting darkness. She was between us and it.

She was, in fact, several feet off the ground.

I could feel the tug in my own chest as the charm around her neck worked to protect her.

"Not all magic?" Quinn suggested, his voice still ragged. He stood more normally now at my side, looking on.

"What? What has happened?" Scarlet was still on the ground.

Twenty paces away, Sakura blazed. Her magic slipped from her control, and a wave of crackling, sparking energy crashed over our shield. I stumbled, but held on, barely.

Scarlet cried out again. "What was that?"

"Gods," Quinn added, looking unsettled himself as he helped me straighten. "Do we need to move?"

The idea was a practical one, but not feasible in the moment. With my concentration divided between the shield and watching Saki, the added strain of moving wasn't wise. I remained stationary. Quinn moved around me to help Scarlet up.

Saki blazed again, and this time the energy went straight up into the sky, obscuring the stars. She was drawing on her anger, I knew. Most likely she was focusing on the apparition as the reason we were all disturbed. But given how much anger she was carrying towards herself, I could not help but worry.

The apparition roared again, and this time Saki's magic coalesced. It started as a wide and uncertain circle, but it grew smaller, intentional. It was a net closing around the creature. She was trying to corral it, to hold it in place. Why,

243

I did not understand. But she must have seen something about it the rest of us had not. She was the only one of us who had stood ground against it.

The creature seemed to waver as the magic closed around it. Then it winked out.

I let my shield drop in surprise. This was premature, a mistake. Saki's magic collapsed on nothing, and another wave of it rolled past us. Fortunately, this one was only strong enough to leave us unsteady on our feet. Her force had been much more controlled this time.

Even so—it was confusing. What had happened?

I was certain Quinn and Scarlet were alright, if winded and confused, so I made my way past them. I reached Saki just as she reached the ground.

"I don't know how it did that," she said, looking up at me. "It just disappeared."

"I saw," I told her. Of its own accord my hand was on her arm, her shoulder, turning her to face me, seeking for injury. "We can discuss it later. How do you feel?"

"Alive." Saki grinned up at me, her eyes reflecting starlight. The fire had been blown out. Gingerly, she held up one finger to my upraised palm. A spark of energy arced between the two. The effect was like being zapped by a children's toy. "Maybe don't get too close yet. I'm definitely still not normal. But did that ever feel good! Aside from the fact that it didn't work," she added, her brief and playful smile fading into a frown.

My Sakura.

"What *was* that?" Scarlet, supported by Quinn, had joined us. She was neither relieved nor admiring. She was, as the phrase has it, spitting nails. "That was more than all the

Witches of the department combined. That was dangerous. You could have *killed* us! How are you allowed on the streets?"

Sparks flared in Saki's eyes, and the air around her crackled. She did not move. While Scarlet's response was unfortunate, I was certain that her own experience—having her magic suppressed suddenly by a foe she was ill-equipped to face— only made her more vehement. Saki, on the other hand, was masking pain. I had watched her do so long enough.

"On the contrary," I said, drawing Scarlet's attention. "The fact that Sakura wielded such power does not, by necessity, mean that she endangered us. She knew that we were shielded. She was simply meeting a circumstance which has challenged and upset us all."

"That's it in a nutshell, isn't it?" Quinn ran his hands through his hair, which remained windblown after the dissipation of Saki's magic. "That was *much* more than any of us anticipated. Saki and I had seen the thing before, of course, but it didn't quite seem so trivial and *mortal* today, did it, Scarlet?"

"It was still only a creature," she snapped back. "It was solid."

"I actually agree," Saki said, focused on Quinn rather than the Witch. "It didn't have magic. It wasn't using any, at least. That's why I don't understand . . ."

She glanced up at me again, and I inclined my head. Since she was as well as she could be at present, it was time to discuss other practicalities. "You confronted it, it stopped in place. It tried to scare you, but you unleashed your magic instead, trying to capture it. Then it disappeared. Correct?"

Saki nodded, and Quinn offered, "It might have seen what you were doing, Saki, and decided to escape."

"Teleportation is possible with the right item, even for

something that has no magic," I agreed.

Saki remained frowning. "But why would a *creature* have something like that?"

"It could also be a pawn, still," Quinn added. "Maybe someone else is controlling it, saw what was going on, and called it back. That wouldn't go against your divinations, would it?"

He glanced at Scarlet, who reluctantly agreed. "Nothing I've learned contradicts that. But—it took my magic. How—?"

"That could have been another item," Saki mused. "Or some kind of protective field?"

Scarlet stared at Saki. Whether or not she was aware of the attention, Saki continued gazing thoughtfully into space. Quinn caught my eye and shrugged.

"We've scared it off for now, anyway," he said.

"I agree that there is little else we can do tonight." I watched Saki, wary that she might offer to try to trace the creature magically. Though she clearly had energy to spare, I thought that the concentrated effort involved in tracing was perhaps one step too far. Saki looked up with a faint, wry smile, as though she knew what I was thinking. Of course. I carried on. "Scarlet, I appreciate that you have had a bad shock, but your magic has not been taken. You will make a full recovery, I am certain. The best thing we all can do now is rest."

Scarlet shifted on her feet, almost as though underwater and unable to make sense of her location. "One wonders why you all even need me."

"It was your idea to go up the mountain. Getting cold feet?" Saki spoke with her dangerously sweet tones, but I could not help but feel it was better than their arguing.

Scarlet replied through gritted teeth. "I'll see the case

through. And I will make a *full* report to the Department. Goodnight."

She stalked off to her cabin, and Quinn looked from her to us with one eyebrow raised. "I will say, this has been far more exciting than I expected. Let us see what tomorrow brings, shall we? And *stay safe.*" With a salute, he left us as well.

Saki watched them go for a moment. "You know, I almost thought that maybe she *knew* we were . . . close, and she screamed on purpose. But that was pretty bad, wasn't it?"

"Far too much for her to have arranged, I think," I agreed.

Saki caught my eye, and her self-deprecating smile was a delight.

"I also think that it would be prudent to be seen going into our own cabins, nonetheless," I added. To admit as much made my heart skip. It was tacitly acknowledging the fact that I might otherwise want *not* to go to my own cabin. And while I didn't normally care too much for others' opinions of my conduct, it was clear that resolving this matter with as little drama as possible would require effort. "But may I walk you to your porch?"

With a soft giggle, Saki agreed. "Oh, alright then, Mister Manners. Not still worried about me, are you?"

She reached her hand up to my elbow, delicately laying her fingers over my sleeve. There was a slight tingle, nothing more. We turned and began walking back the way we'd come, and for a moment, I savored the silence. It was only once we'd reached her cabin that I spoke.

"You are worth it," I told her softly.

Saki turned on the first step, and I did not need starlight nor firelight to read the warmth in her expression. "Marcus . . . thank you."

"You are always welcome, my sweetling," I said sincerely. "For tonight, I hope you take care of yourself, and rest well. As Quinn said—we will see tomorrow what fate brings."

Chapter Twenty-Nine: The Woods

❧❧❧

Sakura

It turns out there is one circumstance in which I enjoy hiking: spite.

Well, to be fair, when we were about ten minutes into the hike, I realized that I could also enjoy it if: I was alone with Marcus. But "alone with Marcus" was a circumstance which made just about *anything* bearable, if not enjoyable.

In this case, though, it wasn't simply a matter of hormones. We set out from the far end of the lake, with our packs and our sticks and our large, trompy boots. I'd fed everyone breakfast and locked Lulu up, much to her dismay. It was still early, an earliness I thought I'd sworn off when I left the Pomegranate. But—that was part of what made it nice. The lake was misty, the forest alive. Birds called and flew above us. Though we had no trail to follow, the trees were just wide enough apart for a single file line, and the little green shoots everywhere were thriving. No curse or creature could be obnoxious enough to mess with this peace.

That was what I thought, at least, and Marcus was as calm and quiet as ever behind me. *We* blended in rather well, I thought. It was Quinn and Scarlet who were causing trouble, for once.

"The trees and vegetation here are younger than elsewhere in the forest, so we must be close," said the detective in front, who was determined to solve the mystery of the mountain via logic and geological science.

"But I am telling you, the energy is *stronger* over to the right," said the Witch on his heels, practically breathing over his shoulder, determined to divine the way to the top and thereby prove her magical prowess.

"'Over to the right' is a sheer cliff, which shows no signs of ever having stairs cut into it—"

"You can't possibly know this landscape as well as the deities and spirits did—"

"It's still a physical mountain, and as such it has to make *sense!*"

I fell back a pace, letting Quinn and Scarlet work this one out themselves. Over my shoulder, I told Marcus in a low voice, "I think I see why nobody has made it to the top in living memory."

"Hmmm."

I twisted to look at him. His head may as well have been in the clouds, birdwatching, for all the attention he was paying to the rest of us. I doubted he was actually thinking about woodpeckers and sparrows, though. "Marcus? Are you okay?"

251

"Saki." His eyes met mine like he was coming back from far away. "Yes, sweet one."

I liked this new habit of his, calling me sweet nicknames, really I did. But the tone he used was just a little sad. I narrowed my eyes at him, bumping into a tree as I tried to keep walking forward. It mostly hit my backpack, so I played it off. "What is it? What's bothering you?"

His mask flickered, a sign I recognized. I was seeing something he didn't want to, or know how to, put into words yet. Well, he could figure it out. I wasn't climbing a mountain with confusion in front of *and* behind me.

"The stillness," he said at last. Which was actually a tiny bit funny, because as he was saying it I was tripping over a rock, and Quinn and Scarlet were several paces away now arguing over a map. None of us were still. But Marcus was clearly serious. "I do not sense anything."

"Did you think you would?" I asked. He'd never offered to lead the way up the mountain, so I'd assumed he'd forgotten it. And he didn't have a sense for the creature, not really—since it wasn't a ghost, and divine power tended to respond only to other divinities, unless specifically called upon. I knew that much—he'd reminded us just this morning. Quinn had been all worked up about us just walking past the lake for some reason, and Scarlet had started a fight with him about legends and heroes. I'd mostly ignored it.

Marcus just held my gaze. The pendant hanging from my neck grew warm.

He's that worried?

I stumbled backward, and this time fell flat onto my butt. But I didn't fall far. In fact, as Marcus knelt in front of me, his hand on my knee, it felt rather like I was sitting in a chair.

Quinn looked back—then rolled up his map. "Ah. It looks like Saki found what we're looking for."

"I did?" I looked back at Marcus. Stairs were nice—maybe—but I was still more interested in whatever was bugging him.

"I'll be more focused," he said softly. "I promise. But take care, Saki. If you feel divine power pulling at you, let me know."

As he helped me up, I turned to look behind me at last. It must have looked like I'd tripped right into a scruffy bush. But from right next to it—well, inside it, really—I could see the outline of one stone stair, and then another—and then another, hidden by moss, and more still obscured by a rock outcrop and a clump of trees. A promising trail, it was not. But it did look like it was headed up.

"Maybe you're the true owner of this property after all," Scarlet said to me as she joined us.

I tilted my head at her. She hadn't spoken to me all morning, and I'd been happy to leave it at that. But, for as begrudging and dismissive as she made this sound, it wasn't so bad.

She scowled at me. "Sometimes that matters. For the magic. For the Reflection Pool. I just hope you're prepared, that's all."

"Sage advice for all of us," Quinn cut in. He also cut in line, jumping nimbly past me so that he was on the stairs ahead of everyone else. "Shall we, then?"

Slowly, awkwardly, one by one, we did.

We—okay, mostly *I*—huffed and puffed up the ancient stairs. It turned out that both Quinn and Scarlet had been a little bit right. The staircase was more or less where Quinn had thought it would be, directly behind the lake, but it didn't go straight up into the mountain. Instead, we were climbing the cliff sideways, sort of. There was Scarlet's energetic cliff face to our left, and—as we left the shrubs behind, and the trees began to thin—a sheer drop to our right.

I'm not too worried about heights normally, but I kept well to the left. Using my magic last night had been alright, but still quite iffy. I could still feel a lot of unease lurking just beneath the surface, that "under the skin" area which Marcus had so rightly pointed out after kissing me into shock. So putting up a magic handrail was tempting but probably not a good idea. Given my luck—or rather, my emotion—it'd be just as likely to toss somebody off as to save them.

By the time we reached the landing at the top of the stairs, I was breathless. And *very* displeased to discover that this was only the first of many, many landings which zigzagged up the mountain above us.

"It's clever construction, really," Quinn said, completely normally. He stood there as if he'd only stopped so that *we* could rest, because of course he didn't need to. "The stairs are all but invisible from the lake side. They blend into the formation. This particular type of rock tends to form—"

"Please." I interrupted him with one hand up. "No geology until this is over and I'm back in my cozy cabin."

From nearby, and acting just as unbothered as Quinn, Scarlet tossed a careless glance my way. "Made a nice new little home for yourself, have you?"

Ouch.

Marcus came up behind me, setting his hand on my shoulder. Rather than reply to Scarlet, I tucked my head against his arm, just for a moment. He was right.

One way or another, we'd make it through.

And so it is said that the Gods Themselves hid 313
away Mount Hallow and their Temple there, to
obscure the terrible deeds which had taken
place during their reign. Unable to face the
shame of it, they set monsters and spells to
guard the temple forevermore. Any who sought
knowledge would find themselves cursed to
and never again to wake or rejoin the

Chapter Thirty: Hats

Marcus

There were twelve staircases.

It was comforting to me that the ancient symbolism was still present, even if none of the *presence* that I had expected was. But then, what did a symbol matter, if those it had once communicated meaning to were gone? When they paused to catch their breath, Scarlet, Quinn, and Saki spoke of mountain creatures and blister prevention, not of deities.

Saki might have been keeping track, though. When we reached the top of the twelfth staircase and found ourselves looking out over a deep, impassable chasm, she gave me a particularly curious look.

The others gave me little time to speak, however.

"Aha!" Quinn rubbed his hands together. "A way to discourage seekers of faint heart, I see. A test!"

"Not everything is an ancient booby trap," Scarlet told him. She stepped up to the stone edge, her arms lifting, her sleeves billowing in the cold breeze. "The bridge probably just wore away over time. I happen to know a spell that's perfect for this. Allow me."

After rummaging among the small pouches on her belt, she produced a vial containing several small rocks and a feather. This she set at the cliff's edge, and, standing over it, she began to focus her magic. The red-and-violet hue streamed out from the vial and her hands to venture across the chasm, faint and thin as it reached the far edge.

Saki caught my eye, but again said nothing.

Scarlet's hair lifted around her as she continued to focus, murmuring the words of a conjuring spell to herself. The outline of a narrow bridge began to form and take root on the ledge in front of her. But when she looked up, her spell complete and her attention shifted, that outline collapsed into nothing more than sparkles in the air. At her feet, the vial shattered.

"What? That shouldn't have happened," Scarlet protested, to no one in particular. "That's supposed to be a foolproof spell!"

"You'd certainly want it to be," Saki murmured.

I saw her point. Trusting oneself to a magical construction over such a drop might prove a risky business.

"I'll do it again." Scarlet was determined, pushing back her hair.

Fortunately, Quinn intervened. "Hold on. Save your energy for when we really need it. Consider: if that was a foolproof spell and it just failed, isn't it possible the chasm *is* booby-trapped, and it is also protected against magical solutions?"

"If that's the case, why not test it with shadow witchery?" Scarlet said the words like they left a bad taste in her mouth.

Quinn cocked an eyebrow at Saki. I watched her too. I did not know, in all honesty, if Saki's magic would work where Scarlet's had failed. I also did not know how she felt about the idea of a "test."

Saki, for her part, kept her gaze on the chasm. "If it was me, I'd probably float across the chasm rather than *make* something. It's not exactly the kind of method you'd want to experiment with."

"There we have the problem with shadow witchery in a nutshell," Scarlet commented.

Saki spared her only the briefest glance. "There are other ways to test it beforehand, though. Sometimes it pays to have a reason to learn to be careful."

She walked away from our little group—as far away as she could. She was dangerously close to the edge, so close that I wanted to walk after her, put my hand on her. But I stopped myself. I knew why she had made this choice. She wanted us well out of the way.

Without words or artistry, Saki cupped her hands in front of her chest. By the sixth staircase she had donned the gloves Quinn had provided, bright pink fluffy mittens. On the seventh staircase, she'd assented to wearing the matching, charmed hat. Its pom pom wobbled in the air as she looked down at her hands. It was only when she moved her mittens that the rest of us could see the small ball of black power within.

Saki let it hover in front of her, taking one deep breath. Then she sent it out across the chasm.

The little ball made it halfway before crackling, flaring, and winking out.

"Even *more* dramatic an answer," Quinn commented.

"Typical," Scarlet muttered.

"And that leaves me." Quinn talked over the Witch with a by-now practiced ease. "Let's see if we can discover the key to the puzzle, shall we?"

As Quinn began inspecting the rocks at our feet and even the scrubby trees nearby, Saki made her way back to me. Scarlet moved away, as though plagued by a bad smell.

For a moment we stood together in peace. Meanwhile, Quinn got down on mittens and knees and peered upside down over the ledge.

"You're just going to let him do that?" Saki asked me.

"I do not think I could stop him," I said.

She shifted more fully to face me, setting her mittens on her hips. "You're sure you don't know anything that would be useful here?"

And there, of course, was the root of the problem. To her, I admitted, "I'm not sure either way."

Saki frowned as she did whenever anything did not make sense, an expression I found quite charming. But even though it endeared her to me, I had not meant to cause it. I cleared my throat. "I had some—memories—or only vague ideas. But I really do not know if there is anything here which Quinn could uncover."

Quinn himself was now several paces away, his plaid hat engulfed in the lower branches of a tree as he tugged at its trunk.

Saki tilted her head to one side. "You mean all your memories of this place faded?"

"I mean," I said, "that I have never been up here."

259

"What?" This time, both Saki and Scarlet rounded on me, speaking in unison.

"I could have told you that," Quinn commented. He had given up on his tree to lie on his belly and inspect the earth again. "Easily. There's a special type of blandness in his voice that he uses when he doesn't have experience with something. He could patent it, it's so obvious."

"Yes, thank you, big words for someone with their nose pressed into the dirt," Saki replied. Her eyes never left me. "*You* have some explaining to do. Why have you been so worried if you didn't *know* there was something bad to expect?"

"Why didn't you tell me this when I was casting the bones?" Scarlet added.

I faltered under such a combination of questions. "I—I know what this place was for, and I knew I was not welcome. That was enough. Why should it matter, what I know, when you have other sources to rely upon?"

"Because you're *here*." Saki stepped forward, poking me in the chest with one mitten.

"I could have asked completely different questions if I had known," Scarlet said, in rare agreement. Like the others, she had opted for a matching hat and mittens. Hers were black: she had chosen them on the fourth staircase. The three of them made a strangely coordinated and comfortable-looking crew.

"And another thing," Saki added, reaching for Quinn's discarded backpack and holding it out to me. "Put on your hat and gloves. You look cold."

Scarlet broke the fragile peace. "He's a god, he doesn't get cold."

"Look at him, he looks cold," Saki repeated irritably.

I hadn't thought of it.

"I found something," Quinn announced from the ground behind Scarlet.

Scarlet and Quinn settled on their knees, brushing a thin layer of dirt and moss from the rock below. The spare set of winter wear beckoned from Quinn's open pack. Saki remained staring at me as I donned red mittens with fluffy trim, and a thick red hat with tassels. The hat would have been easier to put on if I hadn't put on the mittens first. I had very little experience with winter wear. I also suspected that Quinn had selected this set with Scarlet in mind, not myself. But nonetheless the charm woven into the yarn was effective. I could feel my fingers again, and I realized that Saki had been right. I had been cold.

"Ye are welcome should you let your fears die/And respect the power of the realm of Sky," Quinn read out from an inscription carved in the ground before the ledge. Dirt and roots and the grime of centuries filled the once-pristine grooves. "'Sky' is capitalized. Does that mean anything to anyone?"

"Yes," I said, with a sideways glance at Saki. She put her warm hand on my elbow as I went on, "I believe it is a warning as well as a direction. The chasm is only traversable by divine power."

"But the legends say this is where heroes come to become divine," Scarlet protested.

"That's sort of a cruel trick, isn't it?" Saki asked thoughtfully. "If people are coming up here trying to *find*—or earn—divinity? But to get to the top they have to have had it already?"

"As far as I know, the peak of the mountain was not

261

originally meant as a place of ascension," I told her. "That is merely part of the legend which has arisen in the last few hundred years. It was first a meeting place."

"For the divine only, far from prying mortal eyes," Quinn surmised. "What do you think, Marcus? Can you get all of us across, then?"

I glanced down at Saki again, thinking of her comment earlier. *You'd want it to be foolproof,* indeed. I could not let her fall. I had to be certain.

And despite my doubts, as I re-read the inscription over Quinn's shoulder, I was. I was certain. A curious confidence filled me, as solid as the stone which answered my call.

"That answers that," Quinn declared as the bridge formed in front of us.

Saki looked up at me, taking my hand in hers. "Come on. We can go across together."

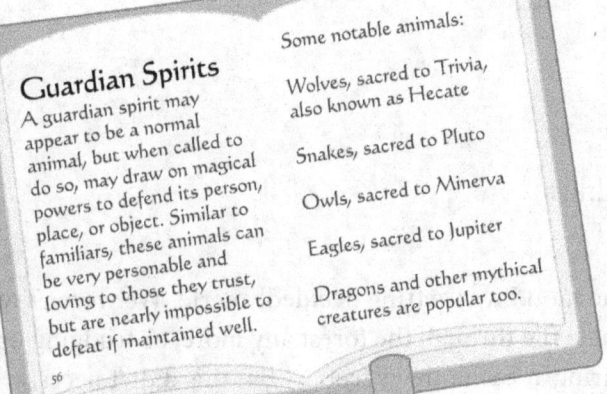

Guardian Spirits

A guardian spirit may appear to be a normal animal, but when called to do so, may draw on magical powers to defend its person, place, or object. Similar to familiars, these animals can be very personable and loving to those they trust, but are nearly impossible to defeat if maintained well.

56

Some notable animals:

Wolves, sacred to Trivia, also known as Hecate

Snakes, sacred to Pluto

Owls, sacred to Minerva

Eagles, sacred to Jupiter

Dragons and other mythical creatures are popular too.

Chapter Thirty-One: A Reveal

~~~
❧◦❧
~~~

Sakura

The mood was getting decidedly eerie. We weren't walking single file through the forest any more, or trudging up stairs staring at each other's feet . . . but this didn't necessarily feel better.

On the plus side, Marcus's bridge took us to a definite path on the other side. It was steep—almost as steep as the stairs, ugh—but it was paved in stone, and wide enough to walk two or three abreast. I remained beside Marcus, holding his hand—or should I say, he remained beside me. I wasn't setting any hiking speed records, that's for sure.

But I will admit, Quinn had been right about the hats and gloves.

And the snacks. We each had a magical thermos, and the honeyed green tea in mine was a huge help. Sipping tea made things less weird.

And that was the thing—they *were* getting weird. Even I, who had never even dreamed of summiting a mountain before, could tell.

Snow carpeted the ground to both sides of the path, but the trees were in bloom. No birds sang, but bees buzzed by. The cloudy sky seemed to be all around us, but it was a shifting pastel haze, impossible to pin down. This was strange enough, if fitting for an ancient divine site.

Worst was that, as the path curved along the chasm before turning upward, we noticed abandoned picks and anchors.

Quinn was the first to see one. He and Scarlet were a few paces ahead, and he pointed out a bit of old iron lodged into the rock face below the path ahead. "Someone was industrious."

"And probably unfortunate," Scarlet added.

My stomach turned. I know I'm not always a ray of sunshine myself, but it was . . . *something,* to really see the legacy of this site I'd inherited.

The next one, Quinn just pointed to. It was a rotted pack leaning against a tree several yards from the trail. He glanced back at Marcus as he did so, and I'll admit, I tightened my grip on Marcus's hand.

"I do not believe the forest to be enchanted at present. Not in a, hmm, *dangerous* way," Marcus told us quietly. "Nevertheless it is better to be safe."

"What, you think someone was drawn off the path by some kind of illusion or something?" Scarlet frowned, not at Quinn for suggesting it, but at the trees. Her expression said pretty clearly, I *wouldn't bother being distracted by those.*

I thought it was a very reasonable suggestion, myself.

Myths and legends were full of magically and potentially-harmfully tempting fruits, forbidden forests, and disorienting landscapes. The fact that we then noticed some discarded old wooden hiking poles, and later one half of a ripped snow shoe, only went to prove the point.

But . . . how had anyone made it to this side of the chasm?

I glanced up at Marcus, and he shrugged. "The mystique of the mountain has always been strong."

"Strong enough to inspire wildly determined—or reckless—behavior," Quinn added, glancing back at us.

Scarlet stopped abruptly. "Did anyone see that?"

"See what?" Quinn was on the case, staring into the forest.

"A floating light," Scarlet said, her voice a little shaky for the first time. "It was moving between the trees. It was *moving*."

"We've already seen orbs down at the lake," I said, not really trying to keep the boredom from my voice. Still, it was nice to stop and get a breather.

"We did watch one for quite a while on the first night, and it never came close," Quinn said. "Let's keep an eye out here, though. Just in case."

We set off again, everybody peering into the woods like comically bad spies in a play.

"There's another," Marcus murmured.

"Two," Scarlet announced. "Two on this side. I saw them together."

"Isn't this a pretty normal thing you'd run into at ancient sites?" I asked. Needling her a bit, true, but also, I just didn't understand her worry. Orbs were very common manifestations of energy. Sometimes they were ghostly, sometimes they were traces of spells, but even so, what could they really do? It wasn't like we were facing another monster.

"Most sites don't have the power this one does," Scarlet snapped back. "Not to mention the power *you're* carrying around. If anything were to happen—"

I finally caught sight of an orb floating off to one side. As I watched, it floated into a flowering branch. The flower just *popped* out of existence like it had been pruned.

"Yikes," I said involuntarily.

Marcus halted, his hand squeezing mine. "What did you see?" I didn't have time to answer him.

"Orbs ahead," Quinn called.

"Something like *this*," Scarlet continued, as though she'd called it. "I prepared containment spells, but not this many!"

"Still, if you *could* capture one, and we could do some tests . . ." Quinn was watching as more and more orbs danced across our path.

Scarlet produced a small brown sachet. She whispered a few words into it and threw it at an orb to her right. The orb flared and swallowed the sachet, which fell to the ground several paces away . . . out of a different orb.

"Fascinating," said Quinn. "What if you try—"

"Quinn," Marcus interrupted. "Come here. Everyone, stay close."

I agreed more with Marcus's idea than Quinn's. The orbs were thick now, thicker than the trees, and they were all around—and getting closer. As Quinn walked back, joining us, the silver bubble of Marcus's shield raced around us. But *what*, I couldn't help but wonder, would we do? We couldn't just sit in a bubble surrounded by glowy omnivorous orbs all day.

Scarlet had her divining bones out, and her eyes glowed violet. "They're protective. The energy—it's guarding the mountain."

"Spirits?" Quinn asked. He hadn't been nearly this calm the first time!

"I don't think so . . ." Scarlet frowned. "I can't tell. This answer doesn't make any sense."

I looked up at Marcus to find he was already looking at me. "If they're guarding the site, and the site belongs to *us*, then . . ."

His frown deepened. "I do not wish to test it."

"But we have to do something," I pointed out.

"Waiting *is* something," he replied.

"For how long though?" I hooked one finger under the chain supporting the pendant he'd given me and held it up, reminding him of its presence. "I'll be alright. Right?"

He wavered. "I am not certain—"

"So I'll send out just a tiny bit of magic first. That's me, part of me, so it should count. We'll see if it gets swallowed. Okay?"

Marcus hesitated. Behind us, I was dimly aware of Scarlet whispering to Quinn, *"Are they always like this?"* and him replying *"Yes, but at least this time they're using words."* I ignored them. Marcus finally nodded.

I moved to the edge of the bubble. Orbs were hovering just beyond it, now in a softly bouncing wall. I put one mitten against Marcus's shield, willing my own magic to move past it. It did—a little blip of black bobbed its way out onto the path.

I think the four of us were all holding our breath as we watched it approach the nearest orb. But no one could have guessed what was coming.

Lulu hopped out of the orb. Wearing a flower atop her head.

She bopped my magic ball with her nose, just like she had the day before, when she was stuck in a wall. Then she looked our way and bleated.

Quinn just about fainted.

He was on his knees, muttering to himself about goats—whether it was good or bad things, I couldn't tell. I left him with Marcus and Scarlet. I didn't think twice. I ran right through Marcus's bubble.

"Lulu!" I scooped her up, caught between shock, disapproval, gratitude, and awe. "Lulu, what are you doing here? Stop it!"

Lulu bleated again. The orbs shivered, and began to recede.

Marcus had dropped his bubble when I turned around. Scarlet was helping Quinn to his feet, but Marcus was already on me, his hands around my waist, at my back.

"Don't ever do that again." He bent to bring his face to mine.

"But Lulu," I offered by way of explanation. I held the little goat up to him. He spared her a long-suffering glance. "She's wearing the flower I saw disappear," I added gleefully.

Turned out, not only did I have a pet—I had a very strangely magical one.

"*Neither* of you are to do that again," Marcus declared.

Lulu nuzzled his shirt.

"We're alright," I assured him, since his hands were roaming like he was expecting to find some secret injury on my shoulder or hip. "But very sorry. Right, Lulu?"

She snorted.

"She'd better be sorry," Quinn remarked. He was still rubbing his chest as he and Scarlet joined us. "She nearly gave me a heart attack. Why didn't anyone know that the guardian spirit of the mountain was this adorable little goat?

You could have saved me a lot of trouble when I was trying
to protect her from monsters!"

I glanced up at Marcus, who shrugged, baffled.

Scarlet crossed her arms as she watched us all. "This makes
it official. Weirdest. Case. Ever."

Be ye ware of the
creature of the pool,

It and its fellows
sup upon hearts
untrue,

And should ye
make it up the
mount,

Ye'll find trouble
ye'd rather be
without!

Chapter Thirty-Two: Stone

Marcus

To me, this conversation was not finished.

Power still hummed through me. I hadn't taken down the shield; Saki had gone *through* it. If I hadn't already been convinced she was my match, that would have done it.

Using that leftover power, I lifted Lulu from her arms and deposited the goatling safely with Quinn. Then I let the stone beneath us come up, forming a wall that circled Sakura and me, giving us a moment of privacy. Quinn would understand.

Saki's hands were already on my chest. I didn't trust myself to stand, so I knelt, pulling her with me. She settled on my knee as I kissed her. In that moment of quiet, I was no longer frustrated but relieved, my lips caressing hers, my arms around her reassuring me that she was indeed whole.

"Marcus, you big softie," she whispered against my cheek.

I could feel her smile. "I told you, I'm fine. Not that I mind being at the bottom of a well with you—I don't. But you didn't have to do this."

"I'm not fine," I whispered back, holding her closer.

"I see that. I'm sorry." Saki wriggled in my arms, kissing my cheek before leaning back a little to give me a gentle look. "We're almost there, and I doubt we're in for any more Lulu-themed surprises. We'll be more careful. Okay?"

I knew she was right, but I wasn't ready to let her go.

She chuckled softly. "Well, I'm glad to know you took it to heart when I said to stop being so polite. By the way, I didn't know you were so good with stone. Not that you aren't all-powerful and all that, I'm sure . . ."

She was teasing me. At last, I was able to laugh quietly at myself. "I am *not* all-powerful, as you well know. None of us ever were. That was the point . . . I didn't know either," I admitted. "It is easier, up here. There is more power in the air, and indeed, in the stone."

"That makes sense, but even so." Saki was watching me steadily, her pink cap tilted over her blue eyes. "I think you *are* a lot stronger than you let yourself be.

"And on that note," she added, "we do have a lot still to do, and I don't plan on being on this mountain in the dark."

I smiled, acquiescing, but spared one moment to kiss her fluffy hat before getting up. What worried me most was, to her, a reason for hope. It was one of the mysteries intrinsic to who she was. As she herself had said: a miracle.

The stone fell away from us easily. Saki let her hand drift down my chest before stepping away to retrieve her goatling from Quinn. The touch filled me with warmth.

"This isn't a good idea, is it." Scarlet captured my attention, not asking a question so much as announcing herself. "This is a terrible idea, isn't it?"

I regarded her solemnly. "The Department's mission is to see that ancient magicks are dealt with responsibly."

"*Artifacts,*" Scarlet insisted. "Vases, amulets, the odd statue. Sure, occasionally a shrine dug into the mountain or an old forgotten ruin. But never the entire top of a mountain. Of *Mount Hallow.*"

"I share your reservations. I have had my own reservations from the beginning," I said. "However, we have met each trial so far and succeeded by virtue of who is in our party."

"A god and a goat, mostly," Quinn remarked cheerfully, walking over to join the conversation. Saki followed, with Lulu in her arms. "I do like to think we all played our part," he went on, "but I'd be lying if I said what's ahead doesn't concern me."

"There's no way to know what's ahead," Scarlet said, clearly exasperated. "Divination isn't working—none of the answers I get make any sense!"

"Sure they weren't just trying to warn you about a tiny goat?" Saki asked.

"*None* of the questions I ask get clear answers," Scarlet replied with venom.

I interrupted. "Quinn. What is the reason for your concern?"

"I think of it this way." Quinn lifted one hand as though to count reasons off on his fingers, and effort stymied by the fact that he was wearing mittens. "We made it past the lake and up the stairs—arguably, none of that was a test; it was simply difficult. We made it over the bridge—that *was* a test. We made it past the orbs, or guardian spirit." He nodded politely at Lulu, who still wore her flower crown. "So that's two tests. But isn't *three* the magic number?"

He looked, not at me nor at Scarlet, but at Saki. "What?" she asked. "The place didn't come with an owner's manual, if that's what you're looking for."

Scarlet loudly scoffed.

Saki considered her for a moment, and then set Lulu down. Both Scarlet and Quinn stiffened, as though afraid. I did not think they had reason to be. I had faith.

"*I* think," Saki began, carefully, "that everybody is here for a reason—including Lulu. And whatever trials are left, we'll only get past them if we're on the same page. But I never introduced myself properly, did I?" She walked up to Scarlet and held out her hand. "Hello. My name's Sakura, but when we're friends, I'd like it if you called me Saki. I'm a shadow witch who's trying hard not to use magic because I lost my trust in myself. I know I hurt your friend, and I'm very sorry. I know I ran away and that wasn't the right choice. But I'm here right now and I can only deal with one thing at a time. I'm here because I made a mistake and I'm learning how to make things better."

Scarlet's face changed as Saki spoke. The derision and disbelief at Saki's unorthodox introduction faded at the mention of a friend. Anger flashed, but that faded also, into a suspicious thoughtfulness.

"You're *here* because no one else could have handled a site like this, much less seen it for what it is. This kind of magic chooses its people, that's what we say in the Department." Scarlet's voice was sour, and as she reached to shake Saki's hand, the gesture was cold.

Even so, Saki smiled. "I'm not sure if it's me or the site

that's cursed, or both or neither, at this point. But it isn't just mine. It's Marcus's too. And Marcus is very good at shielding people."

The meaningful look she gave me went straight through my heart. Was this, then, the true reason that she had wanted to give me partial ownership in the site?

All three of us stared at her. Scarlet spoke. "You know that your magic has essentially overridden his twice now, right?"

"Oh, that wasn't his full strength." Saki didn't miss a beat, didn't falter. "Was it, Marcus?"

"I . . ."

"Marcus has been hiding," she went on. "In fact, we all have. But it ends now. I've been hiding my magic because I was ashamed that I failed the people I loved most. Marcus doesn't want to draw attention from the deities who used to meet here. Quinn doesn't want to leave his friend to something he doesn't understand. And you, Scarlet, don't want to admit you'd rather it was *you* Trent fell in love with. Right?"

She beamed back at the varying degrees of shock on our faces.

"How—" Quinn recovered first. "How did you know?"

"I didn't *know,* but I could guess. Because I know myself and how much I love my friends, and how I'd feel in your shoes," Saki told him. "It's really not very hard. It's not detective work. Everybody's shadow has to do with love in the end."

Scarlet was far less impressed. "How *dare* you? Those aren't your secrets to guess. It's invasive and reckless—"

"Yes," Saki said simply. "It is. But I said I was a shadow witch, not a sage or a saint. I'll bear the consequences if I'm wrong. And under normal circumstances I'd let you keep your secrets, whether you're aware of them or not, but this isn't normal. We have to be able to leave these things behind. Right?"

She was looking directly at me. She was asking me as a partner, seeking my opinion. The others had clearly given theirs.

But there was something else in her eyes, a spark. She was challenging me, too.

My sweet witch.

As I held out my hand to her, I could see it glowing. A clear bright light. She had been right. Of course.

"My Sakura," I said to her, my voice echoing, a divine power I hadn't used in centuries. "You have always known my answer. It is inevitable."

Inevitable. Inevitable that I should come here. And that she should be the one to show me how.

The light from our clasped hands spread, swept over the ground. Quinn jumped to hold Saki's shoulder, and Lulu leapt to lean against her leg. At the last moment, Scarlet reached out too, her hand on Saki's arm.

Then the light grew all-consuming. I kept my eyes on her. I couldn't let myself think of anything else.

When the light faded, we had reached the mountain's peak.

The Temple of the Ascension

Legend has it that if a hero reaches the Temple, they will be rewarded with the Nectar of the Gods, and thus gain immortality. But none have ever seen this place and lived to share the tale . . .

Chapter Thirty-Three: Hallowed

❧⁓❧

Sakura

I'll be honest with you. Scarlet and everyone had been going on about the top of the mountain, and ancient temples, but I hadn't expected to actually *find* one. I mean, I had figured that it was either long gone, or all just a metaphor. If we had found a picnic table and a tea house, or even an empty crater and a bunch of rocks, that would have made a lot more sense to me.

But I was starting to understand that Scarlet was really not one for a metaphor. Which is sort of ironic for a Witch so concerned with divination, when you think about it. Frankly, I was starting to like her for it.

Her hand left my arm the moment the ground beneath us felt solid again. And she was the first to understand. Marcus's eyes were still locked on mine, and I don't think even he knew exactly what this place was.

"It's the temple," Scarlet breathed, like she'd been allowed into the most holy of holy places. And honestly—maybe from her point of view, she had. "This is the Temple of the Ascension!"

"I doubt it was called that back then," Quinn said reasonably. He let go of my shoulder—his grip had really been almost painful—and dusted himself off as he looked around, like this was just another day on the job. "How about . . . let's see . . . 'The Meeting Place of Day and Night?'"

Marcus was still staring at me. If he stared for one moment longer, I'd forget about all this temple and curse stuff, and just kiss him. But right in time, he shook himself. "It wouldn't be called that," he said absently to Quinn.

"Tell that to the ancient stone carver," Quinn retorted. "Or, given that this site was for the divine only, some ancient god?"

I turned to look, at last. It was all around us, in fact. Marcus had brought us precisely to the middle of a tiled circle on the ground. Maybe it had been colorful once, but now it was cracked and faded. Tiles in indiscernible patterns stretched out across the entire floor of the temple, which turned out to be a large circle, with huge, evenly-spaced pillars surrounding us. The pillars more or less stood in their right places, but whatever bits of wall or ceiling they had once supported were long gone. In fact, all that remained was parts of a decorative rim that had once connected them all, running along the tops of them. Beyond that, the sky was opalescent.

Quinn was pointing to a section of that decoration, where the carved letters were actually legible. Scarlet had left us and was pacing the floor, getting right up in each pillar's business, one by one. After a moment of panic, I located Lulu still standing between my feet.

"I don't understand," Marcus said softly. He'd joined Quinn, and was looking where his friend pointed.

I wasn't sure I understood either. Just to be sure of where we were, I walked to the edge of the temple and peered out. I'd half expected the view to be pearly nothingness, like the sky above us, but in fact it was aggressively clear. Mountain and forest and city and sea rolled away from under my feet in shocking and *extremely* tiny detail.

Just as I started to feel sick looking at it, Lulu bleated. Gratefully, I picked her up and carried her back to the others.

"This feels even higher than the mountain top looked," I told them.

"Because we're in the realm of the gods now," Scarlet replied. Her excitement bordered on girlish ecstasy.

As nice as it was to see another side of her, I had to disagree. "Most gods deal with things down on the ground. Or beneath it."

"Beneath the ground was *Pluto's* domain," Scarlet said promptly.

"It could be both," Quinn offered. "An in-between. A liminal space. Don't you magic-users like that kind of thing? In any case, I'm more interested in how we got here. Marcus, could you have done that at any point? Or do you think Saki's, ah, *demonstration* was perhaps the third trial? Letting fear die?"

The look Marcus gave me was nothing short of adoration, and despite everything else going on, I blushed fiercely. "You can sort out all the narrative details later," I told Quinn. "Right now, shouldn't we be worried about some kind of curse or something?"

As one, we looked at Scarlet. Even Lulu seemed to be paying

attention. At this point, that would be the *least* unlikely thing to happen.

"It's no use," Scarlet said. She held her bones out and let them fall into her free hand. Every single one landed with its blank side up. Even Quinn, our resident logician, whistled in surprise. But for once, Scarlet seemed unbothered. "Every sign I was getting down at the lake pointed to an imbalance up here. But now that we're here, I don't feel it. It could be that, by using divine power to get us here, Marcus dispelled it somehow . . ."

"That seems too easy," I said, eyeing him for his response. Given that we'd all been afraid to get here magically because it would make a disturbance, I doubted that all our troubles were over so quickly. By the stiffness in his shoulders and the tightness of his mouth, it was clear to me that Marcus agreed.

"Agreed," Quinn echoed. "I'd say it's best to be on high alert. And it may behoove us to investigate the ruin a little more."

We all nodded, and started to spread out. For just a moment, before we were distracted, I caught Quinn's eye. He sent me one last self-deprecating smile, and a wink.

I do want to understand, his expression seemed to say.

You want to understand the unknowable?

No, I thought, dreamily. *Maybe some things can't be understood. But that's Quinn for you. Quinn would want to know anyway . . .*

And then the shiver made its way throughout my whole body.

Who had I just been talking to?

The temple floor suddenly felt uneven. Like it was waving, or tilting, or something was coming up all around us. I tried to react but I couldn't move or speak. So I thought furiously. My wards on myself were still very poor, it's true. Any magical being could have reached out to talk to me without words. Any magical being with lots of power, that is, and not very much concern for modern etiquette, and—

And maybe a reason to worry about why we're here.

"Quinn! Scarlet!" I cried. It felt like breaking up through water—or ice.

In the distance, Lulu bleated.

I turned in slow motion. Quinn had crumpled to the floor. Fainted? It was impossible to tell. And beside him—was Lulu *carrying* Scarlet to him? No, surely that wasn't right. I blinked and tried again. Now Quinn and Scarlet were both on the floor. Neither was moving. I couldn't see their eyes.

But my goat, my baby goat who still had a flower stuck on her head, was standing in front of them both. And she looked directly at me as orbs filled the air around them. *Good,* I thought. *Get them out of here.* Out of here and away from what, I still didn't know.

Lulu bleated once more. She wasn't leaving, and neither were our friends. But the orbs were closing down over them. In fact—the orbs were making a bubble around them.

Had she learned that, I wondered, from Marcus?

As if in answer to my question, one tiny little orb floated out from the rest, and bopped its way over the uncertain floor until it came to rest, lightly, on my nose.

There was the feeling of a bubble bursting, and then I was free. I could move again, and breathe and speak. I looked at Lulu once more, but I knew she was perfectly safe, she and Quinn and Scarlet, cocooned in a bunch of orbs.

Weirdest case, indeed, I thought, for Scarlet's sake.

Then I turned. Marcus, the person I was most worried

about. He was just a few steps away. But he wasn't moving or speaking either. In fact, he was glowing.

It was the sort of moment where you're confronted with the actuality of your choices. Sure, when you're sitting in your cabin eating a sandwich by the fire, it's all very well and good to say you're in love with a god of the dead. No big deal that sometimes he moves a little slowly, or answers a question with some unearthly perspective. It's cute when he makes end tables out of nothing and talks about traversing dimensions like that's a regular work trip, because for him, it is. At times like that, choices are easy. Even when you're trying not to make them.

But *then* you find yourself in a temple literally gods-know-where and that adorable man who holds his teacups with both hands and likes to make stained glass window art is now hovering several inches from the ground with a stony expression and light pouring from his eyes, and the wind is rising and you can tell you're right at the edge, where something really bad could happen. Something that really does trip the line between life and death.

You would think that, in those moments, choices are harder. But I can tell you that they're not. Actually, they don't even exist.

Without a single thought, I hurled myself at Marcus.

```
~~~~~~~~~~~~~~~~~~~~~~~~~~~~~~~~~~~
NOTES FOR PROF MYRTLE'S CLASS
DIVINE SYMBOLS:

JUPITER:    ♃
JUNO:                    MARS:      ♂
CERES:                   MERCURY:   ☿
NEPTUNE:   ♆             VULCAN:    🔥
VENUS:     ♀             APOLLO:    ☉
MINERVA:                 DIANA:     ☽
                         VESTA:
```

Chapter Thirty-Four: Ghosts

Marcus

You have come to the threshold, the voice said. *At last.*

I didn't understand. Had Janus always known that I would break my promise?

You must go through.

I didn't understand that either. There was no one on the other side.

Everyone else was gone. But Janus's power brought the place alive. The pillars, one for each of them—one for each god. Once more, they lit up, their symbols blazed. The sky overhead wheeled, night and day colliding. The mosaics on the floor, the decorations in the stone, they were all as they had been on the first day they were made.

But there was no one else here.

No gods. I was sure of it. Even Janus's power, the energy of doorways and gates, was little more than a protective remnant. The voice which spoke to me was only an echo through time.

You must accept the consequence.

That, I understood.

But I was terribly afraid. It was, perhaps, even more frightening because no one else was there.

Then the energy of the temple shifted, and when it came back into focus, Sakura was there. She hit my chest as though she'd come running from a distance, and wrapped her arms around me. "Marcus," she cried. "Marcus, what is it? Did we trigger something?"

You made this choice alone.

"Marcus?"

"I—I don't know what to do," I admitted. "I don't know what will happen."

Energy rose up from the floor, a wisp of light. It pulsed, ghostly, and then shimmered a deep, violet red. In the next moment it split into twelve, and at each pillar now, an outline of an ancient deity sat.

"*Pluto,*" said one, "*we warned you what would happen if you came back here.*"

"*We can not have you interfering any more,*" said another, striking its staff upon the ground.

"*You should know better than to become involved in our affairs,*" said one standing behind us. "*Your domain isn't here. It's below, and you should stay there.*"

"Oh, my." Saki was still holding on to me. "This is what you were afraid of?"

That she could see them was troubling, but when one faced her and answered her, a chill ran down my spine. "*Pluto made a promise never to step out of his place again,*" the divine image

287

said.

"Tell her what will happen now you have broken your promise," another added.

"Yes, you have brought unease and ill fortune onto this land," said the first. *"You know what your punishment will be. Tell her."*

I couldn't see Saki—couldn't bear to look at her. Though with one arm I tried to shield her, I kept my head up. "I—"

"Still haven't got a way with words, have you?"

"Coward!"

"Stop that!" Saki shouted at the image who had spoken, before addressing all of them. "If you want him to speak, then let him speak. The rest of you be quiet. We don't need any commentary from the peanut gallery!"

The images shivered, their weaponry glimmering. I held her too tight.

"After what happened with Proserpine, I promised—I promised the Twelve that I would not become involved in any further disputes," I managed at last. "I promised, as they say, that I would not step out of my place. And if I did— the penalty—if I stepped out of my place, I should lose it altogether."

"You will be stripped of your powers and your role," said the first image.

I could feel Saki startle. "Can they *do* that?"

The question, I must confess, had never occurred to me. Who would doubt that they could? Surrounded by them, in all their glory—even if it was only echoes of bygone days. Of course they could. That was why they had created their Council. To wield great power—all their powers, combined.

"I wonder," said one, *"will she still waste time on you?"*

I wondered as much myself.

"You're horrendous," Saki told them. "Don't be ridiculous. I'm *glad* you're all just shadows. You don't deserve to be holding court any more if this is how you run it!"

"Saki," I pleaded. "Don't antagonize them. They're right to be angry. I broke my promise—"

"I don't see any of *them* worried about stepping out of their 'place,'" she replied, now straining against my hold, ready to step away.

"Don't," I begged her.

"We could take your life," said the first one. *"We could consign you finally to your own realm, death."*

"Just you try!" Saki retorted, breaking herself free so that she stood before me. Her magic began crackling around her, a blackness not even this divine spectacle could cover over or deny. I wished briefly that she could be free of it—that in letting go of me, she would lose grip on this reality and be returned to the harmless ruin. But the others had taken note of her now, the images were watching her. They were keeping her here, too. And now it was she who warned them. "Anything you do to him I'll just undo. You try sending him to the underworld and I'll bring him back!"

"Shadow witchery!"

"Such meddling is not to be borne!"

"You think you can face down us, *mortal?"*

"I may be mortal, but I'm a whole lot more solid than any of *you*," Saki returned grimly. "Go on. Either come at me or get out of here and *off my property*!"

It happened too fast for me. An awful light hurled through her. The sharp sound of something breaking rang through the circle around us.

But—Saki still stood.

289

Her pendant.

I understood. The protection charm I had made for her had broken. It had not been strong enough. And now, she was unguarded.

I moved in front of her, and the next lightning bolt went through me.

The shock was intense, but once it passed, it was nothing. It was as she had said: they were shadows.

They were *shadows,* memories. They were of my realm. Which meant they could only do to me what *I* believed they could do. My Saki would be safe—I could keep her safe. And at last I could say to them everything I had long wished to speak.

"I am here," I told them, allowing the divine energy to flow through me and echo through my voice. At last. *"My place is where I choose. I will make a place for me, and you can not take it. And when you find yourselves in my domain, as you do now, your actions will come back to you and you will feel the weight of them, the shame. But I will exact no promises from you, carry out no punishments. I am not like you, and I am glad."*

At last.

290

Hey Saki—
I know you might not want to hear from me right now, and that's okay. But I feel really bad about how things happened. I've been thinking about it a lot. You left so fast. There's a lot of things I don't understand but I don't think it's your fault. And for what it's worth, I'm really sorry.

Trent

Chapter Thirty-Five: Lightning

❧

Sakura

Okay, all that I said about feeling the *actuality* of your choices?
Yeah.

Well, facing down a bunch of gods and threatening to do the impossible—namely, bring back the dead, undo what's been done, and so on—definitely brings that home in a new light.

But I didn't regret a bit of it. And, gods above—not those ones obviously—*my goodness,* when Marcus stood up for himself, he was just about the most marvelous, most wonderful thing in any universe. The hottest, too.

I *knew* he had it in him.

I stood at his back, ready to beat any of these bullies into submission in case they hadn't gotten the memo already. But Marcus drawing on his divine power set two things in motion, apparently. The first was that the whole setup around us, the light-deities and the magically-restored temple, faded away like a bad dream. We found ourselves back in the ruin, on solid ground.

The second, though, was that we weren't alone.

Another god was standing off to the side. I knew immediately who and what they were, not only because of the faint glow about them, but because they looked exactly like their magic-shadow-image had. Blond curly beard, hard eyes, weird old armor. This one had been the leader of the lot.

I squared up with him, magic sparking in my hands.

"Pluto," he said, much more normally. Though still a bit too loudly. When he looked at me, his sky-blue eyes literally twinkled. "Sakura. Please, be at ease. I will offer you no fight."

"Really? Because that's not what your shadow buddy was saying," I replied.

Jupiter threw his head back and laughed. "You have seen a much younger version of me. I'll be the first to admit I was not a nice person when I was young. But we are different now, all of us, aren't we? Stand down, good Sakura, please, stand down."

I glanced at Marcus beside me. Seeing as he'd just made a very eloquent speech about not holding things against people, I figured I'd better follow his example and play along. I let the magic fade and my hands rest by my side.

"I'm grateful," Jupiter said, observing this with further twinkles. "Truly, you have more fight in you than Pluto ever did! He could learn from you. And indeed, I believe he has."

Marcus shifted uneasily as Jupiter, ancient god of the sky and—given how the magic scene had just played out moments ago—most likely the one who had gone about exacting unfair promises, turned to him. "Why are you here now? I thought everyone had left."

"I'm here because of you," Jupiter told him. "You set off Janus's spell on the threshold, did you not?"

I still wasn't sure I trusted Jupiter, but this was starting to make a lot of sense. I was vaguely familiar with Janus—sort of an old gatekeeper god, guardian of doors and the start of a new year, things like that. *Of course* a god like that would be in charge of noticing if someone just walked willy-nilly into a sacred site (or teleported into it, as the case may be). And . . . it made sense that a god like that might also ask a few questions. Like *why are you here.*

Reminded of Quinn and Scarlet, I glanced quickly around the temple. They, and Lulu too, were still in a little group to one side—but now it was clear they were sleeping peacefully.

"When we all went our own ways, we decided that it would be best to let everything that happened here remain here. You understand," Jupiter told me. I still thought he was being too chummy, but I did get it. He'd already said he didn't especially like the person he'd been, all those centuries ago. He went on, "That's what's so *interesting* about you, Sakura. Janus's spell was meant especially to ward off people seeking too much knowledge. How did a wide-eyed witch like yourself make it through?"

Marcus shifted again, this time like he might put his hand in front of me. I grabbed it and held it in mine instead. "I know there's a lot here I won't understand, and I don't care," I replied. "But even so, what you did to Marcus was wrong."

"Ah. Very good. And that brings us back to the reason we're here now." Jupiter paced a little closer to Marcus, oblivious to the way we both stared at him. "I've been waiting forever for this reunion, Pluto. I'd hoped you would step up ages ago."

"What are you saying?" Marcus sounded understandably baffled. "You told me not to. You told me it wasn't my place."

"And I also said that we should choose destinies by drawing straws, and that marriage vows applied to anyone but me," Jupiter declared, clapping a very uncomfortable Marcus on the back. "You should be the first among us to know we're just as fallible as anyone else. Eh? You, my friend, have seen it all."

"I saw you leave and think nothing of me," Marcus said quietly.

"Yes." Jupiter watched him for a moment, then went on a little more normally, with a little less bluster. "It's like this, Pluto. This promise business, what was the whole point of it? That you might lose your place. Whether or not we could have taken it from you, as your witch pointed out, is another matter. The thing of it is that *you* stepped away from your place. What have you been doing all this time? Hiding. Sure, you've still been doing good work, carrying on behind the scenes, but—"

"Stop right there," I interrupted. "Are you trying to say that this is all Marcus's fault?"

Jupiter's eyes flashed as he looked at me from under heavy brows. Like he'd forgotten I was there until I annoyed him. Well, he could stuff it, as far as I was concerned. Particularly if he was *still* trying to blame Marcus for everything.

"No," Marcus said softly. "Saki, I don't think that's what he means. I think he's right."

"Still, you aren't wrong," Jupiter resumed, acknowledging me. "I made a bad call, and I've admitted it. Came down too hard. But I didn't think it'd come out this way, Pluto. You must know that. I thought you'd *fight*."

"It is not my nature," Marcus told him. There was a long-suffering note in his voice that made me think this was not the first time they'd covered that ground. "I was never like you in that respect."

"I couldn't fathom it then. I'll tell you frankly, it still doesn't make a whole lot of sense to me. But it looks like you might have it covered, anyway," Jupiter remarked, with a pointed look at me. I resisted the urge to stick my tongue out at him. Barely. He continued. "You haven't been owning your true power, Pluto, haven't been holding any stake in your life. Surely you see that."

"I do, now. But it is no longer true." Marcus gave me his own pointed look, and this one was much better. His gaze was warm, his hand tightened on mine. "Saki, I realized it when your pendant broke. I hope you can forgive me. I was so slow to see it, and I put you in danger. You asked me for what you wanted, but I was too shy to do the same. The pendant I made you was weak, half-intentioned. My power faltered because I could not admit that I want you, that you are all my stakes."

Who could be mad when he put it like that? Not that I was going to be mad in the first place, because I knew full well he hadn't been sure how things would go. I beamed at him. He was *so* forgiven. I vowed to myself I'd make him feel it later.

"That's the spirit," Jupiter said. "Are you ready to rejoin the world again, then?"

"Yes," Marcus said, straightening. He was just, I noticed with a tiny bit of glee, just a little taller than Jupiter. "And this place, now called Mount Hallow and Hideaway Lake, belongs in part to me. I trust you have no quarrel with that?"

Jupiter grinned. "That's the reason we all felt it was fine to leave it in the first place. We knew you'd look after it, and Helenia. This is how it was meant to be."

This still struck me as rude, if not downright careless, but then again, many deities are not known for their tender compassion. When you get right down to it, a lot of mythology is terrible. I decided not to try to hold Jupiter to task for all his misdoings. We'd be there all night if so, and I had some things I'd *much* rather do with Marcus. Alone. But since we were still standing there, I made it a point to ask, "And me? It's half mine as well, you know."

"I do know, good Sakura." Jupiter chortled. "Let's have it, then. What about you?"

He was challenging me, straight out. And being challenged by a very-much-present god was a whole lot different than a bunch of nasty god-like shadows. I suppose I could have walked away, could have ceded the whole place to Marcus; he certainly deserved it. But I've never been one to give in to bullies. I held my ground and stared him down. "Mount Hallow's half mine, and Marcus is my partner, and I don't want any trouble from you about any of that either."

"I know what you must think of me, little witch. Don't think I don't agree with you," Jupiter declared with too much good humor. "You weren't in our plans, but I can see you're not going to leave. Don't want you to, myself. You've put on a good show, and I respect that. Let me give you a gift—a bit of good will. Pluto made you an amulet, I hear? And the thing's gone and broke? Trust it to me, I'll put it right."

"You most certainly will not," I retorted. "I like it the way Marcus made it."

"I meant no disrespect," Jupiter said, still amused. "Consider it a gift from me to both of you. Not an improvement, just a—an olive branch, if you will."

I caught Marcus's eye, and he shrugged, as if to say, *if you want to, it's fine by me.*

I narrowed my eyes at him, thinking, *Are you sure? He's probably being annoying on purpose.*

Marcus smiled, that sweet little lopsided look that always said, *sweetling, I know, but I don't care. I've got you.*

"Fine," I said aloud. I pulled the chain over my head, fumbling a little in my mittens. They weren't really necessary any more—the temple wasn't nearly as cold as the mountain itself had been, just another perk of divine power, I suppose. But I was too petty to take them off and admit it. The tear drop had partially shattered, leaving a deep hole in its center.

Jupiter took it from my hand cheerfully. "Never knew a mortal so unwilling to accept a gift. Not saying you aren't wrong, mind. Don't worry, though, you'll like this one."

For the first time, Jupiter dropped all the joviality and actually *concentrated*. For just a moment—a very brief moment—it was scary. The sky overhead went dark. The pillars around us flared. Whatever he was doing, it seemed like he was drawing on more than just his own power to make it work. I could almost feel the leftover energy from all the gods who had come through here, almost feel their gazes looking down at us. Just a superficial feeling, surely. Enough to remind me that Jupiter was once considered the king of the gods, though.

But the moment passed, and he was back to grinning insouciantly through his beard. He held the necklace out to me by its chain, letting the pendant dangle. Marcus's black tear drop had transformed—it was still the same shape, but now it was clear, and hollow. And filled with a golden fluid that sloshed and sparkled as the necklace swung. There was really only one reason I could think of that Jupiter would be offering me something to drink . . .

"A choice," he said, as I took it. To Marcus, he added, "Most of us learned a long time ago that it helps to have someone keeping an eye on you. Someone to lighten the load. So good luck with that, and have fun making this place all it can be," he barreled on, before either of us could blink. We were both a bit wide-eyed by then.

"Wait," I said as he began to turn away. I tucked the pendant away, not yet ready to think about what he meant by *a choice*. Instead I focused on the practical. "Is the site not cursed now?"

"Not to worry. That wasn't ever us," Jupiter assured me. "The mountain's just been restless, that's all."

I clean forgot about the gift and scowled at him. *Just restless?* Is that what he called it? After all our heartache and hiking and divination gone wrong? Ha!

Jupiter gave me a jaunty salute and clearly dismissed the subject from his mind. He clapped Marcus's shoulder one last time. His smile did, at least, seem genuine. "See you around, I hope, brother."

Marcus merely inclined his head.

Jupiter took two, three steps away from us, and then disappeared, leaving nothing but the faint smell of lightning in his wake.

I shook my head. *Brother?* I knew the old myths, but . . . I'd forgotten that particular bit. On top of everything else that had just happened, this was flat-out funny. Or it would have been, if I hadn't been too surprised to laugh. "Talk about a family reunion."

"I hope you do not mind too much," Marcus said, shifting to face me, smiling sheepishly down. The temple around us was blissfully quiet. Finally, there wasn't anything but him. Well, there wasn't anything but him and also our friends, who we'd have to rouse and get home somehow. So we weren't alone quite yet, but even so, I knew my answer. No amount of divine drama would ever matter as much to me as Marcus did.

"Oh, I don't mind." I smiled back. "Just wait until you meet Ryu."

Chapter Thirty-Six: Forbidden

Marcus

Knowing that Saki would be at my side made me feel almost excited to deal with further challenges. But as it turned out, Quinn and Scarlet—and the indomitable Lulu—were already rousing themselves.

Saki and I joined them as soon as we heard the uncertain groans. Saki knelt beside Scarlet, and Lulu hopped unsteadily onto her shoulders. The goatling was still wearing a pink blossom between her small horns.

"Oh, no." Scarlet reeled as Saki reached for her. "Why do I feel so awful? My head is killing me!"

"Really? I feel a bit faint, but otherwise fine," Quinn commented as I helped him to his feet.

"I think I can solve that mystery," Saki said. "We all tripped a divine alarm system, and then it started manifesting Marcus's fears. But all the power here is faded, so in order to manifest anything it needed more magic. It started drawing on yours, Scarlet."

She glanced up at me to confirm this. The thought had indeed occurred to me, but in the aftermath, I had forgotten it. The red-violet tinge to the divine echoes. That had been due to Scarlet's power.

But it had not been Scarlet herself directing the energy. This much was clear from her confusion and exhaustion—and it correlated with what I knew. Divine places could be dangerous for mortal magic users. The energies were too likely to draw toward each other and combine. It was a danger I had never specifically stated, because Saki had her amulet and I had assumed Scarlet might know already, due to her line of work.

"It couldn't have," Scarlet said, going on to prove that she was indeed aware of the possibility by adding, "I have—charms against it. Wards."

"Yes, you had an awful lot of wards up, didn't you," Saki said quietly.

The two were still sitting on the floor. Lulu was watching Scarlet just as carefully as Saki was.

"I have to, in my line of work," said Scarlet warily. One hand was still held to her temple.

"You know how important it is to be all buttoned up," Saki agreed.

Quinn and I exchanged a look. Neither of us, it seemed, knew where this was headed.

Scarlet broke, with a ragged, exasperated sigh. She looked away from all of us. "Yes, okay, fine. I used the bones to cast forbidden spells and learned your name. But that's all I did.

Trent asked me not to do anything more. So what, you think this is some kind of punishment? Is that why you dragged me up here?"

"This is not a place of punishment," I said, surprising myself. I certainly had thought of it that way. And I was not averse to the idea in this case . . .

"You dragged yourself up here," Saki reminded her. "And, no. For the record, I don't think it's some kind of divine punishment. I think you brought it on yourself. I'd take another look at your bones, if I was you."

Scarlet frowned for a moment before reaching for her belt. When the bones tumbled from their pouch into her hand, every one of us could see that something had happened. Each piece was scorched and cracked.

"Oh." Scarlet stared down at them. "Oh *no!* How did this happen? Did you—you did this—"

"I really didn't," Saki said, looking at the ruined bones with a bland expression on her face. "I bet you Janus did. The old spell here didn't want anyone figuring too much out. It might have just cracked them, if you hadn't ever asked them forbidden questions. But those spells are supposedly forbidden for a reason, right? And they leave a mark. Not on the outside, but in the inside. On the inside, your bones were rotting. By breaking them, the spell here let the rot out."

"Oh, my gods." Scarlet spoke to herself, her growing panic evident. She began rifling through the pouches at her belt. "My wards. All my charms! Everything's broken—it's all been turned—it's all *gone!* What have you done?!"

"I'm trying to tell you, it wasn't me. You made your own choices," Saki said.

Scarlet ignored her. I leaned down, touching Saki's shoulder, and she took hold of my hand as she stood up. Lulu managed to maintain her position, which left only Scarlet on the ground.

"Maybe we should—give her a moment," Saki told Quinn and me.

"I don't feel quite ready to tackle another hike, myself," Quinn said easily. "I say, that was some reasoning. Are you certain about all that?"

"Yes." Saki watched Scarlet for a moment, meditatively, before looking back up. "I don't know if you could see it, Marcus, but I could see there was sort of a tinge at the edge of all the magic going on. Until Jupiter showed up, the real one, I mean. So in the back of my mind I was thinking, how could anything possibly draw on Scarlet's power? Only if all her wards were down. And why would that happen? Not just because she fell asleep—she would have planned for that. *I* would, if I knew I was going to an ancient temple that might have traps. And not just because it was powerful, either—I felt something drawing on my energy too, but it was just a tug, nothing more. I was just fine focusing on Marcus. So— something of Scarlet's must have gone wrong, or broken. And—I know it sounds ironic coming from someone like me, but, that *is* the consequence of forbidden spells. They corrupt your tools. They can corrupt *you*. That's the whole point."

"I follow you," Quinn told her. Then he glanced at me, his expression knowing. "Marcus?"

I had been staring at Scarlet, who still sat on the ground, furious.

"Even though she did it, it only worked because I had my own wards down, like you said," Saki told me softly, leaning into my arm. "She didn't do anything—violent."

I wasn't so sure the same could be said of me, if we continued lingering on this topic. And what then, one wonders, would my brother Jupiter think?

"Also," Quinn said, "what's this about gods showing up?"

My friend did know me well. I allowed myself to be distracted, helping Saki give him a brief summary of what had occurred. Curious, she asked him, "Did *you* notice anything? Anyone—speaking to you before you fell asleep?"

"Not a thing," Quinn told us. His eyes became distant. "But I will say—I had a very peculiar dream . . ."

At this point, Scarlet stirred once more. "Get me out of here."

"Gladly," I said.

But Saki put her hand on my chest. "We *all* need to get back home. And I don't know if you all have noticed, but I think night has fallen. We'd better stick together, because of the dark if nothing else. And—now that we're not worried about using magic—"

She looked back at me, and I inclined my head. "I will transport everyone to the lake."

"So it won't take a moment," Saki told Scarlet, rather more kindly than I would have. "But you should probably stand up."

Scarlet refused any help, and it took her several moments to collect all the bits of broken bone which had scattered around her. In my professional acquaintance with her, I had never had any reason to consider her or her methods. In the confusion following her use of Sakura's full name, I should have thought harder. I could have confronted her myself. Had I done so, a large part of the trouble we encountered at the temple would have been prevented.

Perhaps it was fitting that I did not, but even so, I took a lesson from it. A growing determination to act when necessary. To let myself *see* when, indeed, it was necessary to act.

Scarlet seemed to know she would not be well-received at present. She focused what little of her attention she would give us on Quinn, holding on to his arm as he held onto mine. Which left my right side free for Saki and her goat.

She was smiling up at me. There was relief in her eyes, and warmth. As I let my arm circle her, I let myself relax. She was right, my sweet Saki; she was right to be relieved. We had come a very long way.

When I step between places, it takes no time for those I bring with me. I knew this. But for me, the in-between is a place where there is no time. With the key that is my divine right, I can linger there. And for just a moment, I did so, realizing all that had happened . . .

And feeling amazed.

My Sakura—she had done all this. Not done it herself, perhaps; but she had wrought and faced changes which to me had been unimaginable. It was by virtue of her strength and her faith in me that I had come back to myself. And as we stepped onto the lawn before the lake, gratitude swept over me.

It was, indeed, night time. The stars shone in her eyes as she looked up at me. Lulu now safe in her arm, and her hand warm upon my back. All I wanted was to carry her into the little cabin she had made, and stay there until I was certain she knew how very precious she was.

But my friend Quinn, while very knowledgeable and clever, can sometimes be as annoying as he is astute. "So, what now?"

he asked.

The question was a blow. I had no idea. Would Saki stay, now? Surely she wouldn't want to leave right away. The inn wasn't set up, wasn't even made. But she was much more confident in herself—she had reclaimed so much, and it was good to see. Did that mean she considered her work here done?

"I'm leaving," Scarlet announced.

"A commendable effort, but one which will be complicated by the fact that it is far too late for the gondola to be running," Quinn observed.

"You can stay here one more night," Saki agreed. "Both of you. We can figure out all the other details in the morning. For now, we should focus on food and rest. We could—"

Her eyes met mine again, and my heart leapt. But I did not know what she meant to say. Sometimes her meanings were clear; this time, she had been interrupted.

Behind her, the surface of the lake broke. Droplets arced through the air, scattering across all of us as an unseen creature breached and once more disappeared.

"That's *it*," cried a particularly wet Scarlet. "I'm so *done*!"

Quinn seemed more amazed than alarmed. "What *was* that?"

"Marcus? Did you see it?" Saki asked.

"Yes." The familiar power hummed around me, and for an instant I closed my eyes in gratitude. "I would have told you, Saki, but you said you did not want to know. I have encountered this particular creature before."

"But it's not the monster, or an apparition. It stays in the lake," Saki reasoned, slowly. "It's not what we saw last night, or before?"

"That's right." I smiled faintly down at her. "It appeared to me in the rain. It does not mean any harm. Perhaps it was simply reacting to what we've done. It gave me the idea for your charm."

Saki's eyes narrowed. "It gave you the *idea* . . . not the magic itself?"

"No." Despite Scarlet, despite Quinn, my smile grew. "Sakura, sweetling. It only gave me the idea of suggestion. The only magic in that charm has ever been yours."

Chapter Thirty-Seven: Monster

Sakura

Well, this was turning out to be quite a day of revelations, wasn't it?

But I find that's how these things go. Once you finally get hit over the head by fate (or divinity or whatever power is out to get you at the moment) and start seeing things a different way, pieces begin coming out of the woodwork to fall into place.

And this was a big one.

It meant nothing to Quinn and Scarlet, obviously. They were completely adrift, though Quinn was putting up with it in his usual amused and watchful manner. My mind was racing. Had there never been a protective spell in the butterfly at *all*?

Sure, I'd never *felt* anything in it. But I'd assumed that was

311

because my own magic was so wonky . . .

"The two of you are going to make me *sick*," said Scarlet.

"An unwise protest, seeing as their cabins are all that stand between you and a massive lake creature, and a goat wielding orbs, and a monster," Quinn reminded her. "Did we deal with that, by the way?"

No. We hadn't. Nothing and nobody at the temple had said anything about a monster in the woods.

"Marcus," I said softly. "You had your moment. Right? You think it's time I had mine?"

"Anything you wish," he replied, his face grave but his eyes so tender and encouraging.

"Okay. Take Lulu."

I handed him possibly the best little pet anybody ever had, and I turned to face the lake. It seemed like the right thing to do. The creature of Hideaway Lake had accepted us. It was time for me to accept myself once more.

I took off my silly pack and the mittens and hat, which admittedly had grown on me. I laid them down in the grass, and stopped paying attention to what Quinn and Scarlet were doing. I even let Marcus and Lulu fade from my mind. They'd be perfectly fine. That much, I knew.

I closed my eyes. That little butterfly was still in my hair. But if it wasn't there to protect Marcus, then its purpose, I decided, must be as my guide. I thought of it, and let all the worries fall away. So many worries had piled up! Visions of the hurt I'd caused. Fears of conversations I hadn't yet had. Accusations, condemnations I'd hurled at myself. Rules I'd tried to build up, wards to protect others from me. I let every single one of them fall away.

And in their place . . . wings did grow.

But this wasn't just about me. I opened my eyes again to find I'd risen in the air, and I was hovering over the lake. Right at the heart of my new home.

Magic was surrounding me, palpable in the air. But it wasn't crashing out into people, wasn't *doing* anything scary or unpredictable. It was there, just as it had always been. I took a deep breath, and found I could admit it. I was powerful. And I was . . .

Sad. I cast the feeling out over the mountain, and the rocks and earth answered. Grieving for the ways life changed— and didn't. For realities that weren't the way we'd hoped. The loneliness in me was echoed by the loneliness of the mountain itself, left alone for years upon years, alone and misunderstood.

The anger of it rocked me next. It was mine, my own anger at the way things had played out, but it rippled through the water and whispered through the trees, too. Anger that anyone dare misunderstand us. That we *had* been left alone so cruelly. I could feel the magic blaze through the air but I held steady. Because I knew that under the anger was hurt, and that under the hurt was love.

Love. The feeling settled, a peace that ran through me and out across the mountain, like watercolor ink racing over a black and white page. I was aware of every hue and line of the landscape, every creature's heart beating, every memory and hope. We were all held together in that moment by the magic itself.

And there was one creature who didn't belong.

It *was* monstrous. And I knew exactly who it was.

Just to scare him, I lifted him up. Magic he couldn't fight or disable, magic that in fact he could barely see plucked

313

him from his little hiding place behind the final cabin. He squirmed and wriggled. I'd always known he was a bug.

The monster was a lot less scary when it hovered helplessly above the water in front of me.

"You're *crazy*," he cried, from under his shaggy creature-suit and mask. "Put me down! What are you doing? Who even *are* you? I didn't do anything wrong!"

"Hello, Bertram." My words, my grin shivered out along the magic, over the water below. "You're looking awfully well. Tired of ironing and offices, are you?"

"I don't know what you think you know, but you don't know *anything*," he shouted back.

"You'd certainly like it that way," I agreed. "I heard Marcus had to intimidate you into sharing anything at all. And you were so hoping I'd be easily scared, weren't you?"

"I'm not—you're not—*Sakura?*" he sputtered.

"Were you expecting someone else?" I was amused. "The ghost of your old boss, maybe, coming to get you? What would she think of you trying to take over her empire, Bertram?"

He was still struggling, flailing really. Funny when you think about it. What was he hoping to achieve? Possibly nothing: he was clearly focused on himself, as always. *"It should have been mine anyway!"*

"Yes, you've worked very hard, haven't you." I let him flip himself over. The magic wasn't going anywhere, he wasn't going to escape. But he got a very good look at the water below.

The deep, dark water *quite* far below.

"Gods! Oh, gods!" Bertram was clawing at the air now, as though he might climb his way out of the trap he'd found himself in—the trap he'd set himself up for. "Whatever you want, just don't drop me!"

A heartfelt plea, even if it didn't follow the conversation we'd been having. Well, it wasn't much of a conversation anyway. I knew everything I needed to for the moment.

I considered the water. I wouldn't hurt him. But we might see if his monster suit was waterproof . . .

"Please!" cried Bertram. "Don't drop me, don't leave me here!"

A scaly back broke through the ripples below, round, smooth, large. The creature of Hideaway Lake. I'd seen just a part of it now, slipping through my magic.

And as I saw it, I understood. I wouldn't drop or leave Bertram. But I had done both in Belville. And I'd done both to myself. And I'd been flailing just like this fake monster ever since.

But there was still time.

Magic wrapped around Bertram, cocooning him at first, then binding him. I sent him safely to the water's edge, before I followed, landing gently in the grass.

And then with a conscious breath I released my power, and the awareness of the mountain faded. The black sparkles, the wings, the energy of it all lapsed back into me—and back into the ground. Though I was no longer performing any kind of spell, a little sense of connection remained. I could feel, rather than hear, a tapered tail ruffle the cold water behind me.

And then I felt Marcus's arms around me, and I was wholly back within myself.

Bertram was still yelling. Scarlet was yelling. He'd once disabled her magic, after all. Quinn was laughing and quipping as only he would. Lulu was bleating in the background, triumphantly.

And Marcus, Marcus was holding me. I said the first thing that came to mind.

"Closure," I told him.

His arms were so warm and solid. "You found it?"

"Sort of," I said, collecting myself. "More like—I see it now. The way to find it. By letting yourself be hurt and then letting yourself heal."

"Hmm." Marcus settled me closer to his chest, watching the others over my head. "Like shedding a skin. Tell me, Saki, did you also see the creature in the lake? What did it look like to you?"

A funny thing to ask, maybe, but I smiled against his coat. I knew exactly why he was asking it. "You know what it is. I told you, this is your site too."

"Mmm," he said.

"And that means," I added, looking up with conviction, determined to start a new habit and do things right, *all* the way through, "that we both have some visits to make. Loose ends to tie up. Give me a moment, let me find my purse . . . I just need that address. I think I know someone who can help."

Chapter Thirty-Eight: Denouement

Marcus

My Sakura was right, as so often happens. And though it meant I had to wait before I could get her to myself, it proved to be a very interesting exercise.

She asked me to find and bring back two people. When I duly returned, I found that she and Quinn had set up a fire by the lake, and dragged the benches into a semi circle. Scarlet sat on the farthest one. Lulu sat on the same bench, watching her.

"Thank you," Saki told me, her expression and her tone so much more at ease, confident. Even without the fire beside her, she seemed to me to be glowing. To my companions, she added, "And thank *you* for coming. I know it's late. This won't take too long, but we need you to see something . . ."

She stepped aside, and Quinn assisted her in pulling the

mask from Bertram, who sat on the ground still bound.

To my left, Professor Myrtle gasped. And to my right, the young police officer Herakles took out his notebook and pencil.

"Pluto warned us something was afoot, but I'll need you to start from the beginning. I know better than to be surprised, with *you* involved," he added to Quinn.

Quinn, in his turn, grinned broadly. "Oh, it wasn't me this time, Herc. You can thank Sakura for this one."

"For physically catching him, at least," Saki said wryly. "But I'll need you to fill in gaps. Officer, Professor, I'm sure you both knew this place was supposedly haunted? Well, it turns out there are some things—like the mysterious lake and the occasional orb—that are intrinsic to the site. But there *was* something here that never fit the legends. Something that was running around at night chasing people, scaring them, and even stealing supplies. Quinn?"

"The important thing to note," Quinn told the police officer, gracefully taking over, "is that the sightings began in the fall. Shortly after construction began, yes, but more importantly, *after the trial concluded.* Saki herself didn't know the results yet—they weren't yet public—but those closest to the accused, those who would find themselves spending months making all the arrangements, *did* know. Didn't you, Bertram?"

The man on the ground didn't look up.

"I spoke to several employees working on the project—I'll give you their names," Quinn went on, still largely addressing Herakles. "They spoke of terror at night and missing materials—materials which, by the way, are now sitting in the station."

For the first time, Scarlet stirred. "*That* was why you wanted me to check over those that first night?"

"Materials that are stolen is one thing," Quinn said. "Materials that go and come back are another. Why bring things back? Either the thief had decided that they liked Sakura and wanted things to go forward after all—or the thief had *never actually meant to prevent construction*. And in that case, what would the hauntings be for? Not to prevent the project. So, they must be to scare off the project's *owner*.

"By starting things slowly, in the fall, Bertram was able to sow the seeds before Saki arrived," Quinn went on. "This served two purposes: first, he hoped to instill *more* fear in her when the time came, because a long-standing haunting is more menacing than a night or two of disturbance. Second, and even more important, it meant that everyone here would be aware of the haunting and would join in warning her off, thus saving him from having to incriminate himself."

Saki set her hands on her hips. "No wonder you didn't feel like you had to tell me right away," she said to Bertram.

"In fact, he asked *me* to warn her," I offered.

"Right." Quinn nodded, rubbing his hands together briskly. "With stories of hauntings coming from every angle, they not only blended with the legends and seemed more plausible, they also obscured the fact that only one person was involved. Bertram. When Saki and I investigated the cabins, I couldn't help but notice that there was one set of footprints which had created a trail going into the woods. When we tried to follow it, who should appear but the monster himself?"

"Wait," Saki said. "You knew his lair was back there? Why not say so, so we could look for it in daylight?"

"I didn't need to say so, because I thought our Department representative would take care of it," Quinn said, glancing at

Scarlet. "Or rather, I thought at the time that the orbs, as well as the monster himself, were protecting the woods."

From her position on the bench, Lulu bleated. It sounded not unlike laughter.

"I thought it best to neutralize any actual ghostly threat first," Quinn said. "But when Scarlet got here . . ."

"Yes, we know what happened then," Saki said. But in the next breath, she tilted her head. "Although—he didn't come out and attack that night when you were out here divining, did he? Why was that?"

"*That* was what convinced me we were dealing with a purely human threat," Quinn said. "The answer is simple. He wasn't prepared to deal with Scarlet. Were you?"

"Ughh," was all Bertram had to say.

Officer Herakles was still scribbling furiously at my side. "Miss Scarlet? Does that strike you as true?"

Scarlet flipped her hair over her shoulder and paused as we turned to her. Eventually, she admitted, "I was focused on the divine aspects of the site."

"She didn't have to know he was there to be intimidating," Quinn added more helpfully. "The first thing she did when we all got back here was put up witchy shelters, lanterns, and velvet cloths. Bertram might not have realized how magical our friend Sakura is—particularly since she was doing her best *not* to be when she first arrived." Quinn inclined his head to Saki, grinning, and went on, "But with Scarlet, it was impossible to miss. So it was no coincidence when we met Bertram in the market the next morning."

"Buying an anti-magic charm," Saki reasoned, her eyes widening. "Which means he probably *did* recognize you! So much for your reporter cover!"

"A charm is one thing. But he couldn't have bought anything at the market that let him teleport," Scarlet was quick to argue.

"That, he didn't have to buy. That was just good old-fashioned theft from an employer," Quinn said, glancing at me.

I nodded reluctantly. "Minotaur Enterprises had a long-standing interest in teleportation artifacts. Bertram was sent to me several years ago for . . . something I did not sell, but nonetheless it should have occurred to me that they would remain interested, and would collect other magical devices for the same purpose."

"Okay," Officer Herakles said over his notebook. "So I have, he was threatening the workers, probably stealing supplies, maybe stealing artifacts from his boss. But why?"

"We'll give you a copy of the instructions for the land," Saki told him. "You'll see that basically, if I gave up my rights, they would resort to Bertram. It's not true any more, though," she added to Bertram's bowed head. "You think I didn't know to change that first?"

Ah. Another reason she had wanted me to sign paperwork. When she lifted her head she caught my eye, and she winked.

"So it was all for nothing?" At my side, Professor Myrtle spoke. "Oh, Bertram . . . And yet now, you're staying?"

"Yes, I'm staying," Saki replied. My heart thrilled. She went on, addressing Myrtle this time. "And I wanted you here to know about all this in case Officer Herc runs into any trouble. I know you hinted that Minotaur was paying people at Town Hall not to be interested. Well, that's ending now. Herc, the way I see it, you and the town should have full authority to charge Bertram. Myrtle, if they say it's out of their jurisdiction, we may need your help. And also, I *do* want a historic marker and official recognition for the site. We're going to keep ownership of it, mind, but it's important to know it'll be protected, too."

This time Myrtle's gasp was a happy one. "And—you'll work with the University? The students?"

Saki's gaze lingered on mine, amused. "One thing at a time. Let's focus on wrapping this up, for now."

Officer Herakles looked up from his notes. "With everything you've told me—and the fact that you've got him *in* the suit—and testimony from the witnesses you mentioned, Mister Doyle, I think that about wraps things up. It's enough to take him down to the station now, at least. Anything to say for yourself, Bertram?"

The captured monster shuffled uncomfortably on the hard ground. Finally he grimaced up at us. "Think you're so clever, don't you? But it wasn't greed. It's not the stupid resort I wanted. The Temple—that's what matters!"

From her dark corner, Scarlet laughed hollowly. "It's not what you think."

"You've *been* there?" Bertram's eyes went wide. "But—but—"

"Yes, we've been there, and we're not any more divine than we were before, if that's what you're wondering," Saki said. "Also, no one's buying your excuses. If you wanted to get to the top of the mountain for fame or power, that's still greed."

Bertram scowled. "You have no idea what it's like to work for someone who never thinks about *you*. I was going to—I was going to show her . . ."

"You'll need to rethink your methods," Quinn remarked. "Is that all, then?"

The monster on the ground remained quiet.

323

"Excellent," said Saki, cheerfully. Again, she met my eyes, smiling. "Bullies usually *do* run out of things to say once you've held your ground."

Saki,

Luca found some research on Mount Hallow he wanted to share, so I'm including it here. We're thinking of you. Love, Red

Chapter Thirty-Nine: Seeing

Sakura

Before he left, Officer Herc pressed a bundle of papers into my hands. I honestly had no idea what they were, but I decided to hold to my new maxim of *one thing at a time.* I could read them later, when there was light and everything else had been settled. Meanwhile, Marcus escorted Herc and Bertram, and Quinn as well, down to the police station without a complaint. I was tempted to joke that he ought to start charging for trips, like Gwyn. But the look he gave me as he left made me forget about all that, and just focus on what might happen when he came back . . . *That* was a loose end I was looking forward to.

My happy bubble burst, though, when I turned around and realized that Scarlet was still sitting at the bonfire with me and Lulu.

"Congratulations," she said, meanly.

I walked over to her bench, letting her tone wash past me. "You and I have to talk, too."

"Save it," she said, sounding supremely bored and—maybe just a little—vulnerable. "All this talk of teleportation reminded me. You know what I have that *didn't* break? The one thing that was charmed to always work, in case of emergency?" Though her voice broke, her gaze remained flinty as she held up her hand, showing me a black ring. "My one get-home-free ticket. I think I'll be using it. Just remember I was right. It *was* the Temple that was the source of your trouble . . . aside from yourself. See you never, I hope."

And before I could get another word out, she'd taken off the ring, tossed it into the fire, and disappeared.

I settled heavily on the bench beside Lulu, deflated. "That's how most of those artifacts are," I told the goat, not sure if I was unhappy or relieved. "They've got a single spell trapped inside. Break it and you're gone, but that's it. Definitely only for emergencies. I wonder how Bertram's worked? I guess Officer Herc will find out."

Lulu nibbled at my sleeve, and I gazed at the dying fire. Unhappy, definitely. I'd meant what I said to Marcus: bullies talked a lot less once you held your ground. And I hadn't had the chance to officially hold my ground against Scarlet. I was going to have to face her tomorrow.

Her, and probably her Department too. And then—Belville.

"But I'm coming back this time," I whispered to Lulu. "That's the difference. I've made my choice, and even if it hurts, I know I'll be coming back."

"Sakura?"

It wasn't Lulu, suddenly developing a capacity for speech—

of course not. It was Marcus, looming out of the dark, sudden but also constant, adorable. I stood up on the bench, ignoring the way it rocked over uneven ground. Lulu bailed, but I leaned forward, flinging my arms around Marcus's shoulders. We were finally alone.

"Sweet Saki," he murmured, his hands skimming over my back, his mouth finding mine. "My sweet soul, my butterfly."

"Does that make you my serpent?" I pulled my head up, my nose brushing his, teasing him. Unable to wait for his answer, I kissed him again, savoring the way he tasted, the way his heartbeat felt against mine.

"Anything," he said softly, after a long moment.

I paused, laughing at him, at the thrill of it all. "My partner, apparently. Even the gods know now, so it must be true. Are you okay, Marcus? With everything that happened?"

"I have you," he said, pulling me closer, his lips brushing mine. "Everything else that happened is passed."

"Fair enough." I chuckled again, kissing his cheek. "But I'm not okay with the way things are. Not at all. There's far too much you don't know. Did you know I'd face dozens more gods and monsters for you? And that the way you finally spoke up back there was so incredibly hot? And that you're *totally* forgiven for the amulet thing, I didn't expect it to be perfect—"

"Mmm. Wait," he rumbled against me, now amused too. "You thought I was hot?"

"*That's* what got your attention?" I pulled my head back, grinning at him. "Carry me home, and I'll show you."

Challenge accepted. He didn't say it aloud—he didn't need to—his expression clearly did. Not to mention the fact that he immediately had my legs wrapped round his waist, and we were already in the cabin. In the bedroom.

"Lulu is downstairs," he murmured. The star lights twinkled as he started kissing me again.

"Good. I've been waiting *forever* to be alone with you," I whispered back.

We both heard the crash of a chair falling over, but this time, we ignored it.

It wasn't until much later that I realized I was *starving*. I poked Marcus, who lay sleepily beside me. "I know it's probably the middle of the night, but . . . Did we ever have dinner?"

"Mmm. No," he said, as though his memory was as hazy as mine was.

"We'll have to be better about that when we're running the place," I told him lightly.

"Sweet Saki. We *are* running the place," he pointed out, shifting onto his elbow. After leaning over to kiss me, he added, "What is your decree? Is it time for dinner, or breakfast?"

I laughed. "Breakfast is easier. We can have some now, and later, too. Come on."

He followed me down the stairs, the noise waking Lulu, who had eventually given up and claimed her spot by the fire. She was bouncing as she joined the parade to the kitchen. I probably was, too.

For a while we worked in happy silence, hands drifting over each other, *mostly* focused. "I think we'll definitely need a bigger kitchen," I admitted.

"I see nothing wrong with this," Marcus protested, his voice low and easy. He kissed the top of my head as he squeezed past, searching for a knife for the bread. "But I do think you could use a larger bedroom."

So we were playing *that* game? Delight trilled through me. "I've always wanted a bay window to sit in."

"And a suite for Miss Lulu," Marcus added. At his heels, Lulu bleated adoringly.

"A really large bathtub," I added to the list, sighing at the thought.

Marcus passed behind me again, and lingered this time. "I would like that."

I laughed. "You're incorrigible. This is a wish-list, not a scandal in the making."

"Hmmm." Marcus sat at the table as he sliced bread for us, and for a moment was quiet. When he looked up, he was a little more serious. "Saki, you've said twice now you don't mind about the amulet."

"True both times," I chirped, flipping our omelet.

"I have been thinking. I meant it to be a gift for you, but as I said, I—I didn't wholly understand what I was trying to give."

Was he thinking about this because he'd taken my wish list comment seriously? I slipped the omelet onto one large plate, both touched and thoughtful. The answer came to me as I joined him at the table. "Darling. You're adorable. But I don't think gifts are what either of us need." I looked up, and he was watching me with a deliciously curious expression in his dark eyes. I grinned. "We're working together, right? So it's a two way street. Not just giving, but receiving too. I know I've been bad at it also, I thought I didn't deserve anything, I was basically overwhelming myself with shame. But . . ."

"But," he concluded, his voice going rumbly again, "perhaps once you've finished your breakfast, we can practice another way."

And so it was *much* later in the morning than usual when I was finally ready to face the world again. I put on my amulet, and I put up my wards. I'd forgotten how comfortable they felt. I lingered in the mirror, looking at my reflection, not because I was scared but—because I wanted to remember how this confidence felt.

Marcus wanted to come, of course. But this was a battle I needed to fight alone. Besides, a ride down the gondola was a lovely excuse to catch up with Gwyn. And by the time I'd made it down the mountain and across town, I was fully ready.

"I knew you'd be coming back," Scarlet announced, when at last someone pried her out of her office and brought her to me in the lobby.

"You can tell them, or I can," I informed her.

She had the grace to blush, at least. "It wasn't really related to the case. If you must know, I did it *before* you all came here. So it's really not releva—"

"Your immoral actions caused a magical backlash that put every single one of us in danger at a divine site," I interrupted, rising to my full height. I hadn't brought Marcus along, but I was conscious of myself drawing on his example. "I believe it *is* relevant."

Scarlet deflated. "It's not like I want to take on more work right now anyway. Not until I craft a new set of bones."

With this dubious message of contrition, she accompanied me to visit the head of the department, where at my insistence she made her report. Her *full* report. Something about it— maybe the heavy smell of ancient parchment in the air— made me remember that bundle of letters Herc had given me. *Somebody's been looking for you,* he had said. It hadn't even

331

registered at the time—I'd had other things, other Marcus-shaped things, on my mind. The papers were still in my purse, hanging at my side. Without thinking I put my hand down to feel them, as though by touch I might be able to see if they were full of anger or worry. Instead, a sprig of dried lavender among the envelopes and edges brushed my fingers. *Trent.*

"The reason the divination ritual went wrong." I said it aloud, interrupting Scarlet's description of how terribly powerful I was and how awfully uncontrolled and how she had made a mistake but I shouldn't be allowed to go free, either. Somewhere in all of her talking about me, I heard that little note of truth. That little bit of something relatable. And because I could relate to it, I suddenly saw what had happened. In the dark, rich, meant-to-impress office, lavender crumbling in my fingertips, I turned to speak to only her. "Trent's true love ritual. You liked him even back then, didn't you?"

Scarlet licked her lips. "I never said I liked him. *You* said that. This is why—"

"It's why you were scared he might see someone else," I interrupted firmly. "Right? You couldn't bear that. So you tried to influence the ritual, didn't you?"

For once, she was silent.

"But it backfired," I said softly, "and that's why it showed him *me.*"

Not because of anything about me, or anything I was. Not because of Trent or because he misunderstood. Merely because of people being afraid to ask for things they want. Merely because people—and their spells—make mistakes.

I could see it very clearly. Because it was *exactly* what teenage Saki might have done.

Scarlet's complaints fizzled quite a bit at that. She was summarily dismissed from the office, and placed on leave. But the head of the department asked me to linger.

"This business about shadow witchery . . ."

A shot which, only yesterday, would have hit home. All they had to do was hint at it, and I understood that I should feel ashamed. Well, not now. No longer. I put my hand to the amulet under my clothes, and said as evenly as I could, "Ancient and magical sites chose their own guardians. Isn't that what you and your Department believe?"

THANKS FOR THE COOKIES! HOW DID YOU KNOW PEANUT BUTTER WAS MY FAVORITE? I CAN SEE IT'LL BE HANDY HAVING YOU AROUND. GLAD THE SCARY PART IS OVER! LET ME KNOW IF YOU

TO: SAKI
FROM: GWYN
+ THE BOTS

Chapter Forty: Love

⤧⤧⤧

Marcus

On the street outside the gondola station, I encountered Quinn. He carried a coffee cup in each hand; he had, it seemed, been waiting for me.

"It's been a whole day," he commented. "I hope you've descended to town because you realize you owe me a recap."

I accepted the coffee, amused, and had to admit he had a point. "Please forgive me for 'holing myself up.' It was not my intention. Saki and I . . . had much to discuss. Yesterday afternoon, she made a visit to the Department. Afterward, she said it was time to return to Belville and settle her affairs there. She left by the evening flight."

It was difficult to admit. I had not been without her a whole day, and yet I felt her absence keenly.

Fortunately, Quinn knew how to remain light. "The

Department building's still standing, from what I hear. You two opted not to go for scorched earth?"

I gave him a reproving look. It was mid-morning already, and there were many people around us, tourists and locals alike. It would not do to cause alarm. "What happened was not the fault of the Department."

"Spotty oversight, one might argue," Quinn remarked. "If Scarlet did forbidden magic for the sake of a friend, what more was she doing? If they investigate, they'll find more. I'd lay a wager on that."

"They will investigate," I assured him. But the word made me think of other matters. As we strolled down the street, I asked, "What of your own plans?"

"Still moving forward. Soon." Quinn sipped at his coffee, and deftly avoided a cart of freshly-baked bread traveling in the opposite direction as we walked down the street. "Officer Herc has everything well in hand, and made contact with the other witnesses yesterday. I've made my final statement on the case, and am no longer needed. Not to mention that Professor Myrtle has already made several visits to Town Hall. I'm sure they'll be in touch soon, if they haven't reached out already. No doubt justice will take its course.

"Listen, Marcus," he added, "I'm well aware of my failings. But—even so—you *are* my oldest friend—not just in age, but in terms of how long we've known each other."

I smiled at the joke. "Since that is the case, you should say what's on your mind."

"Just that she was right, you know." Quinn looked up at me, thoughtful despite the crowd around us. "I *have* been worried about leaving you behind, and at such a dodgy site. Now that you and Saki have cleared it of hauntings, that's by the by, of course—"

"You played your own part," I reminded him. "If not for you, we would not have consulted Scarlet and gone to the temple at all."

"Thanks for that, dodgy as the honor might be," Quinn replied with a little bow. "In any case, I suppose the case is over now. Right?"

I eyed him with amusement. "Shouldn't you, as the investigator, be the one to determine that?"

"An investigator who was knocked unconscious for half of the big reveals," he reminded me.

"All you missed were personal matters." I glanced ahead of us, taking in the people, the buildings. Behind them, the harbor and the sea. The mountain. This was my home. I had a stake in it. "Yes, my friend, I believe we can safely say that the hauntings are over."

"That's a relief." Quinn nodded and we walked in silence. Before we had made it far, he added quietly, "I *was* worried about you, you know. But I'm not any more."

"I thank you for it," I told him sincerely. "And I agree that you no longer have need to be."

At that, he grinned. "Excellent. In that case, what do you say to sending me off with a glowing endorsement? Maybe a letter of recommendation or two? And if you happen to know any other lake monsters that might need investigating . . ."

I laughed. "I do not make it a habit to keep track of lake monsters, and I would advise you not to do so either."

I left Marcus in a good mood, and completed my shopping with a spring in my step. I even rode the gondola back as well, taking advantage of the opportunity to talk to Gwyn. She was every bit as supportive and interesting as Saki had said.

When at last I was left to myself back at the lake, I considered the pile of construction materials. It did them no good to sit unused. Saki had plans, of course, and her sketches . . . but, she *had* made me a partner in the site, and she had made a point of her trust in me.

The building part was my favorite.

After the strange power surges and stresses of the days before, it was calming to work on building the lodge. Everything I needed was right here; it was only up to me to arrange it. I tried several different versions before I felt I'd got it right. A welcome counter was needed, surely, with a nice airy lobby. And the restaurant, the bar—a nice, long bar, with plenty of shelves for ingredients. And windows everywhere, opening onto a wraparound porch. Who could come here and not want to appreciate the view?

By the time I was done, I'd placed the very last of the construction materials. Everything had gone into the new lodge, and I had to admit, I was proud of myself. It was just the sort of place which Saki would make cozy, warm, and magical. She would love it.

She would love it—I certainly hoped so. Yet I realized as I stood there that I hadn't yet told *her* how I loved her. She certainly deserved the words, and more.

And this would be the perfect place to share them with her. I had built this place, and now all I could do was wait.

Travel between Belville and Helenia was no simple matter, after all. I could have loaned her my key—I was more than willing to. But she wanted to do it her own way, and I could understand that. It would be easier to deal with a past lover, or potential lover, without the current one hanging around, either in person or via magical artifacts. I was at ease, thinking of her there, knowing she'd return. Though I was a little curious to visit in my own right one day. To meet all the friends who had been such a part of her life.

And so several days passed. But something in me had changed, certainly, for I was no longer content to sit *all* day. I decided to fix up the path between the station and the cabins, and the new lodge, as well. I'd told Saki that my affinity for stone was due to the divine power surrounding the temple, but that turned out to be only partially true. The stone around the lake responded just as easily, rising to the surface and forming cobbled paths. I felt a camaraderie with it, in fact. Stone knows what it is to be quiet for millennia, and to watch over the dead.

I was just finishing the path by the last of the cabins one afternoon when I heard the creaking of the gondola, far behind me. And as I turned, I caught sight of her at last.

Her eye was drawn immediately to the new lodge building, of course. She went to it at once, forgetting her luggage, scarcely remembering to wave goodbye to Gwyn. In the bright, cool light, looking brighter and lighter herself than I had ever seen her, Sakura paused on the path and considered her new inn. Her hands at her mouth did not hide her wide smile.

With a step, I was behind her. What a joy to know that this meeting would be so different from the first!

Before I could surprise her, she whirled, knowing she would find me there. "Marcus," she cried, delighted. "You did this?"

I smiled. "Would you like to inspect it?"

"I can't wait," she said, an emphatic *yes.* Indeed, before I could say anything more, she bounced on her toes and raced for the door. Lulu raced at her heels.

I followed them more slowly, letting the love I felt fill me, enjoying the sun over the stone path. As I climbed onto the porch I found the door open and Saki already inside, gazing up at skylights and beams with an expression I knew very well. She was already making lists.

But I had to tell her, now.

I picked her up and set her atop her new counter, already flushed. "As much as I'm sure you'd like to begin decorating, there is something I must say to you. If you'll allow it? Here, you are a queen in her domain."

Saki leaned back on one hand, the sky blue of her traveling cloak reflecting her eyes. In her free hand she toyed with the pendant around her neck. "Is that so?" she asked, mischief in her smile. "Not a goddess?"

I glanced down at that pendant, the golden spell it contained. "I am not sure that is exactly how it works," I told her honestly. "But you can be mine. You already are one, to me."

She reached up then, her hand at my cheek. More gently now, she chuckled. "No, I'm only human. We both know I make lots of mistakes. But at least, for now, I've fixed all the ones I can."

"But that is your strength, sweet soul." I leaned in, unable to resist, repeating, "That is your strength, and you have reminded me to see mine. I am still learning from you how to fix my own mistakes. I am still learning—"

It was the warmth of her smile that interrupted me, and the light in her eyes. She already knew.

"Say what you want, then," she dared me.

Sweet Saki. Of course she knew.

"I want *you*," I told her. "I want a life with you, a present life. I love you. I want to be more than your business partner, more than your friend, more than—"

By that point, she was laughing sweetly. "Dearest, you were always much more than that to me, and I just was too afraid to say it too. I love you too. You're my miracle."

Overcome with relief, I kissed her at last. Holding her face to mine, claiming all her attention. It was only when my hand had dropped to her skirt, her knee, that we heard the crash echoing from somewhere in the lodge.

Her wide eyes met mine for a heartbeat. Then she grinned. "Let me guess. You built this place with a bathroom?"

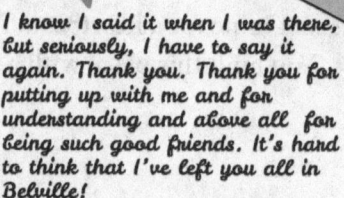

Red,

I know I said it when I was there, but seriously, I have to say it again. Thank you. Thank you for putting up with me and for understanding and above all for being such good friends. It's hard to think that I've left you all in Belville!

But that brings me to two important points. The first is that I happen to know somebody who can travel anywhere in the blink of an eye and is very curious about the Pomegranate. So we may come by and check in on Glacial and Mel! But in the meantime, you and Luca MUST come to our new inn. Opening day is Ostara. You'll be VIPs! See our sign included here.

All my love,
Saki

Epilogue

Sakura

When Ostara came, we were ready. Just barely.

It seemed too good to miss. The chance to open our inn and take in our first official guests on the spring equinox, a day of springtime and new beginnings? I just couldn't pass up the symbolism of it—besides, I figured it might bring us an extra little bit of luck.

That said, we'd done a pretty good job of creating luck, ourselves, I must say.

I grabbed my pendant, still full of golden liquid—a choice for another day—from my dresser and slipped it over my head, the last touch. My dress was adorned in butterflies, another special touch I'd been saving for this day. I was excited for Marcus to see it—excited for everything, honestly. I hopped down the stairs, and didn't even care.

Lulu was already in the kitchen, munching at a pile of fresh greens. We had our snug apartment in the upper levels of the lodge now, and the cabin we'd first lived in was due to be rented out today. Marcus's cabin was, too. He often spent his nights at the lodge, after all.

He glanced up from the kitchen counter, where he was measuring out tea ingredients. When he saw me, he set everything down.

"Saki . . ."

"Go on," I said, grinning as I did a little twirl.

"My sweet butterfly." He gathered me up and kissed me, not stopping until I was laughing and gasping for breath.

"Okay, okay, enough," I cried, though of course I'd known he might react that way. It definitely had not gotten old. "I have to make breakfast, and cookies, still, remember? We can't have people show up and not get anything to eat."

"Hmm. After all your decorations and arrangements, I think any guest will be hard-pressed to come up with something to complain about," Marcus said. He did let me go, though, and returned to making his tea.

"You say that, but I know you're being extra careful too." I smiled at him over my shoulder. "Special iced tea?"

"I thought it only appropriate," he said. "Green tea, with hibiscus flowers and lemon balm honey."

"A perfect way to start off on the right foot. A *calm* foot." I gathered eggs and veggies from the icebox, using my magic to make sure the door was closed, and took over the counter space beside the burner. It wasn't until the peppers and onions were sizzling nicely that I risked looking at Marcus again.

"Yes?" he asked.

I smiled ruefully. "Are you nervous?"

"I am immortal and considered by many to be above daily

344

affairs. I am of another realm entirely, some might say." He gave me his own lopsided grin. "But yes. I am nervous."

"Good. Me too," I told him, bouncing on my toes again. I couldn't help it. The energy had to go *somewhere*.

"Was it like this when you opened the Pomegranate?" he asked.

I nodded as I poured eggs into the pan. "Yep. It doesn't get any better, no matter what you do."

"Then perhaps we should be glad." As he passed me on his way to the sink, Marcus kissed the top of my head. "It means we care about this place."

"And you," I added over my shoulder. "I love you."

"I love you, too," he replied.

Lulu bleated.

Though our first arrival wasn't due until the afternoon, I insisted we eat breakfast on the front porch. It was one of my favorite places—but then, I also loved the side porch, which stretched along the restaurant and had the best view of the lake. And I loved the bay window in my apartment, which had the perfect view over the front door of the station. And along the other side of the lodge, Marcus had already started growing a garden and built a freestanding patio with a breathtaking view of the city . . .

I had maybe too many favorite places.

We ran over our plan as we ate. I would run the front counter, and Marcus would help people to their cabins. Later, he'd take over the bar. Both the bar and the front counter had access to the kitchen, which was perfect, because we could take turns keeping an eye on things. And if these first few days went well, we could think of hiring people; Gwyn had already promised to refer a few of her local friends . . .

It was strange. In thinking of Gwyn, it was almost as though I could hear the gondola wires groaning. Or—

I paused in the middle of cleaning up our plates. Marcus, sitting with his back to the station, didn't catch it at first.

"Maybe she's delivering something?" I offered, when it became clear that *yes,* I was hearing the gondola.

"We have everything we need," Marcus said, twisting in his seat to look.

Something was definitely arriving. And if it wasn't supplies, then . . .

Gwyn docked her gondola, and *people* spilled out. A group of them. And at the very front of that group—

"Ahoy, there!" A familiar figure swept the hat from his head in a grand gesture of greeting as he strode down from the station, hailing us. Lulu stuck her head out between the railing to bleat at him. "I hear this is the best, *least* haunted inn in all of Helenia!"

"Quinn Doyle!" I set down my plates and leaned over the rail to yell back. "I thought you were gone?"

"I was! And I came back to stay at your lovely inn," Quinn declared as he reached our front steps. "You didn't really think I'd let the occasion slip by, did you?"

I rolled my eyes at him. Actually, I laughed. Marcus was laughing at my side. And behind Quinn, a dozen visitors—or more. Eyes wide with astonishment, just as mine had been when I'd first arrived.

"Welcome, everybody," I called. "Welcome to the Hearthstone Lodge at Hideaway Lake!"

About the Author

Elle adores cozy tales, matcha, and above all, learning new things. As a hopeful romantic, she believes in the value of stories as safe havens and inspiration. She currently lives in New Jersey with a grumpy tortoise and a three-legged cat.

Find more stories of Sakura and her friends at **ellehart-ford.com**. And while you're there, sign up for Elle's newsletter to get bonus material, behind-the-scenes sneak peeks, and terrible jokes!

Also by Elle Hartford

The Alchemical Tales, a cozy mystery-meets-cozy fantasy series, includes:
  The Carousel Capers (prequel story collection)
  Beauty and the Alchemist (book one)
  Cold as Snow (book two)
  Mermaid for Danger (book three)
  Cry Big Bad Wolf (book four)
  Cinders to Dust (book five)
  Death Pulls the Strings (book six)
  A Thousand and One Alibis (book seven)
  Tangled Up in Murder (book eight)
  Labyrinth of Crime (book nine)

A spin-off series of cozy fantasy romance, Pomegranate Cafe Romance, includes:
  Worthy in Love (book one)
  A Tale of Rowan and Daisy (extra novella)
  Strong in Love (book two)
  Steady in Love (book three)
  Sweet in Love (book four)

A cozy fantasy spin-off series, Marine Magic, includes:
  How to Care for Cursed Fish (book one)
  How to Treat Talking Beasts (book two)

And a noir-meets-cozy spin-off series with reporter Leo begins:

The Silver Deck (book one)